THE YOUNG AND SECRET

BY
ALICE GRANT ROSMAN

THE WINDOW
VISITORS TO HUGO
THE YOUNG AND SECRET

THE YOUNG ~
~AND SECRET

BY
ALICE GRANT ROSMAN

MINTON, BALCH & COMPANY
NEW YORK   1930

Printed in the United States of America by
J. J. LITTLE AND IVES COMPANY, NEW YORK

TO
ETHEL AND LANCE MATTINSON

THE YOUNG AND SECRET

THE YOUNG AND SECRET

CHAPTER I

i

THE first present for Una Swithin's nineteenth birthday was bought by her Aunt Marion in Florence rather before the event, and inadvertently, as gifts from such relatives are likely to be. A strange young man was actually responsible, but the elder Miss Swithin never discovered that—she was one of those women who never discover anything— and when she saw him again she actually recognized him as a friend.

She had been wintering on the French Riviera and had gone into Italy for a change of tongue rather than for any more practical or æsthetic reason. She spoke a little of many languages very badly but, being English, quite well enough to persuade most of her friends that she was a cosmopolitan. As this was her aim in life, she never made the fatal error of calling foreign places by their English names. Genova, Il Vaticano, Le Boule Miche, flung into a conversation gave it, she had found, quite an air.

She loved striding up and down the corridors of the Rapide or about the lounges of hotels, talking fluently to porters and officials while her fellow Britons looked on in wonder, and the same instinct constantly led her into little shops where she would bargain volubly with the pirate in charge, and prove herself the better pirate by emerging empty-handed in the end.

It was a harmless vanity and if this afternoon in Florence it betrayed her into a piece of unwarranted extravagance, this was soon transmuted into generosity. Miss Swithin's mistakes always became virtues as soon as made; so her digestion was excellent and her outlook cheerful. She was constantly described as such a bright woman.

It was a golden day in the city of flowers. The iris were raising their blue and white banners along the Arno and the wind blowing down over the orchards from Fiesole was drowsy and sweet with the scent of almond blossom. Tourists were swarming. In and out of the Uffizi, the Bargello, and the Pitti Palace they strode, till their heads were giddy with madonnas and their aching feet carried them on mechanically. They would not really see anything, but tonight they would write eager post cards home about Raffaello—he would never be merely Raphael again —while that prince of jesters perhaps laughed among the spheres.

Miss Swithin of course would have seen no occasion for laughter. She was kind to the tourists, giving them advice in Anglo-Italian which was as impressive as it was confusing. They thought her a personage and were convinced she knew Florence from end to end. So was she, but this was a delusion. She had passed the Ghiberti gates often enough, and thought they wanted washing, while the delicate leaves almost quivered in the wind and the birds rose from them as though alive. She had never entered the Medici Chapel because she disapproved of the family; and she vaguely believed Fra Girolamo to have been an artist, which would have been considered clever of her in the right circles. In short, she knew Florence as so many people know the cities of the world, merely as a geometrical pattern of roads and bridges leading from one house or hotel to another.

With a glow of conscious satisfaction in this knowledge, she had set out after luncheon for a brisk walk down the Lung'Arno and suddenly caught sight of two young people from the hotel to whom she had given some help that morning. They wanted souvenirs and she had advised the Ponte Vecchio, but here they were actually going into Sponelli's, a different matter altogether.

Feeling impelled to go to their aid she hurried on, but they were too quick for her, coming out with their little parcels as she entered the shop and too pleased with themselves even to notice her.

Done out of her piece of knight-errantry, Miss Swithin could not merely retreat, so she bore down upon Sponelli and proceeded to bargain about various odds and ends she had no intention of buying. The old man could speak English, but she was not the woman to stand that from any foreigner, and when after a moment someone else entered the shop, the battle was on.

Tony Corcoran had come pelting down the Lung'Arno eager with purpose. He at least knew what he wanted and he fidgeted round Sponelli's customer, keeping an eye out for it, while he took in with delight the sharp-nosed, vivacious old girl in her preposterously Bond Street clothes looking as though she might pounce at any moment.

"Mrs. Polhampton," thought Tony, pleased with the imaginary name, for he had an impish taste in such matters.

Next moment he saw the object he was seeking, lying almost under the lady's nose. It was an intaglio ring of white onyx set in Florentine silver, and it seemed clear to him that her argument, which he could not follow, had nothing to do with this, for she was fingering a large medallion horrible to see.

He put out an unobtrusive hand to take the ring and Sponelli nodded and said, *"Si, si,"* for this young signore had been looking at it the day before and had almost been persuaded to part with three hundred lire for it.

Then Mrs. Polhampton pounced indeed. She was outraged that this ungentlemanly young man should snatch an article she was deigning to consider. She had never been so treated in her life and wouldn't put up with it for a moment.

"No, no, no," she cried to Sponelli's *"Si, si,"* caught the ring up off its velvet cushion and put it on her finger, pouring a flood of questions on the old man from which Tony's limited knowledge of Italian could only disentangle the sinister word *"prezzo."*

Oh, lord, she was going to buy it then?

Sponelli did his best for Tony, who had talked

English to him yesterday. He was not proof against the subtle compliment of that.

"*Cinque cento cinquante lire, Signora,*" said Sponelli, putting the price up without the turning of a hair.

"*Si, si,*" said Miss Swithin briskly, produced the notes as though she had come here for no other purposes, and walked with triumphant dignity and the ring on her finger out of the shop.

"Oh, but look here, I say . . ." exclaimed Tony.

Sponelli shrugged his shoulders. It had been a profitable sale, and what could he do, his expression seemed to say, against a signora like that?

As there was clearly no help from this quarter, Tony turned to regard the retreating form of "Mrs. Polhampton." He had set his heart on the ring and perhaps she would part with it, though the price was more than he had any right to pay. The old cat had pounced by instinct he was certain. *She* didn't want the ring, and there she was pausing outside to unfurl a sunshade. It was Fate.

Miss Swithin, having spent a large sum on an article somebody else evidently wanted very much, felt she had been clever; so she regarded Tony as he came out with affability.

"Too bad you were disappointed," she said, "but you see one needs a knowledge of the language to strike a bargain with Sponelli. And it is quite a bargain, isn't it?"

Tony saw his hopes departing and mischief prompted him.

"I don't know so much about that. It rather depends upon the point of view—but perhaps you are not superstitious?"

"Not in the least, but why?"

"Oh, well—a Medici ring, you know. Some mighty queer things were done in medieval Florence, don't you think?"

Miss Swithin, who had vaguely supposed the intaglio to represent Julius Cæsar or Mark Anthony, both so Shakespearean and therefore respectable, took off her glove and regarded the ring with a faint sense of discomfort. But still . . . a medieval ring . . . it must be valuable then, for this young man seemed to know what he was talking about.

"You don't happen to have been born in May?" inquired Tony hopefully, continuing to embroider.

"Certainly not," said Miss Swithin, as one seeing a sinister implication in the question.

"What a pity! No evil influence from it if you're born in May, so they say, and although one doesn't believe all these tales, it's just as well to be on the safe side. I," finished Tony with an insinuating smile, *"was* born in May . . . the Medici month, you know."

"Oh, really?" Miss Swithin had never heard of the Medici month (neither had Tony for the matter of that) but she was now quite cheerful again and drew on her glove with decision. The mention of May had been fatal, for she had remembered her niece Una's forthcoming birthday. And what more handsome and generous gift than a genuine medieval ring? She decided to suppress any mention of the Medici as not quite suitable.

"Next time you want anything, if I can help you you must let me know," she said with an affable nod. "I am at the Cosmopolis. *Good* afternoon."

She was gone with the air of a personage whose identity would be common knowledge, and Tony looked after her, mournful and raging.

"Damn Mrs. Polhampton!" he said.

ii

"I'm no good, old thing," he wrote despondently to his sister that night. "Since I've seen the real stuff, Michelangelo, Donatello and a few more, but especially Mike, I see I shall never come within a thousand miles of them, and the sooner I come home and get a job the better, though God knows who's to give me one unless it's a tombstone merchant. What is the use of a footling little talent like mine?

"I spent the morning in the Medici chapel, studying Lorenzo the Magnificent. The old scoundrel sits up there with his chin on his fist, planning intrigues and villainy on the grand scale and I don't wonder the young bucks followed him. I'd have done it myself. The fellow's alive in stone and you'd swear he'd be getting up and coming down for a chat in half a minute. Pity he doesn't. The world could do with a few chaps as thorough as Lorenzo nowadays, and besides, look what he did for art.

"I've been kicking myself all the afternoon for losing a rather quaint and decent little souvenir of him, all through the damnable necessity of counting the cost. It was an intaglio ring of white onyx, not genuine, of course—you couldn't hope to find a Medici ring knocking about Florence in these days, but the stone had been carved by a bit of a genius and he'd got the pose of the head. You couldn't mistake it. I was offered it for three pounds odd yesterday, but couldn't make up my mind whether I ought to spend the money. Hobnobbing with Lorenzo this morning cleared the air a bit. 'After all,' he said, egging me on, 'you can always go home and rob a few banks with me to aid you,' and so on and so on. Fact was, Kit, I'd grown superstitious about the ring. When I slipped it on, though I could never actually wear it, or any other such bauble, the onyx grew fiery like an opal. I believe they do on some people—matter of health, no doubt, but of course it's supposed to be lucky and I could do with a pack of luck just now. So I decided to blow the expense, and sprinted off to buy it after lunch. I'd actually got my fist on it, too, when a prancing old catamaran by Mayfair out of Bond Street literally snatched it, whisked out her money and the thing was done. I could have strangled her and I did throw out a few hints about dear old Lorenzo's sticky past, but you couldn't move her. She's that kind, peak-nosed and bent on doing the clever thing, and I only succeeded in making her think she'd got a medieval treasure. Don't know who the woman was, not an English resident . . . she hadn't the flavor, nor yet the usual traveling Briton. I call her Mrs. Polhampton because she looks like that, and I'm modeling her *en pounce,* my swan song, before coming home to begin a career of crime, tombstone variety.

"Tony."

iii

Tony's letter and the ring for Una actually traveled to England by the same post. It was weeks before the actual date of the birthday, but Miss Swithin felt it would be better to get rid of her purchase at once, not that she was in the least superstitious about it, in spite of the informative young man, but, as she wrote to Una's father:

"One can only get rare things like this by chance, and I don't care to keep anything so valuable at the hotel. Some mighty queer things happen in Florence, so it seems better and safer to let the child have it at once. The ring is said to bring particular good fortune to anyone born in May, and although one wouldn't have her believe such nonsense, still it did seem as though I were meant to buy it for her, coming upon it as I did, when her birthday was so much in my mind."

By the time she had finished her letter, Miss Swithin was not only persuaded that the ring was of great value, but that she had been inspired to buy it, and in this satisfactory state of mind she sealed and registered it and sent it off.

Surely Una's parents would be impressed by such a gift, she thought. In common with the rest of the family, she had felt it necessary but very difficult to impress them, ever since her brother Jeremy's spectacular marriage to the beautiful Lady Anne Challice.

CHAPTER II

i

THE title was actually of little importance, for Anne's father had been a commoner raised to the peerage for political services.

The first Challice about whom anything was known made a fortune out of jam in the fifties and, seeking ease rather than aggrandizement, bought himself Wenlock, an estate in Hertfordshire, presently marrying a lady of impoverished family who were only too glad to hand her over to him willy-nilly. Though self-made, he was an unpretentious fellow. He was kind to his delicate, nervous little wife, did not expect her to bear him twelve children after the fashion of the time, made a hobby of pedigree dogs, and eventually bequeathed Gilbert, his only child, Wenlock and twenty thousand pounds.

By the time her son was conceived, poor little Mrs. Challice had come to adore her jam-maker, but she would have been amazed to know that by so doing she was helping to produce a future peer of the Realm. Gilbert developed graces unshared by either of his parents, like so many children born of love. As a promising young Liberal, he married in the early nineties the daughter of his political chief, a beautiful girl who survived only three years, leaving him with one daughter Anne.

Anne Challice was a golden child. She had her mother's looks and her father's graces, added to which the old jam-maker's sense of proportion still magically survived in her. As a nobody her photograph would have been much in demand as representing a perfect type of English beauty. With her father's mounting political eminence, little Anne, Miss Anne Challice, and finally Lady Anne became the darling of the illustrated papers and the great sentimental British public all over the world.

She and her father were firm friends, but he never told her that he allowed them to push him out of the way into the peerage on her account. The young century was suffering from growing pains and change was in the air. Victorianism was being swept away; there was talk of national health insurance; women were demanding votes, with stones and hammers to enforce the argument; the tango had come in and the square dances had gone out; the Irish question was once more raising its tempestuous head. Gilbert Challice at fifty felt old and ill, while Anne grew lovelier every day. His views were changing and he could not compromise; politically he was done. He took the peerage they offered him with an obscure feeling that it would be a protection to the one being for whom he cared.

Anne, used to the world to play with, was charmed. She tried on his robes and told him he was a wonder to make her a lady at last, and he never realized that she would have been equally pleased if he had refused the honor. Such a gesture would have delighted her grandfather in her.

It was her father's sudden death that threw her into Jeremy Swithin's arms, for there seemed something solid about Jeremy that set him apart from the host of young men with whom she had flirted gayly through an enchanting first season, and most of whom she had known for years.

Jeremy had swum into her ken more or less by accident and was clearly dazzled at being there. He was shy and inarticulate before her at all times, and more than ever in the face of her loss, and this was grateful to the girl. . . . She had always been a self-contained creature.

Swithin at this time was a promising junior at the Bar, but most of Anne's circle knew little else of him, except that he was presentable and had played cricket for his university. His family was prosperous enough, but unimportant. Swithins had been merchant captains, civil servants, and for several generations solicitors of good standing, with solid houses in the suburbs and sons at St. Paul's. Jeremy took a scholarship from his school to Oxford, where he made useful friends without seeking them, and finally came down with a Law prize to eat his dinners in the Inner Temple. His own record and his father's influence eventually got him his chance with Joseph Drew, K.C., and it was at the Drews' house that he met Lady Anne Challice.

Their engagement, three months after her father's death, was a thunderbolt to Mr. Drew, who thereafter looked upon his junior with increased respect. This young man would go far. He was evidently out for the main chance. Mrs. Drew, however, disagreed with this verdict and said so. Having no family of her own to distract her, she had an insatiable sympathy for all young people, who never knew it but called her "a fright," "a scream," or "priceless" as the catch-words of one generation succeeded another. "The boy's lost his head and his heart and small blame to him," said Mrs. Drew, and she was right.

Jeremy was madly in love and almost equally appalled at his own presumption. Anne's money was actually a reproach to him, for how could he hope to provide for this dazzling creature as she had a right to expect? At last he took his difficulty to the family. (In 1910 the Family as a definite entity had not ceased to exist.) The Swithins, male and female, sat in council and agreed with Jeremy. Such a definite increase in Swithin importance must be paid for. Certain sacrifices were made, Jeremy was given a legacy in advance by his father, who also bought for the young couple a house in Palace Square, which was within a stone's throw of Kensington Gardens.

From that moment the Swithins felt it incumbent on them to live up to Jeremy and his Lady Anne. Anne, who of all things was no snob, was at first amused and presently bored by them, for they were so dull, poor dears, and to her dullness was the unforgivable sin. Jeremy's people became in time a source of constant friction between them.

But in the first year or two he was too happy to care what she thought about his family or anyone else. He adored her and Anne loved and mocked

him, and her friends accepted him into their world
as a matter of course. Then Una came.

Jeremy had wanted a child, but for weeks before
the event he was in terror, and later when for a
time Anne was seriously ill and the doctors told him
there must be no more children, he breathed a sigh
of relief. He almost hated in a shamefaced fashion
the little dark-eyed scrap of humanity so unlike
either of its parents, but Anne was delighted with
the creature and called her a changeling. Jeremy,
watching her with anguish, wondered how he should
bear it if she grew too fond of the baby and he was
shut outside.

The Swithin women came one by one in their best
clothes and gave Anne much excellent motherly advice; but she, lying in her twin bed (which they
thought so new and strange and very advanced of
her) with her golden, burnished hair bound round
her head, laughed at them and said the baby was to
be a spoiled child like its mother and have a lovely
time. She knew they would go home and talk her
over doubtfully, hoping for the best.

She grew well at last and the clouds departed. On
Jeremy's consciousness the baby Una for the first
few years naturally obtruded very little.

ii

Then War came; Europe was split asunder, and
Jeremy joined the army that was soon to embrace
the whole young manhood of England. In those
four years of blood and slime, chaos and death, he
knew a deeper torture because he was parted from

Anne. She might be ill, dying, she might be sad. She might cease to love him, for who was he to hold her? She might love some other fellow. His brief leaves were filled with the agony of the parting to come. He was never wounded, though twice he was ill, and he achieved no glory, but in the third year of the War, some real or fancied aptitude for routine got him sent to divisional headquarters. Things were easier here, but that did not bring him peace of mind. Newspapers would come and there she was suddenly looking out at him.

> "Lovely Lady Anne Swithin, who drives a
> motor ambulance from the hospital trains
> in London three nights a week."

or

> "Lady Anne Swithin and her little daughter,
> Una, entertaining convalescent Tommies at
> Wenlock, her ancestral home."

The last phrase would have amused Anne, but Jeremy saw nothing funny in it. To him she would always remain part of the glitter such a term conveys to the less fortunate world, though it had no bearing on his love for her.

Anne had let Wenlock a year or two after her marriage, but she lost her tenants during the War and for a time did open the old place up for the benefit of the soldiers, until the drain on her resources became too great. Jeremy, so jealously anxious to pay for everything, never guessed how Anne had from the first lavished her own income on their home, but she had her grandfather's money sense and by the time he was demobilized Wenlock was let again and she felt financially stronger to meet the costly years ahead.

The War was over, he came home, they were together again. Anne's golden hair was short now, her frocks shorter and simpler than of old, but the glow of her beauty remained. Lovelier than ever, Jeremy thought her, and for a moment, with his arms about her, breathing her sweetness, his tired face pressed against the soft cool texture of her cheek, he felt the strain of the four past years drop from him and he was young again.

"You were a darling not to go and get killed," said Anne. "Don't let's recognize the next war, shall we?"

Then she had missed him. He was in heaven.

But the door was pushed open cautiously and Una came in, gazing with polite astonishment at her father and mother.

At seven she had developed at least one Challice quality. She had her mother's beauty of limb, though she was unlike her in everything else. She was a tall child, her straight dark hair cut like that of a medieval page, her great dark eyes looking out solemnly from the pale oval of her face.

"Here's your changeling daughter," said Anne. "Come and speak to Jeremy. I think she'd better call you Jeremy and me Anne. Would you like to, sprite?"

"No," said Una.

They laughed, but she didn't care for their laughter. She felt valiant and proud, filled with a sense of exaltation which was to accompany this incident in her mind for years. Everybody called her mother "Anne" and what was the good of that? She wasn't going to. She, who had never refused her mother anything, had done it now—an act at once desperate and magnificent.

Anne of course flirted with her daughter, as with everyone else, unconsciously however. There was no need to challenge Una's adoration, for it was plain enough. When her mother talked nonsense to her or sense that was more than nonsense to the child, she would sit and gaze at her with serious delight, watching her laughter, her bright hair, her changing face. Una had awakened early to a sense of beauty, and for years Anne's comings and goings in the house were to govern all her secret pleasures and affairs. She was not a demonstrative child and she was unobtrusive. She was quite happy watching Anne through the banisters, from behind a curtain or from the nursery window.

Anne, her arm tucked in Jeremy's, was laughing down at her ridiculous daughter so firmly refusing to call her "Anne" and suddenly a smile blazed back, lighting up the odd little face. Jeremy's heart turned over. These two were friends. They shared together something in which he had no part. He was shut out. The old torturing jealousy of the child rushed back upon him, and as though fighting it off instinctively, he exclaimed:

"Come and talk to me, Una."

He lifted her to his knee and she sat there politely but without effusion. He tried to amuse her but he felt awkward and absurd and didn't in the least know what to say, for how could he hope to gain her attention with her eyes fixed upon Anne? He wanted to be looking at Anne too, he wanted her to himself. For months, for years, he had been dreaming of this moment, of the heavenly quiet and peace of his home, but now he said restlessly, as thousands of other home-coming men were saying for reasons equally nebulous:

"Let's go out somewhere."

That phrase was to be the index to a whole social era.

Anne was quite willing to go out, though the perfect little dinner she had planned for him must be wasted thereby. She did not even tell him of it, nor of the fight she had had with the Swithin women not to turn his home-coming into a dreadful family reunion.

"We'll dine somewhere jolly and then dance, shall we?" she suggested.

Yes, they would dance.

"But not too jolly," amended Jeremy wistfully. "I don't want anybody but you."

So Una was sent back to the nursery and they ran upstairs eagerly together. Jeremy felt happy now like a boy. Getting into his evening suit again was an adventure in itself, with the dressing-room door open and Anne a distracting figure in her silken slip moving busily among her powder pots. Jeremy sniffed the familiar scent of them blissfully, and the dreadful years behind him became a fantastic dream.

iii

Anne, golden from head to heel, in a shining tissue frock, bought specially for Jeremy, stopped him on the landing in dismay.

"You've left your scarf and it's a new one I bought you. What a blind creature! Besides, it's cold, darling. You really must go back for it."

She had bought him a scarf and he hadn't even seen it. He would have been so hurt if she had overlooked any gift of his that he wanted to kick himself, and he rushed off and found the scarf, returning with it in his hand, eager to tell her it was the most beautiful scarf in the world—any extravagant nonsense, to make it up to her.

She had gone slowly on downstairs and was waiting for him halfway, humming a gay tune and looking back. In his hurry Jeremy stumbled against the long curtain that hung before the landing window, and felt something move there under his knees. He stopped short in bewilderment.

"Good God, what's that?"

A small dark head came out. His daughter gave him a fleeting glance, then, the curtains tucked under her little chin, returned to her game of watching the golden figure on the stairs.

Jeremy ran on after his wife with a new feeling of discomfort. It seemed to him that there had been actual triumph in the child's glance, but he was giving her credit for an intelligence outside the limited experience of seven years. Anne on these occasions was merely a composite of all her nursery heroines, going forth to incredible adventures. Jeremy was no more important than the footman who would presently open for her the dazzling doors of the golden coach.

"Una's up there behind the curtains. Oughtn't she to be in the nursery or somewhere?" he asked Anne.

He knew he should have sent the child upstairs, but he was shy of playing the parent suddenly.

"She'll be all right," said Anne. "It's bedtime and they always love scuttling about, but nurse is very reliable."

The car was waiting and he got in beside her, put his arm round her like a young lover and in the blessed darkness held her close.

"You're mine," he said. "All mine."

Una was forgotten.

iv

To Jeremy it was like a honeymoon evening. Anne was so lovely and gay and she was all his. She had eyes for no one else, though admiring glances followed her as usual. He forgot that this had been happening all her life and so could have little significance for her. He was filled with the pride of a conqueror. He was a lucky devil.

They danced; they had always danced well together; and the realities he had left behind became unreal and this world and this moment the only things that mattered. There were cabaret items between dances and even the mildest of these delighted him tonight. He felt tireless and wanted the evening to go on forever. A girl who had been singing produced a basket of favors and flung them broadcast among the audience. One fell into Anne's lap—an absurd black cat with up-standing tail and staring yellow eyes.

"It's for luck," exclaimed Jeremy delighted, "our luck."

Anne laughed, set the beast up on the table and twirled its whiskers.

"It will do for the changeling," she said.

Una was back between them and Jeremy on a sudden felt tired.

If he had seen the presentation of the cat next day he would have been easier in his mind, for Anne's gifts were always casually bestowed—there was no ritual about it—and their charm to Una was that of any occasion that brought her mother into view.

But Jeremy, seeing old Drew, who welcomed and even made much of him, and facing the prospect of presently getting back to work—a strange, impossible, yet necessary prospect—had the wretched cat in his mind all day. He was appalled at his jealousy of the child; he knew it to be contemptible, and at length going home, he plunged into a toy shop and bought her the largest teddy bear he could find. He would not have it sent but took it with him in the taxi, arriving at his own door with his burden and feeling a fool.

"Aren't you absurd," said Anne, "coming home with a bear under your arm?" But she sent him off to the nursery to deliver the gift in person and he was grateful for that.

"There now, what a lucky little girl to have such a kind father," exclaimed nurse. "You must thank him nicely for his beautiful present, Miss Una."

Nurse was showing off to the master, of course, for Una at seven was capable of the minor courtesies without any such prompting.

"Thank you, father," said Una, clasping the animal round the middle.

"Not many little girls have such a big bear as that," proceeded nurse, the Greek chorus, "and most little girls would give their daddies a big kiss, if you ask me."

(Dam' the woman. Why couldn't she hold her tongue?)

Jeremy put his arm round his daughter and lifted her off her feet. Una looked surprised though pleased about it, but the bear slipped from her arms to the floor so that she had to be put down to rescue him. This seemed such a pity that she sat him in a chair, kindly however, lest his feelings should be hurt.

"Why, he quite fills the chair. Did you ever?" said nurse admiringly.

Jeremy punched the bear in the stomach in search of a squeak that was not there, but Una's look of astonishment told him this had been a mistake. Rather helplessly he held out a hand to her.

"Come and tell me about all the other presents you've had today," he invited.

"I haven't had any other presents today," said Una.

"Oh, yes, Miss Una. You're forgetting the lovely

pussy her ladyship gave you only this morning. Such a tail it had, too."

Una had not forgotten, but it had never occurred to her to regard this as a present. It wasn't, she was sure. Presents came from aunts and grandmothers and people and had to be thanked for, an embarrassing business. Still it was no good arguing with nurse, so she smiled confidentially at her father, and explained:

"It was just a little cat."

Jeremy bent down suddenly and kissed her.

Just a little cat! Wasn't that a tribute to his much more magnificent present? He was almost a stranger to his daughter—this cursed war—he had four years to make up and he must buy the little soul heaps of presents.

A new era was opening for Una also.

CHAPTER III

i

THAT era was more than eleven years old on the morning when Una Swithin, her dog Tim at her heels, ran down to breakfast, unaware of the little parcel from Florence which had come for her by the post.

She would have gone more soberly had she known about it, and the spring day which was making her heart and her step light and calling her out, would have lost some of its glory, for she had developed in these years something of a present-complex. She hated the sight of one.

Una had long ago ceased to watch her mother from behind the window curtains. Even before she was of an age to be self-conscious about it, she had discovered that in her father's presence it was inadvisable, and to do it in his absence would have seemed disloyal. Not that she ever spoke of this. It wasn't wise, she had found, to speak of anything much to anybody. This was one of the odd, secret responsibilities she cherished towards these two who up till now had made her world.

If Anne had ceased to be a nursery heroine to her daughter, and Una had learned to guard her smiles, Anne had suffered little in the change. Secretly, Una thought her entrancing, a privileged, unchallenged being who could be as absurd as she chose, and she wished her father could see it like this. She was dreadfully sorry for her father, whose jealousy she had sensed long ago, while misinterpreting its cause. Carefully, she was always trying to hide from him the fact that he was the odd man out.

Of these sentiments, however, Jeremy and Anne suspected nothing. Una had never ceased to be an entertainment to Anne, who, looking not a day over thirty, could well afford a grown-up daughter. It amused her to take out this tall, thin, laconic child with her cropped dark head and solemn eyes, though she did not overdo it, as she knew perfectly well Jeremy thought she did. Una, who had come out last year, had her own small car and her own friends, and if these were the children or young brothers and sisters of her mother's friends, it was not surprising, the Swithin cousins being what they were.

Jeremy was considered an almost fanatically affectionate father, and even Anne laughed at him because he seemed unable to bear the girl out of his sight. Jeremy, conscious of the truth and untruth of this, was maddened by her laughter. Irritability had grown upon him year by year; he was increasingly difficult to live with and miserably knew it. He was too much aware of Anne and himself to wonder what Una thought of it all, but he still guiltily bought her presents at all times and seasons, though he knew Anne could afford to buy her more and probably did while he knew nothing about it.

In one such preposterous mood of reaction

against himself, he had refused point blank to let
the child be sent to school. This sacrificial folly
seemed merely selfishness to Anne, who gave in only
after a long and bitter struggle. It was their first
serious quarrel and the subject was never reopened.
Anne would have thought it useless and Jeremy
could not go back. He had set his own snare.

ii

The dining-room was flooded with sunshine. In
the plane trees outside the window the sparrows
were busily singing in the April morning, and there
were daffodils on the breakfast table. Una coming
in, in her yellow sweater and short brown skirt,
looked one with the young season, and Anne thought
with pleasure :

"She's quite a beauty, the funny darling."

Her parents were both there before her, unconscious of how, morning by morning, Una contrived
that this should be so. Very carefully, as usual, she
measured out her greeting, an exact share of smile
to each of them, though it was hard to avoid the
infectious little twinkle in her mother's eye. Anne
was full of the fun of being alive on such a lovely
day, and it would have been jolly to laugh with her,
but father was so touchy in the morning and ten
to one he would think they were laughing at him.

"There's a parcel for you, Una," said Anne.

"Oh !"

For a second her frightened little old great-grand-
mother at Wenlock looked out of the girl's eyes.

"It's a present from your Aunt Marion," added

Jeremy, quickly and jealously. "Something she bought for you in Florence."

"I wonder why," said Una in a regretful voice. She might have known it was a present and she didn't want it, whatever it was. Christmas and birthdays were bad enough, without having things dropping out of the skies like this.

"It's for your birthday in advance," said Jeremy. "I've had a letter—where is it now?"

He proceeded to read Miss Swithin's letter and Una, pushing the obnoxious little parcel aside with relief, began her breakfast. Later on, however, he cut the string for her and undid the wrapping. Una, seeing there was no help for it any longer, opened the box and took out the onyx ring. She tried it on, but it was too large for any but her first finger, so she concealed the fact hastily and held it up for her father and mother to see.

"Rather quaint," said Anne. "I wonder if it is really as valuable as all that."

"There's no reason for Marion to lie about it that I know of," flared Jeremy at once.

Anne, knowing her sister-in-law better than that, smiled inwardly, but men were all idiots at breakfast, she thought, so added with the best of intentions:

"Then perhaps you should put it in the bank."

"Nonsense! Una will wear the ring. I'm not going to have Marion's feelings hurt, and you'll write her a nice little letter of thanks, won't you, Una?"

(Yes, of course, that was another thing. "Dear

Aunt Marion, thank you very much for the pretty ring you sent me, which I like very much. I hope you are enjoying Florence. . . ." Oh damn, why were letters to aunts always such imbecile things to write?)

"And tell her not to forget your party on the 17th. She is sure to be back in England by then."

"But Jeremy, it is to be a young party this time. Marion would be bored to tears," expostulated Anne.

"Why should she be bored? Marion is never bored, and besides, she will expect to be asked. She always has been in the past, so why not now?" Jeremy was up in arms in a moment.

"Yes, I know, but Una is not a child any longer and it is absurd that her birthday should be made the occasion for a dreadful family reunion."

"A—*what?*"

One look at her father's face sent Una flying to the rescue.

"*Must* I have a party?" she inquired wistfully.

"Of course you must, you heathen child. It's a social obligation. You've been to so many things and hospitality must be returned."

"Besides, the newspapers will be getting restless," said Jeremy bitterly. "Your mother's photograph has not appeared anywhere for at least a week."

"Really?" Anne was laughing at him and trying to make him laugh, but of course he would never see it. "I shall have to look into this. I must advertise the family, mustn't I?"

"Do I ever court advertisement through my

wife?" thundered Jeremy, throwing down his nap-
kin.

"Darling, you couldn't court anything—even me."
Anne got up, kissed him lightly on the head in passing, and went gayly to the door. "Come along, Una,
leave him to growl in peace," she said.

"Let the child alone. Why, good lord, I never see
her for a moment and you have her day in and day
out," exclaimed Jeremy.

Una, who had half risen, dropped back into her
chair with shaking knees. She wished they wouldn't.
She couldn't help being sorry for her father, though
she knew he was absurd, but now she felt a traitor
to her mother sitting here.

At last she rose cautiously, as the door opened
and a maid came in.

"Tim's waiting for his walk," she said, and fled
with her dog, so that neither could feel aggrieved.

iii

Between the buses racing to town ran Una and
Tim with the wind in their faces. Kensington Gardens received them, but not the more gardeny-part.
They liked better the place where the old trees
marched through the grass sedately, real, country
trees, for this had been country when they were
young. Today they were rustling their new green
dresses and Tim, entranced by the moving shadows
on the grass, ran them to earth triumphantly.

"Rabbits, Tim. Catch 'em, boy," encouraged Una,
but in spite of the stillness and the lovely scents of
the young world, she had to admit to Tim it was a

hollow sham this morning. This wasn't really the
country. The scene at breakfast and the forthcoming
party lay heavy on her heart.

A young party would have been rather jolly, even
if Mab and Herbert Swithin had to be invited, and
they were a pair of whited sepulchers if you liked.
Her mother was quite right, thought Una secretly,
these family reunions were dreadful, because it was
always the Swithin family. There were no Challices
left, and what relatives her mother had, through her
own mother, were casual, satisfactory people, who
said to you when you met, "I say, aren't we ump-
teenth cousins or something? Let's go and hunt up
a cocktail." And if you said you hated cocktails, they
didn't mind at all, but said: "What about a gallon
of ices, then?" The Swithins would be shocked if
you admitted a liking for cocktails, and disbelieving
if you denied it. They wouldn't actually say so, perhaps, but they had a way of looking at each other
triumphantly, as though they had always known.

A wave of repulsion suddenly enveloped the girl
as this look, which she had seen so often down the
years, took on for the first time a concrete meaning.
They hated her mother, she was sure, and how could
they dare, and why didn't her father understand
it? Grandmother seemed to think it absolutely improper that the mother of a grown-up daughter
should be still lovely and full of fun, and Aunt
Herbert and her whited sepulchers were always
hinting about money, and Aunt Fanny was convinced her sister-in-law knew dukes and duchesses
and was offended because she was not asked to meet

them. Aunt Marion, when she came back to England, it is true, went to the other extreme and gushed effusively about "dear Anne," but Una, to whom endearments were private things, except those uttered in derision, viewed this devotion with distrust, as youth must view the easy phrases of middle age. Aunt Marion, moreover, with her habit of dropping, ostentatiously forgetful, into French, German, or any language but her own, was a source of embarrassment to her niece, who was not of an age to be amused by the pose and in its presence suffered agonies of shame for the poseuse.

Una, thinking of this habit now, sat down on the grass against one of the friendly trees and sighed. It would have been splendid, she thought, to uphold her mother about the family reunion, to put her foot down and demand, as her right, an ordinary party such as other people had, but of course she couldn't hurt her father's feelings like that. If they left it to her, she would have to pretend she wanted the family.

"Don't let them ask me," said Una in a panic. "I wish the beastly birthday was over. Let it be over."

But the vague powers she addressed were not going to oblige her like that, she knew. She could not even hope to be ill for the event, for she was almost disgracefully healthy and never caught cold. Unless she went to bed and said she was ill and refused to get up! She didn't see how they were going to prove she wasn't ill, if it came to that; but it seemed a boring prospect and she dismissed it after a moment and whistled to her dog.

Tim came and sat before her with a benevolent air, his perfectly laundered coat ashine in the sun, his long, wise head on one side. He was a beautiful creature, but to Una he was something more than that. Although she did not know it, another Challice quality was coming out in her. The old jam-maker at Wenlock had bequeathed her his instinct for dogs, and Una, bringing home a disreputable stray, and fighting tooth and nail to keep him, had been certain of his quality from the first. To the odd, shy girl, torn by her conflicting loyalties, Tim seemed sometimes the one stable thing in an unstable world.

"I wish we could go away to the country and have a dog farm, don't you, Tim?" said Una, wistfully.

It was an old cry, an old dream, that misty stronghold to which her thoughts retreated in times of stress, and all the sweeter perhaps, like most castles in Spain, because so unlikely ever to become concrete. Tim alone was in her confidence about it, and now, answering the manner rather than the matter of her exclamation, moved nearer to give her comfort. A smile broke over her face and she put her arm around him, seeing as she did so the ring upon her finger glowing faintly as though the old dead stone had awakened to life upon her hand.

"Rum! I'm sure it was white before," she said in a tone of surprise, and for a second a faint thrill passed through her; but Aunt Marion was a poor instrument for magic and her promises of good luck were empty words. Hadn't her gift brought trouble and dismay already?

Una took off the ring and showed it to her dog.

"Do you believe it's lucky, Tim?" she asked him in a scornful voice.

Tim, however, yawned, rolled over, and buried his nose in her frock. His views on onyx rings might be nebulous, but he had learned infinite wisdom in chasing the clouds from the face he loved, and it was a laughing child who called him a lazy rascal and presently raced with him over the grass.

CHAPTER IV

i

MRS. POLHAMPTON wouldn't pounce.
Tony looked at the little clay figure of his
swan-song in despair, for the comedy of his subject, though clear as crystal in his mind, had eluded
him in execution, and wasn't this merely another
depressing proof of his incapacity? Instead of Mrs.
Polhampton he had produced the personage.

"Yes, I know," he nodded gloomily to the picture of Lorenzo nailed to the studio wall, "you've
flung fellows into the Arno for less than this, and
quite right too, old cock."

He took up the figure and carried it to the window in a threatening manner, then of a sudden held
his hand, and looked at it instead. Miss Swithin in
miniature returned his glance, affability in every line
of her.

"I bet she'd be delighted with you," he thought.
"That's the kind of thing that would happen."

There might be money in this too—sculptured
portraits of nobodies-in-particular, family groups in
bronze or marble, guaranteed fadeless and inde-
structible.

Tony, just in the mood to be enchanted by the
horrible idea, saw himself rising to heights of afflu-
ence and success, but the creator in him defeated the

clown and pulled him down to earth again, for the curse was on him. Success after all is a prisoner for life in the soul of the artist who may never see her face and live. And to do a thing with ardor and delight and find it acclaimed by thousands of fools incapable of either, would always confirm Tony Corcoran's worst suspicion. It must be pretty bad.

His stay in Italy was drawing to a close, for funds were low, and the fellow sculptor who had been glad in an emergency to let him the studio at a nominal rent, was on his way back from England at the moment. Faced with the problem of his already inflated luggage, he saw that Mrs. Polhampton was destined for destruction, unless he could do a deal with the original for the onyx ring.

The very absurdity of this inspiration rather pleased him, for, the serious work of past months being set aside, and his departure from Florence imminent, he was at the mercy of any mood—a dissatisfied, unsettled creature. And more than ever he wanted the ring. Because it had turned pink on his hand? Certainly not. As a link with Florence and Lorenzo the Magnificent? Ridiculous. Too much of the present-from-Eastbourne in that idea. Actually he now wanted the ring because Mrs. Polhampton had snatched it from him and she had snatched it because he wanted it, two idle, childish reasons, but human and therefore formidable.

"Yes, you're a sweet thing," he said scornfully to the little statue. "I wonder if she'd pounce on you."

Vanity and cupidity would probably run neck and neck in a woman of her type, he thought, and it

would be interesting to see which would win in the
end. Vanity, of course. She would want this pretty
image of herself, and in order to possess it, she
would soon be persuaded to sell him the ring.

"I'll try it," said Tony, wrapping up Mrs. Polhampton and seizing his hat. He did not know the
lady's name but he knew her hotel. Hadn't he been
invited to call upon her? And he saw himself walking through the gilded portals of the Cosmopolis—
or was it over them you walked?—displaying a
little image to the concierge and demanding to see
the original. Being a foreigner on the eve of departure had its uses. You could be as bizarre as you
chose. Besides, "Allah created the English mad."
The concierge, or whatever they called the fellow,
would know the sentiment even if he didn't know his
Kipling.

ii

Tony swaggered forth on his adventure, which
was beginning to amuse him mightily. Crossing the
Ponte Vecchio he nodded to the bust of Cellini as
one swashbuckler to another. Benvenuto had had all
the luck, he thought, living at a time when art was
cherished and couldn't be reproduced at two a
penny, but what ironic hand had set him up here
among the merchants of tawdry filigree and gems—
he who had once worked jeweled magic for popes
and kings? A simple fellow, Benvenuto, going forth
to kill a few enemies before breakfast, then settling
down to fashion a chalice or scepter that centuries
would not surpass, falling from favor to a dungeon
in the Castel'Angelo, and presently pitching the in-

vader off the Castel ramparts into the Tiber—a very handy chap to have about.

Accompanied by the shades of Benvenuto and the Magnificent, Tony felt that his guileful errand couldn't fail. The Cosmopolis was less gilded than he had expected. Tourist agencies listed it as a first class hotel in order to earn a few more guineas from those who fondly hoped to be exclusive even on a tour. At such a place Miss Swithin, despising tours, could afford the best suite and receive the flattering attention reserved for the most important guests.

A tour was awaiting the moment of departure, the vestibule filled with clamor and luggage, but he made his way to the desk at last, said he had been asked to call by a lady whose name he had forgotten, and unwrapped the little image.

"*Si, si*, the lady Swithin," cried the clerk, seizing upon the new English word with relish, "but it ees good, *buono, molto buono*. You have made him, Signore? You are *scultore?*"

"Yes, but I say, send up and ask if she will see me, will you?" said Tony, embarrassed. "Corcoran's the name."

"Hear that?" said a near-by tourist, nudging another, as Tony was led off. " 'Lady Swithin,' the fellow said. It must be Mrs. Herbert Swithin's swell relation. Fancy her and us staying at the same hotel. I wish I'd known, Perce. I wish we weren't going, now."

"Well, we are," said Perce, unsympathetically, "and quite time too. These picture palaces give me the hump."

"Oh, Perce, listen to you—picture palaces. My husband says he's tired of picture palaces, Mr. Jordan."

"Ha, ha! Very good," said Mr. Jordan.

"Perce, I'm going to ask the fellow. . . . Is it Lady Anne Swithin staying here?"

This was beyond the clerk, so he said, *"Si, si, signora,"* hoping for the best. "You have seen the statue of the young *scultore?* She have inspire him. Oh, very romantic!"

"Did you ever," exclaimed Mrs. Perce, nudging anew.

The hotel bus was at the door now and they had to go, but she was consoled for departure by the thought of the letter she would be able to write this evening to Mrs. Herbert Swithin, who was a bit inclined to swank about her titled relative, Mrs. Perce often said.

"We stayed at the Cosmopolis in Florence, quite the best place," she would say, "and what do you think, dear? your sister-in-law, Lady Anne, was staying there too, though we didn't see a lot of her, being out all the time, and you know Perce, he's not one for making new friends. There was a little romance going on, or so I heard. You ask her about a good-looking fellow named Corkran, who did a statue of her, quite inspired him, she did, if you're to believe all you hear. What do you think of Perce's latest? He says he's tired of all these picture palaces, not the movie kind he doesn't mean. They keep real palaces in Italy to hang their pictures in. Perce is quite the wit of the party, and laugh—"

Mrs. Perce, composing her letter to put a some-what arrogant neighbor in her place, felt that there was a lot to be said for travel after all. It broadened your mind something wonderful, travel did, and look at the people you met—well, not actually met, but as good as. Mrs. Perce was determined to be quite honest about it, but now she did seem to remember someone who might have been the much photographed Lady Anne among the guests at the hotel. And besides, didn't the fellow at the desk say she was there? No getting away from that.

iii

So she was Lady Swithin, was she?

Tony, waiting in a little salon, was not surprised to hear it, though the name meant nothing to him. She had married off some poor old Knight, he supposed. She would.

However, the clerk had been encouraging with his *"molto buono,"* and he hoped for another Gilbertian insult in the same strain from the lady, if she condescended to come down.

She did. Miss Swithin was charmed at the prospect of a visitor, and though she could not remember anyone called Corcoran, there was nothing unusual in that. She met so many people in her wanderings, and so seldom troubled about their names. Tony's face at least was vaguely familiar to her, and she bore down upon him with her most gracious air.

"Now this is charming of you, to look me up," she said. "Do sit down and tell me all you have been doing since I saw you last."

Tony, though surprised at the warmth of her

reception, had the presence of mind to seize the opening she gave him.

"I have done one little thing," he admitted modestly. "I hope you won't think it frightful impertinence, Lady Swithin."

It is possible she might have denied the title, had not her visitor at this moment unwrapped the little statue, before which, of course, all such irrelevant matters were swept away. In a moment she had pounced upon it.

"But how wonderful . . . it's me . . . I . . . myself. And you did this? My dear Mr. Corcoran, you're a genius, and what can I say to thank you? You did this for me. Why, it's quite perfect."

Tony's swashbuckling instincts were not equal to the situation and he felt himself floundering helplessly. Impossible to tell her to her face it wasn't exactly a gift when she put it like that.

"Oh, it's nothing," he protested, "only a plaster cast you know. Of course I'm delighted if it pleases you."

"But it's perfectly charming and so unique. What can I do to show you my appreciation? One moment—you must stay and have tea with me."

"No—please no," exclaimed Tony. He was hanged if she was going to get out of it with a cup of tea. "As a matter of fact, I never take it," he said.

"Really? Still, I know what you mean. Tea abroad does seem rather provincial, doesn't it? Then you must certainly dine with me one evening instead."

Miss Swithin sighed inwardly at her own recklessness, for was it thirty or fifty lire they charged for dinner? And there would have to be wine on top of that. But still, a statue and such a compliment! One must do something.

"You're very kind," said Tony, rallying his forces, "but though I am delighted you like the little image, it was something else I really called about. You told me I might, if you remember. I wondered whether I could persuade you, after all, to part with the little onyx ring you bought at Sponelli's the other day—at a fair figure, of course."

"Ring?" echoed Miss Swithin. "Oh, yes, I remember now. But what a pity, I sent it away the same evening or you could have had it with pleasure. I am sorry."

Tony felt suddenly flat and his precious adventure became ridiculous. What a driveling idiot he had been to come near the old catamaran! Well, she could keep her silly image and her dinner too, though she had snaffled the former in the coolest manner.

Somehow he got away, leaving Miss Swithin bewildered, it is true, but charmed beyond measure. What a mysterious young man! What a romantic episode!

It did occur to her to wonder uneasily whether he had expected her to buy the statuette, but no, he was well dressed. One couldn't have offered, and, besides, he had said it was nothing—merely a plaster cast. And he had been so shy about it and had run away. Miss Swithin felt touched, for he must have admired her enormously, and though he was a mere boy, young men did have these romantic passions for elder women. As a woman of the world one had to acknowledge that.

Half shocked and half excited, she hardly left the hotel for days, lest he should call again, but Tony, who would have enjoyed this picture of Mrs. Polhampton, had left Florence for London.

iv

"I'd have been a made man if I'd got that ring, too," he told Kit, perched on the studio table and recounting his adventures, the night of his return.

"Tony, you've worn your socks to shreds," said Kit, who was unpacking his clothes. This was less bathos than cunning, for she knew his habit of chasing rainbows and she had no belief in the pot of gold.

"You wait till I'm walking the Embankment," said Tony to this. "Wonder if they'd take me on as under-ghoul at Madame Tussaud's. I'd love to feel all the great ones of the earth were wax in my hands."

"Have you brought nothing home that is fit to wear, I should like to know?"

"Certainly not, woman. What are you for?"

Kit laughed, and sitting back on her heels caught up one of his disreputable garments to fling at him, but something heavy weighed it down and in a moment she was back with her head in the trunk. There, lying in a nest of shirts and pajamas, with all sorts of soft oddments tucked about him, she found the Singing Boy.

He was shuffling bare feet through the fallen leaves; he was singing; you could almost see the song rising through the little hollow under his throat; he was singing in solitude and therefore gayly, at the top of his voice. A breath and he would have been living beneath her eyes. Kit did not dare to come out of the trunk, and she heard Tony move off in embarrassment and start a boxing match with Whiskers the cat, presently inviting him out on the roof to view the moon.

She might have known it—all this talk of failure. He had achieved something and his mood was simply the desolation that came after. There ought to be an interim occupation for artists, Kit thought, something vital and undodgable such as the domestic jobs most women, artists or not, have to see through, come what may. Men were such rudderless creatures.

A level-headed young woman, Kit would have thought it disgustingly sentimental to be a slave to her brother's genius, but secretly she believed in it, perhaps because she had seen how it had driven him all his life, in spite of the determined hostility of his father. A volatile and rather delicate child, Tony had not been endowed with a nature that thrives on opposition. He could not be at once happy and "agin the Government," and yet in the face of harsh treatment, ridicule and parental scorn, he had held his way, as though impelled by a blind force which he could not withstand. Kit, on the other hand, had resembled her father, but he at fifty was a survival, while at twelve, she was the young woman of tomorrow, a cool little individualist with a passionate sense of fair play.

"Don't you mind, Tony. He's a pig," she had cried fiercely to the white-faced small boy, whose first creation his father had contemptuously destroyed.

Their father, admiring her spirit, had laughed at her and called her a saucy little devil, but this favoritism made Kit more than ever indignant. Thereafter she was a stern though generally silent judge of the constant issues between the man and the boy, and when at twenty-one Tony was enabled by a legacy from his mother to cut adrift, Kit coolly packed up and followed him.

"I'm sick of Richmond and I mean to go in for dress-designing," was the only explanation she gave to Tony.

In spite of his own bitterness, Tony immediately had a picture in his mind of the lonely house she had left.

"Yes, but I say . . . what about the governor?" he had protested uneasily.

"Well, what about him? I want to lead my own life."

Cheerfully and efficiently she had proceeded to lead it forthwith and Richmond saw her no more. She and Tony took the studio in Church Street together, for purposes of economy and because they were good friends, and if she kept an eye on him, she did it so unobtrusively that he never guessed. Sometimes, remembering his father, he thought Kit was a hard little nut, but he knew in his heart this quality kept them together. He could never have endured a clinging vine.

Prowling round on the leads with Whiskers, Tony crept to the window and looked cautiously in. What was she doing in there and what was she going to say? Praise of anything poor he did always filled him with glee, criticism made him argumentative, but when he did surpass himself a little, he hated it to be noticed. It never occurred to him that Kit might be aware of this.

The trunk was shut, the room empty, and the piles of clothes had been carried away. He could hear Kit in his bedroom opening doors and closing them in the definite manner so characteristic of her, and with a sigh of relief he jumped whistling back into the studio.

There, set up in the best corner, where the morning sun would find it, he saw his Singing Boy.

CHAPTER V

i

TONY CORCORAN back in England naturally dismissed the episode of Mrs. Polhampton and the ring to the background of his mind, together with the flowering panorama of Tuscany, the shades of Michelangelo, Lorenzo and Cellini, the acrid taste of Italian wines, and the odd, many-lingual talks with the fellows of his craft he had met abroad. These dreamy splendors did not belong to a workaday world.

When, therefore, he saw the ring again on the hand of a girl in Kensington Gardens, the thing seemed so incredible that the heady atmosphere of his Italian holiday rushed back upon him and he behaved in a manner more incredible still.

"I suppose you don't want to sell that ring, do you?" he inquired of the strange girl.

"I'd love to," said Una.

The incident had at least the dignity of an introduction of sorts. Tony, in an ancient blazer and flannels, with a towel round his neck, was coming up through the Gardens from his morning swim in the Serpentine when he saw the girl and her dog. Una had taken to coming out with Tim before breakfast, partly because she loved these early May mornings and partly through her secret need of being a little late for the meal. At this hour too you had the Gardens almost to yourself and could dispense with hats, which was a double inducement; so what Tony saw was not a sedate young woman of nearly nineteen, but a youngster dressed in the green of the spring trees and joyfully absorbed in a game with her dog.

The grace of the little picture immediately enchanted Tony, the perfect contour of the girl's cropped head, her slender limbs, her complete delight in the moment, as Tim dragged her waggishly along by his lead, laughing in every inch of his black and white body. Una pretended to resist his capture, did resist it, and in that fatal moment, Tim suddenly dropped the lead and was off on affairs of his own, leaving her to fall backwards on the grass.

She sat up laughing, and then became aware of Tony running to the rescue.

"Not hurt, are you?" he enquired, holding out a hand to help her to her feet.

"Not a bit," smiled Una. Shy as she might be in her personal relations, she was too much of her mother's world to be self-conscious, and she accepted his hand as naturally as a child, pulled herself up by it with a "Thanks awfully," and looked round for Tim, the deserter.

It was at this moment that Tony saw the onyx ring and asked his preposterous question.

"I suppose you don't want to sell that ring, do you?"

And Una, recalled to private problems and troubles, answered grimly: "I'd love to."

But the peace of the Gardens was suddenly shattered by the din of battle and the reason for Tim's departure became plain. An Alsatian had also come out to take the air in Kensington Gardens, a piece of insolence which Tim, who owned this territory in his own estimation, was not going to put up with for a moment. With all the valor of his breed he had rushed at the invader and was already down with his antagonist on top of him when Una rushed headlong into the fray.

She caught the Alsatian round the middle and desperately tried to pull him off, but Tony dragged her away.

"Good God, those brutes are dangerous. Leave him to me," he said, and twisting his towel, he lifted it high and gave the dog two hard clouts on the nose. The Alsatian released his victim, and still threatened by Tony, beat a hasty retreat; but Tim lay still on the grass bleeding profusely from an ugly wound in the leg.

"He's killed," cried Una in a dreadful voice, gathering her dog into her arms. The blood poured over her green frock unheeded, and Tony knelt down beside her awkwardly, and put the towel beneath the little creature, tucking the ends of it into her shaking hands. Tim moved, whined softly and at that Una came to life again. She eased her burden on to her knees, examined the wound without a tremor and began to staunch the blood with her handkerchief and then to bind the injury. Tony, helpless and sympathetic, watched her with admiration. Most girls would have shuddered away from the sight of blood, but she was as plucky a young-ster as he had seen. Most girls would have been howling, making a scene, but this affair was, he sensed, too big for tears.

"Look here, we'd better get him to a vet as quickly as possible," he said. "There's one close to my place and it will only take us two minutes. Come along."

Once more he helped her up and, a hand under her elbow, guided her to the gates and called a taxi. Una went without a word. Her face was white above the burden she carried, wrapped in Tony's bloodstained towel; her eyes were dark with trag-edy, but she still kept her self-possession and as he handed her into the cab she said mechanically again: "Thanks awfully."

It was lucky Benyon the vet had his quarters below the studio, though Tony and Kit had been doubtful enough of the benefit in the past. "We live over a menagerie," they always warned their friends, for Benyon, being an enthusiast, gave house room to many strange beasts whose music was sometimes disconcerting.

The old man was at breakfast, but at Tony's hurried knock came out, whisking Una and her patient into the surgery without wasting unneces-sary words. Tony ran upstairs for change, paid the taxi and returned to seek Kit.

"Have a load of coffee ready, old thing, will you? I've a poor little kid downstairs with an injured dog. She's with Benyon and she'll need something to steady her when she comes out."

"There's plenty of coffee," said Kit, "but Tony, your breakfast is just ready."

"Stick it in the oven," called Tony and was off before she could seize him, to wait on the stairs outside Benyon's door.

His mind was full of pictures of Una, pictures that both charmed and moved him and which he was never quite to lose. Side by side with her shape, clear cut and lovely against the trees and grass, he saw her kneeling with the bleeding dog in her arms. The very texture of youth was here, gay, gallant, tragic. The onyx ring was completely forgotten; the Singing Boy was a poor thing of the past.

It did not occur to him that his own vigil was surprising or absurd. He was intimately concerned with this enchanting child and her dog, and from time to time he went and stood with his ear against Benyon's door, listening for any sound that would tell him all was well.

"God, I hope the poor little beggar isn't done for," he thought, and turned up the stairs a step or two, for if so what help or consolation could he hope to be? And yet someone would have to take her home at least, so he returned to his post. Kit came out and tried to entice him in to breakfast, but he drove her away with such impatience that she was amazed. Most of Tony's moods were known to her and they were too many by half. If this was a new one something drastic, said Kit firmly to Whiskers, would have to be done about it.

Remembering of a sudden that Tony had mentioned a dog, Kit saw that Whiskers would have to retire from the scene, so she deposited him in her room with a saucer of milk and closed the door. At that moment she was relieved to hear voices below, and once more returned to the head of the stairs.

Benyon had brought his patient to the door, and, very much the invalid, Tim sat up in Una's arms, his injured leg encased in a bandage-trouser.

"He's all right then?" exclaimed Tony joyfully hurrying forward.

"He'll do, Mr. Corcoran, with care and good nursing," said Benyon, with a twinkle in his eye, "and he'll have both if I'm not mistaken. Now you ring me up, Missy, if you can't manage the dressing and in any case I'll look in tomorrow."

"Thank you," said Una. She was pale still, but smiling. "But where's my taxi? I didn't pay it off so it can't have gone surely?"

"That's all right. I sent it away. You can't," said Tony reprovingly, "leave taxis eating their heads off like that. It's extravagant. And now, before we call another, my sister's going to give you a cup of coffee. You've had a nasty shock."

"Oh, I couldn't let her trouble, really," protested Una. "There will be breakfast at home. Mr. Benyon rang them up to explain why I would be late."

"All the better. There can't be any hurry," argued Tony eagerly. "Come along now. It's all ready and my sister's waiting."

Una smiled suddenly.

"You saved his life and I haven't even thanked you," she said with a rush.

"Oh, I say, rats," protested Tony and at this the invalid stirred and cocked an ear and they were both convulsed with laughter.

Kit retreated to the studio, smiling to herself. Tony's new mood was explained, but being wise, she composed her countenance to welcome the "child" and her dog.

ii

Una, sitting in the studio's easiest chair and drinking Kit's coffee, felt curiously at home. Tony of course, having saved Tim's life, was a being apart—she could not think of him yet in any more ordinary character—but she liked Kit with her curly head and bright, satirical glance, and she liked this odd, bare room with its plaster casts and little statues and the sunlight streaming into it. Though she knew so many people she had always been rather solitary and she had few friends— none, indeed, of her own choosing. The choice had seemed to her disturbed young mind too dangerous and too complicated and likely to defeat the careful neutrality she had set herself to observe towards her father and mother. But these two were strangers and like Tim her own find. They could not be suspected of belonging to either camp and secretly she had determined already to make them her friends.

"Are you artists?" she asked them presently.

"Certainly not," said Tony, from his favorite perch on the table. "And yet I don't know. Kit is a creator in her way. She creates frocks—not just

coverings you know, but garments of personality—
frocks for the frivolous, the ferocious, the fretful,
confections for the coy, gowns for the godless—
that sort of thing."

"He means I design dresses," explained Kit in
her dry way.

"Exactly—for the nobs," continued Tony. "You
know those little shops a yard or two square with
a veil, a rose and a garter in the window, and
AVRIL or some such lie scrawled across it like a
duke's signature, and queues of limousines waiting
outside and strings of duchesses hanging on to the
telephone? That's the kind of place for which Kit
designs, so you see I am connected with the peerage through my sister. Nice, isn't it?"

Una smiled. She knew the place. Avril had made
her coming out dress and Anne often went there,
but she was not going to mention that.

"I know a girl in Avril's," she said.

'Really?" enquired Kit. "Not Roberta Lyne?"

"Um—Robby the Robot. Do you know Robby?"

"We went to the same school and that is how I
got in with Avril," explained Kit. "Luck, wasn't it,
because if you're in with Avril all the other people
want you."

Una remembered Robby Lyne saying one night,
"Things are horribly slack, Anne; so do be an
angel and order a dress. I'll get Kit Corcoran to
design it if you will," and Anne, who knew her
Robby, replying: "I don't believe there's any such
animal." Robby the Robot, without conscience and
without soul, as she and everybody else declared,

was quite capable of inventing a famous designer to keep her job with Avril, Una knew. They said she was mercenary, miserly even, for it was a standing joke against Robby that she would never spend a penny if she could avoid it. Una was rather sorry for her without knowing why, but now she saw wistfully that if the Corcorans were friends of Robby's they might not be so safely outside the camps as she had supposed.

"Robby is rather a scream, isn't she?" she said to Tony.

"Oh, I am not allowed to know Kit's personages," he told her grinning. "Who am I?"

"I don't know her very well myself," explained Kit. "She was in another house at school and younger, but we met again at an Old Girls' reunion. Robby said trade was bad and she was looking for clients because she had a mission to clothe the heathen. When she heard I did dress designs, she asked me to give Avril an option on them, and of course I jumped at it."

"Is an option good?"

"Jolly good for Avril," declared Tony. "She gets all the best designs at the lowest prices."

"Never mind," said Kit. "It's worth it. I've never done so well and I'm grateful to Robby."

Una's heart felt suddenly light and she smiled all over her face. Anybody who was grateful to Robby the Robot certainly belonged to no camp that she knew, quite the contrary, and she decided that this Kit Corcoran was not only a darling but unique.

iii

Tony watched the taxi carrying Una away. He had not even discovered her name, for she hadn't mentioned it and for some reason unknown to himself, he had been unable to ask it. Why hadn't Kit done so? That would have been the natural thing. He saw now that he might have asked her telephone number so that he could ring up and enquire for the dog. Benyon would know it, he supposed, but it would be rather obvious to ask the old man. What an ineffectual idiot he always was!

She was coming round again to return his towel . . . that was one consolation. At the very last moment she had shown it to him, wrapped up in paper for her by Benyon, and had faithfully promised to return it in a day or two. He had been horrified and tried to get it from her, but luckily without success. Bless the towel! All the same she might change her mind and post it. Oh, damn!

He had not mentioned the ring again although he had seen it on her finger glowing as it had done on his own, with a sense of pleased excitement. There was something extremely odd about all this.

"Kit," he called, running upstairs to his long neglected breakfast. "What do you think of it? That youngster was wearing Lorenzo's ring."

"Don't be an ass," said Kit.

"But it was, I tell you. There's not a doubt of it."

"Then there are probably dozens of them about. That's the simple explanation."

"Oh, yes. You'll say it came from Woolworth's next."

"Well, her frock didn't," said Kit.

Tony saw the connection immediately, and began his baked breakfast in a gloomy silence. She was probably rolling, this little girl, and what chance had he then of sculping her and her dog? That was all he wanted, little enough surely, but it was just his luck. One of the idle rich, she was, complete with haughty parents putting their foot down.

Cunningly he said nothing to Kit about the towel, and if she missed it from his room, decided to look innocent and absent-minded, both useful attributes in an emergency. With a bit of luck Kit might be out when she came too, but he would take care to be about. The studio was going to see a lot of him during the next few days.

iv

Una in the taxi alone with Tim at last, buried her face in his furry coat and held him close. The reaction had come and she was shaking all over, for suppose he had been killed—suppose Tony Corcoran hadn't had the presence of mind to beat off the Alastian just in time? Una was convinced she never could have done it, and she had not even managed to tell him how wonderful he was. But she would.

She felt for her little parcel triumphantly. The towel would make a splendid excuse to go back to the studio and she wouldn't trust it to the laundry either. She would get Brent to wash it carefully as she washed Anne's fine laces.

Tim might have been killed. At the thought panic possessed her, panic against a world where she would have been terribly alone. She might have been going home now with Tim stiff in her arms, to find her father and mother no doubt waiting to offer her all the dogs in London . . . as if that would have been any good. They never had been able to understand about Tim, that it wasn't just a dog she wanted, but this dog.

She remembered the young, stray, disreputable Tim of two years ago. She had bought him for five shillings from some little brutes of boys who were ill-treating him in the park. He was starved and dirty and utterly miserable. It was his misery she couldn't bear, for he had spirit enough to fight his tormentors even then; but he didn't fight her after the first moment or two. He snuggled shivering against the grateful warmth of her jumper, whimpered a little, and then buried his grimy nose under her arm.

Their arrival had caused pandemonium in the house. Anne and Jeremy were going to the golf club but they never got there. They were horrified at Una's purchase, threatened her with horrible diseases, called Tim a mongrel and refused point blank to have him about the place. They rang up the Dog's Home and a van was despatched to collect him forthwith, but Una locked herself and Tim in her room and refused to come out. Anne promised to buy her the best Sealyham in London and Jeremy immediately capped this offer by saying she could have a chow or a borzoi. They could not see that it wasn't a present she wanted—above all, a competitive present. She had had too many of these all her life and merely dreaded them. Tim was different and glorious. He was her own.

The van was actually at the door at last. Then Una made amends to the Furies for a sober and well-conducted youth. She was seventeen, but she behaved like a spoilt child of seven, crying, scream-ing with gusto, howling the house down, until Anne and Jeremy, utterly confounded, gave in. What else could they do? In all her life Una had never behaved like this and they were both embarrassed and alarmed. They felt that something ought to be done about it, but in the end nothing was. Anne, her sense of humor overcoming her dismay, left it to Jeremy, and he, immediately suspicious and indig-nant, retreated.

Una alone felt no embarrassment over her scan-dalous behavior, because it had been deliberate, though she was sorry her father and mother should have missed their golf. She was tactful with Tim, keeping him for a long time in the background, and even fighting his puppy ailments singlehanded and telling nobody.

Tim had grown and flourished since then and mongrels were no longer mentioned in his presence, but nobody guessed that more than chance was re-sponsible for his present beauty and perfection. . . except Benyon this morning.

Benyon, thought Una, was a wonderful man, and

over Tim's injury they had become friends. Confidences had been exchanged.

The taxi drew up before the house and, late though it was, Una saw the car waiting, which meant that her father was waiting too . . . for her. She had been hoping he would have gone. She asked Giles the chauffeur to pay for her cab and went slowly up the steps, her dog in her arms.

Jeremy was in the hall, looking restless and apprehensive.

"Oh, there you are, Una? Is the little chap all right? Are you sure? . . . What did the vet say?"

"Yes, he'll be all right in a week or two. It's not very serious," said Una. "I'm sorry you waited, father. I thought the vet had told you."

"Oh, well, I was anxious . . . you are so fond of him," said Jeremy awkwardly.

And Una thought, "I knew it. He was ready to offer me another dog."

She kissed him on the cheek.

"Pay Giles for my taxi, will you, and don't you worry about Tim."

She went on upstairs and met Anne coming out of the little study with a handful of letters.

"Hullo! How is the poor invalid?"

"He's all right. Sorry we've made such a commotion and kept father waiting about."

Anne had been arguing with Jeremy on this head for half an hour. His waiting was both unnecessary and absurd; but something vaguely pathetic about him down there struggling into his coat, prompted her to say:

"Naturally he was worried about the son of the house." Then moving to the head of the stairs she called: "Good-by, Jeremy. Don't be late."

Una was amazed to see her father turn round and smile like a boy. The next moment the hall door banged behind him.

"You may put him to bed by the study fire if you like," said Anne. "I'm glad he's not seriously hurt, for we can't afford to lose the best looking member of the family, can we, Tim?"

Una's old smile suddenly came back. She was shaken, hungry, excited, glad, and her careful impartiality was flung to the winds.

"He isn't," she said, looking her mother in the eye.

Anne, she was sure, had not even thought of another dog.

CHAPTER VI

i

UNA, following her old cautious habit of not allowing Tim to be a nuisance, did not leave him for some days, and much to her surprise, neither Jeremy nor Anne protested, though it meant her cutting several evening engagements at which she was expected to appear with them.

A sudden peace seemed to have descended upon her family. Jeremy was no longer irritable and suspicious; he did not even bring her disconcerting presents, though each night he looked into the little study to inquire for Tim. Una did not connect this pleasant state of things with his sudden smile at her mother the other morning, or dream that he was for the moment happy because he had Anne to himself a little. Such an idea would have amazed her.

Though the young set she moved in was at an age to be more sophisticated than anybody in the world and talked frankly and none too elegantly of the love-affairs of its elders, Una, fond of games and movement, but shy of conversation, was little affected, because uninterested. It never occurred to her to wonder whether her father and mother were in love, other than in the conventional sense of parents generally . . . a kind of domestic neutrality.

Anne, a casual parent in some respects, was perhaps really responsible that Una was still young and unawake to many troubling questions. She would come in late of an afternoon, inquiring: "Well, how's life?"

"Oh, all right," the girl would reply, or "Pretty rum."

"Come and tell me all about it."

But it was she who did the telling. She was a good mimic and Una heard all the gossip, social, political and scandalous, inimitably told. Her paternal grandmother would have been shocked to the soul, but Anne was no fool. The girl would hear these things, whether or no . . . hadn't it always been so, for all the talk of modern young people? Let her at least hear them decently and without malice.

It was inevitable that Anne with her spectacular and much advertised beauty should be libeled and talked about by the people who did not know her but hung, as it were, on the fringe of her world. By her own set, however, she was known to be straight. Preposterous as it might be, she and Jeremy were still in love, they said, and in a sense this was true, though it was an unequal love like any other. Anne did not understand Jeremy's tortures; it was not in her nature, but she was very fond of him and would not have let him down, and she bore with his unreasonable irritability though it grew worse year by year. It never entered her head that his jealousy, having no other outlet, had turned upon Una, that he believed them constantly together and allied against him, and that in some muddled, ineffectual fashion he was always trying to defeat this. Nor had she an inkling of the girl's troubled interpretation of his attitude.

Una, nursing her dog, exchanging confidences with Benyon during his daily visits, and full of her new, secret friendship with Kit and Tony, was happy in the curiously peaceful atmosphere of that week. Desperately she hoped it might continue though she could not see what had brought it about.

One evening when Anne came in to show a new frock before going out with Jeremy, Una asked her suddenly: "Did you get the one Robby wanted you to? You know, she said she'd get some girl to design it."

"This is the one," said Anne, revolving. "Like it?"

"Rather!"

Una's enthusiasm was not wholly concerned with her mother's beauty this time. She was glad Kit's creation was a distinct success.

"I didn't need it, of course," Anne went on. "Wouldn't your father think me an extravagant hussy?"

"Why shouldn't you be extravagant?" said Una.

"No reason whatever, but men always think we are and it is so bad for them to be right."

Una considered this.

"I don't think it would hurt him to be right," she remarked cautiously at last. She meant he so rarely was but Anne supposed this was Una's sense of fair play. The changeling was so wise, like a little owl, and she laughed.

"Then we'll let him be right," she said.

ii

"Like my new frock?" she asked Jeremy later in the car.

"Um . . . is it new?"

"What is the use of having an extravagant wife if you never look at her?" said Anne, teasing him. "This is one of Robby's very special creations."

"Can't stand the woman," said Jeremy, because he could not tell her he was always looking at her and longed to do little else. He could not take advantage of his happiness. His tongue denied him.

"Well, there's no reason why you should," said Anne equably.

"Making a public exhibition of herself. It's all this craze for sensation."

"Sensations are good for trade. Besides one can't judge a person whose world has been smashed to bits."

"All the more reason she should keep quiet," said Jeremy.

Anne did not argue about it. Lawyers, she supposed, saw so much evil that they were cynical by nature; but she had known the Lyne twins, Robby and Bob, since they were children, and their father had been her father's friend. Bob, a good-looking pleasant lad, had become entangled with some woman, who, when he would have broken with her, followed him to a restaurant and threw vitriol in his face. The uproar and scandal broke Mr. Lyne, who went to pieces and finally committed suicide. Robby at twenty-one was left to face it alone, almost penni-

less too, for there was very little money. The
woman was sent to prison and Bob disappeared. In
the years since no one had heard of him and Robby
never mentioned his name. Friends got her into
Avril's and Avril, Anne strongly suspected, used
her without mercy, playing upon Robby's fear of
losing her job with all the cleverness of a scheming
and greedy woman. Yes, there was something to be
said for Robby, though she did court sensation by
changing her face to match every new type of eccentric, dummy figure that appeared in the shop windows. Robby the Robot focused plenty of limelight
on Avril's, and Avril, whose real name was infinitely
less elegant, took care that she should continue to
do so.

"You don't understand girls of that type," burst
out Jeremy.

He spoke savagely but he had not meant to be
savage. He had meant to be tender and to show her
he loved her not to understand. She was his, and he
wanted to carry her away far from such contacts,
from idiot newspapers, from everybody in the
world.

The car drew up before an awning and red carpet lined on each side by a staring crowd. He knew
that was his answer.

iii

Tony wandered about the studio all the week,
though he was sure she wouldn't come and told himself so a dozen times a day.

The May mornings were golden, and by noon

the studio window showed him the little clouds rolling together on the blue grass of the sky; even Church Street, winding away without a beginning or end, seemed to call him out to adventure. When he tried to work his hands made sport of his mind, and he could do nothing right.

He spent restless evenings looking up fellow spirits in Chelsea or, more often, wandering alone in the park where a young moon hung above the trees, turning the Serpentine into a silver sea. Then one evening he met Benyon coming in and threw discretion to the winds.

"How's the patient I brought you the other morning getting on?" he asked.

"The little terrier? Couldn't be better, but it's not much thanks to me. He has a good nurse and although I have been looking in every day, upon my word I shall be ashamed to send in the bill. Still, money's no object there, I imagine."

"Lucky dog, eh?" said Tony with a somewhat despondent grin.

"You're right, Mr. Concoran, and a stray at that, he was, the young lady tells me, though you wouldn't think it to look at him now. Extraordinary girl that. I'd give my head for a young lad or lass with a bit of animal sense, if you know what I mean, to lend me a hand with my job. But, can I get one? Not on your life . . . born fools, every one of them. And here's this young lady with everything she can desire, studying up the care and breeding of dogs for the fun of the thing and, mind you, she's got the instinct. What a waste!"

"Really?" said Tony, eager for more.

"That's life, that is," said Benyon. "So damned contrary. Yes, she's collected quite a goodish little library and she tells me her idea would be to have a dog farm. Well, I hope she'll let me in on the ground floor, that's all, for she'd make a 'do' of it if I know anything. Hasn't stirred from the patient all the week if you'll believe me."

Benyon, smiling benignantly over his glasses, nodded good night and went in, and Tony ran upstairs with a heart suddenly light. So that was why she hadn't come?

Early the next afternoon she was there.

Kit had gone out, bless her tactful heart, and Tony, feeling that Robert Burns didn't know everything about the plans of mice and men, drew his visitor into the studio with a beaming smile.

"I've brought it back," said Una, holding out her little parcel. "Your towel."

"Oh, I say, you shouldn't have bothered," declared Tony. "Still I'm glad you did because here you are. Kit's out, so I'm afraid you'll have to put up with me."

"But I'm not going to disturb you if you're working. *Are*n't you working?" said Una, looking suspiciously round the studio.

"Not a stroke. I was killing Time, but you've saved the old beggar's life."

"As you did Tim's."

"Not a bit of it. Tim is equal to half a dozen Alsatians. You ask Benyon. . . . Come along over here and look at a friend of mine. Sort of patron saint, he is, Lorenzo the Magnificent, otherwise Medici. They'll tell you he was a bad lot, but don't you believe 'em. Lorenzo was a great man."

Una examined the photograph of Michelangelo's statue with a serious face.

"I thought they poisoned people," she said, "or do I mean the Borgias?"

"Oh, I'll let you believe anything you hear about the Borgias," said Tony handsomely, smiling at her with delight.

She was not in green today, but the non-Woolworth dress he remembered had been stained with Tim's blood. This time she was all in yellow like a daffodil, from the soft felt hat pulled down over her eyes, to the pointed, narrow shoes. And he had not been mistaken, her lines were perfect. His Girl and Dog would be a lovely thing.

She had moved on and was standing before the Singing Boy. Her very stillness pleased him, but somehow the Boy no longer mattered and he did not care what she said about it.

"Makes you think of morning in the country," said Una wistfully at last.

"Fond of the country?"

"Yes, I wish I were there."

"All right," said Tony, eagerly. "Come along, there's plenty of country round about and we'll soon find some."

Una laughed in pleased surprise.

"Of course we can't," she said. "I must go back to Tim."

"Yes, I know all about that. You've been sitting

by Tim's side holding his paw all the week," said Tony, reprovingly, "and you'll be breaking down. You don't stir from this studio till you've had tea at least. What sort of host do you take me for, any-way?"

"It's much too early for tea."

"But it won't be later on," declared Tony per-suasively. "I'll tell you what. We'll go and have tea in Kensington Gardens and then you'll be halfway home."

"I'd like that," agreed Una at once. She had her own reasons for wanting to prolong the interview for she had brought something for Tony because he had saved her dog, but she had not yet found cour-age to give it to him. In Kensington Gardens it would be easier, she thought.

They closed the studio and went out together. Tony had always loved the shapeliness of London, the narrow, curving streets and the odd buildings, shabby though they might be, rising with grace to the pale sky; but it seemed altogether the wrong background for this tall child. He saw her instead in "sweet Hellas" running like the wind among fields of asphodel.

"Let us visit the scene of the crime," he said, as they turned into the Gardens.

Una looked at him with her sudden smile. He was ridiculous but what did that matter? He and Kit were her secret friends and he could say and do what he liked.

So they found the place as nearly as they could remember and looked for the bloodstains earnestly but without success; and Tony said he had a good mind to write to the *Times* about it. Historic landmarks should not be effaced like this and trampled over by the vulgar herd. He would also point out the folly of the Government in allowing so many aliens into the country and ask why unnaturalized Alsatians were allowed to walk into Kensington Gardens in broad daylight and attempt to eat British born dogs.

At the end of this oration Una drew something from her coat pocket and held it out to him.

It was the onyx ring.

"I know you wanted this," she said, "so I brought it to you from Tim."

Tony was momentarily struck dumb. Then he laughed and closing her hand over the ring shook it warmly.

"I couldn't possibly let you," he protested.

"Please . . . because I don't want it."

"Nonsense! My dear child, you can't go round giving away rings like that."

"Yes, I can," said Una earnestly, "and I'm not a child. I shall be nineteen this month and I'm certainly old enough to do as I like."

"Really?" asked Tony. "I wish I were. I don't think I'll ever be old enough for that." He smiled at her coaxingly. "Please put it on again. I didn't really want the ring, but it was like one I tried to buy in Florence, and I was so surprised to see it on your hand that day that I asked you to sell it on the spur of the moment."

"Well, it came from Florence," said Una as

though that settled the argument. "I suppose you weren't born in May?"

"Certainly I was. All the best people were born in May. I thought everyone knew that."

"Well then . . . this ring is very lucky for anyone born in May," declared Una eagerly.

Tony for a moment wondered why this phrase sounded familiar. Then he saw the Lung'Arno and Mrs. Polhampton putting up her sunshade outside Sponelli's, and his heart missed a beat. He had invented it himself.

"This argument must now cease," he said in a firm voice, "and you have an appointment with me for afternoon tea, so come along. I'm sorry to seem inquisitive, but I wish you'd tell me your name."

"Una Swithin," she said in surprise. "I thought you knew."

He might have known it; there was no reason to start like that, especially when he had always maintained that human beings didn't "start"—that it was a form of physical jerk unknown outside melodrama. Then she was Mrs. Polhampton's daughter? She couldn't be . . . it was utterly profane. But she must be. Tony, his mind more than ever in disorder, stole a glance at her and saw her walking beside him as naturally as the child she had declared herself not to be.

"It isn't as though I were offering you a present," she said urgently after a moment. "I hate the sight of presents myself, but this is a kind of memento. You saved Tim's life and you may think that a little thing, but it isn't to me. It was rather jolly to think

I had something you wanted, to give you in return.
I don't see how you can refuse it either, when it's
your patron saint."

"Sharp eyes, haven't you?"

"Well, I'm not blind."

Una, having a moment before made one of the
longest speeches of her life, sat down at the tea-
table with a little gasp. They were the first custom-
ers and far too early, as the waiter's bored reception
of them seemed to suggest. He brought them the
worst provender he could find, to teach them better,
but the sparrows enjoyed it, coming down with cock-
ney impudence and eating out of Una's hand. Tony,
watching her, enchanted, forgot that the food was
uneatable and he a very bad host. The surly waiter
might have been Eros himself.

"I think your offering me the ring was the nicest
thing that ever happened to me," he said, "but you
must see that I couldn't take it. There is something
you and Tim could do for me though, if you only
would."

"Of course we will."

"What a reckless girl you are! I might be going
to ask you to commit a murder," protested Tony.

"Well, *was* it a murder?"

"No . . . I want you to let me make a little
statue of you . . . you and Tim, just as I saw you
out here in the Gardens the other morning."

"I knew you did that boy singing in the country,"
said Una in a tone of triumph.

Tony looked at her guiltily wondering if she had
seen his dreadful image of Mrs. Polhampton.

"How did you know?" he managed to ask.

"Well, you kept so dark about it and you must have a studio for something."

He laughed with relief. Girls, he had always thought, talked far too much and saw nothing, but this was one unique. She said so little and she saw a great deal. He was convinced her wisdom was profound and wonderful.

He knew he was asking a great deal, he said presently, about the sitting, but he was a quick worker and Kit would be there to talk to her if she felt too bored. He said this cunningly because he had had a sudden vision of Mrs. Polhampton wanting to come and chaperone her daughter. Yet *was* she the old catamaran's daughter? It seemed incredible. "Is your mother Lady Swithin?" he wanted to say but the question could not be asked like that as though he were a snob or after something. He looked up and saw, neatly against the sky, the tip of the Albert Memorial like a shrine gone wrong . . . a shrine to Mr. Grundy.

But Una, untroubled by the Grundys, was delighted to sit to him as soon as Tim's bandage could be taken off, and thus reminded of the invalid, said she must go back to him and jumped up, the sparrows fluttering round her. Tony paid Eros and went with her to the Garden gates.

"Look here," he said awkwardly at last, "you'd better ask your mother . . . about the sittings I mean. She's sure to think it's like my colossal impudence."

Una smiled a secret smile, looking at him out of

the corner of her eye. As if you did ask your mother or your father either in these days. You had to work things out for yourself instead of putting it on to them. Una had been doing this all her life, asking nothing and telling nobody. He was funny and she wondered why he wanted to make a statue of her. If she had been lovely like her mother, she thought wistfully, it would have been easy to understand. For the first time she felt sorry she was not beautiful.

"As soon as Tim's better I'll let you know," she promised, "and if you really want us we'll come. I've only a few yards to go now, so I'll run while the policeman has his arm out. Good-by."

She was off, and before Tony recovered his wits the policeman had the traffic racing to Knightsbridge, an impenetrable cavalcade. All pedestrians being mad there was little astonishment though plenty of violent language when one of them plunged into the cavalcade and by a miracle came out on the other side alive. But by this time Una had disappeared.

Tony, cursing himself for a fool, turned sadly away in the direction of Church Street. Yet it was not such a bad old world after all, he decided. He began to feel in his pockets for a pipe to salute the world, and in doing so his hand came in contact with something unfamiliar. He pulled the object out and stared at it in stupefaction, though he might have known. It was the onyx ring.

This wasn't real, of course. It was a dream and presently he would feel himself falling through space and wake up with a jump. He stared at the ring to the infinite amusement of a pair of nursemaids passing with perambulators. Their titters restored his senses and he stuffed the ring into his pocket again and hurried on.

He now saw the whole preposterous story of the ring as though set out before him, from that moment on the Lung'Arno weeks ago. It was simply the kind of thing that didn't happen and yet it had happened, chapter by chapter, and what could you make of that? It should not be Lorenzo's image on the stone, however, but some old god whose fun it was to tangle human destinies—"ye gods from whom these miracles do spring."

Tony carefully left the matter of which god, and seeing a public telephone at hand, on an impulse went in.

S . . . Sw . . . Swithin! There it was, Swithin, Jeremy, Palace Square, S.W. No other Swithin in this neighborhood, so it must be correct. And no title either. Lady "Polhampton" then must be some other Swithin, though a relative no doubt . . . not her mother, thank heaven.

Tony, much relieved, called Mr. Jeremy Swithin's number, got it and asked in a nonchalant manner to speak to Miss Una. In two minutes he heard her soft "Hullo!"

"There's magic about," announced Tony, without preliminary.

"Really?"

She knew his voice then? Tony could almost hear her smiling into the telephone.

"That ring jumped clean into my pocket. I can't account for it."

"It must be for luck," she suggested.

"Please, Miss Una Swithin, let me buy the ring in a sane and proper manner. I'm afraid of magic."

"It's the best magic."

"Yes, but we can't have old Tim's life paid for. You know yourself he's a priceless dog."

"Then I'll charge it to your account," said Una in a breathless voice and escaped by hanging up the receiver.

iv

Kit had returned and was entertaining Carstairs on tea and buns with sugar on them for which he had a childish passion. Tony since his return from Florence had several times looked in on Carstairs in vain; so he supposed this visit was the result, though Kit could have undeceived him.

Carstairs was the man whose Pericles had been bought for the Tate Gallery, the coming man in English sculpture, and his judgment was as sound as his criticism was unmerciful. You loved or hated Carstairs. There was no middle course.

"Hullo, Corky," said the visitor. "Have a bun."

"Bring 'em with you?" enquired Tony. "Thoughtful fellow."

"So you fell for Lorenzo, I observe?"

"Oh, yes, we grew very thick, the Magnificent and I."

Carstairs gave a joyous shout.

"Magnificent be damned, my innocent lamb. This is another bloke altogether, nephew of *the* Lorenzo and a chap of no particular consequence. Any tuppenny ha'penny guide-book would have told you that."

"You're a liar," said Tony hotly but without conviction. Carstairs, alas, knew his Italy. He had won the Prix de Rome years ago.

"All right, my lad, read up your Renaissance. The worst of you young men of the present day," said Carstairs from the lofty eminence of thirty-one, "is that you're so darned superficial."

Tony was looking at the photograph indignantly.

"Then what in hell was Mike about?" he enquired in an injured tone.

"L.S.D.," said Kit.

The sculptor turned and looked at her and they smiled but Tony missed the interchange.

"Isn't it the common fate of genius to perpetuate the mediocre?" said Carstairs. "Michelangelo owed the family something, and if he added wisdom and nobility where none was, perhaps the old lad knew his work would endure when all the Medici had passed to dust. And patron or no patron, he did get the chance to illuminate an idea now and then. When you go to Rome . . ."

He was off; the things he knew tumbled from Carstairs in a heap, but Tony was not listening. Ideas! They were always spouting about ideas nowadays, and what did they mean? Tony was convinced he hadn't an idea in his head, only an aching desire to seize beauty when he saw it and mould it with his hands. Superficial, was he? Carstairs was probably right, damn him.

But the other man had finished his diatribe and had strolled across to the window. Casually, as though he had not already examined it under Kit's eager eye, he took up the Singing Boy and turned it about in his large, careful hands. Tony, who had wanted him here for no other purpose, felt his knees turn to water and his heart go down with a thud.

"Better have this cast and send it to the London Group," said Carstairs briefly at last. "You've done it this time."

He put down the little figure and peered at Lorenzo in passing.

"Dam' fine statue anyway," he remarked, "so cheer up, Corky."

CHAPTER VII

i

EARLY on Saturday afternoon Una was getting ready to take Tim for a drive. His wound was healing well and he had already been into the Gardens once or twice, though not off the lead, and had met there quite by accident a young man whose smell was somehow familiar and pleasing. Friendship between them was advancing rapidly.

A born motorist like most dogs, Tim had been trained to keep still in the car, and Una, after an earnest consultation with Benyon on the telephone, had decided the drive would do him no harm.

Anne had gone in to lunch with Jeremy in town, for they were playing golf that afternoon; and Una was almost ready to get the car, when a maid came to say Mrs. Swithin was downstairs, and learning that her ladyship was out, had asked for Miss Una.

"Oh, which one, Turner?" asked Una blankly.

"Your grandmother, Miss."

Una went rather slowly downstairs trying to fight off a sense of disaster. For ten days everything had been so jolly—no arguments, no discords, no presents, and now what was going to happen? She knew her grandmother's habit of descending upon the house unheralded like this and then looking pained and disapproving because its mistress was not in.

Mrs. Swithin was a brisk old woman of seventy-five, as upright as a girl and looking, unlike most people in the world, exactly what she was—an elderly lady with a largish house and garden at Wimbledon. Her hair was white but she had kept her fresh complexion by working all the year round among her flowers, and she considered snails and slugs only less abominable than the Labor Party. No fallen leaf was allowed to lie in Mrs. Swithin's garden; every blade of grass was in place and ribald spirits declared the standard roses were dusted every morning. Flowers blew and faded and their petals were carefully carted away with the dust. To pick one was an enormity.

She was equally a fanatic in the house, and her younger daughter, Fanny, had become a slave to it under her mother's domination. Marion, having inherited some money from an aunt, had broken away from this tyranny, winning thereby Mrs. Swithin's secret respect.

She was not consciously an unkind woman. She was good to the poor and devoted to her family, and if Jeremy were to die penniless tomorrow, she would take Anne and Una into her home without a murmur, as she had taken poor Herbert's pretentious wife and children, until her husband had been unable to put up with their presence any longer. But her mind was inelastic. It had set in a Victorian mould and she could not understand this generation, nor even the one before it. The world was going, she was convinced, from bad to worse. Anne sometimes thought it almost ridiculous that Mrs.

Swithin should be such a typical mother-in-law, but she was a woman who took pride in being typical. To be an individual would have seemed to her a little loose.

Una found her grandmother looking suspiciously round the drawing-room. As a perfect housewife she felt herself preordained to advise and criticize all young wives, and Anne was to her mind still a girl. All maid-servants, as she invariably called them, were alike and the beauty of her daughter-in-law's L-shaped drawing-room did not deceive her for a moment. She was convinced there was dust under the rugs. What else could you expect with the mistress of the house always gadding?

"Well, my dear?" she greeted Una, holding her at arm's length and looking her up and down. "You are far too thin, Una. You want feeding up."

Mrs. Swithin had no patience with the flat figures and brief skirts of the young generation, and was convinced that her granddaughter was under-nourished and under-clothed.

"I'm wonderfully strong, grandmother, really, and I have a huge appetite," declared Una eagerly.

"Your mother should give you a glass of hot malted milk the last thing at night. I shall advise it," said Mrs. Swithin with decision. "The servant maid tells me your mother is out. I'm sorry."

"She and father have gone to play golf," said Una in quick defense. "He always likes a game on Saturdays. He has so little time."

"Yes, poor father. It is perfectly right he should be considered. That, my dear, is a good woman's first duty. You must never forget it. Still, I had hoped that by coming early I might have found your mother in. I see so little of her and I do not often find time for a day in town. This morning, however, I had some business to transact for your grandfather."

"Mother would have waited to see you if you had only telephoned, grandmother. She'll be so sorry."

"I cannot put up with the telephone, child. Nothing would induce me to have one about the place. I am old-fashioned," said Mrs. Swithin unnecessarily and with complacence. "Well, you must just be my messenger to your mother. I want you all three to come to us for a little family dinner on Tuesday. It is my wedding day and until last evening I was afraid we should have to give up our usual gathering owing to your grandfather's rheumatism. However, the doctor thinks it can do him no harm and it may well be our last wedding dinner, so your dear mother must not disappoint me. Grandfather is failing fast, Una . . . oh, yes, daily."

Una felt uncomfortable. She knew her grandmother's habit of hitting below the belt and now, whatever engagement they might have for Tuesday, it would have to be given up, because she had so unfairly said this. And Una didn't believe her grandfather was failing; she did not want to believe it, for she was fond of him. She tried to remember if anything very important was happening on Tuesday night, but her mind seemed a blank and it was a positive relief when, in the middle of her stammering reply to her grandmother, Turner opened the door and announced:

"Miss Lyne to see you, Miss."

Robby the Robot came in quickly. She was always restless and in a hurry.

"Oh, Una, isn't Anne in? How too tragic. Damn! Don't tell me she won't be in because I couldn't bear it."

"She's gone to golf with father," said Una, drawing her into the room.

"Curse!" said Robby.

"I don't think you've met Miss Lyne, grandmother."

"I have not," said Mrs. Swithin with emphasis.

For a moment Una found herself trying to see Robby with her grandmother's eyes. Miss Lyne was certainly the kind of apparition to startle elderly ladies from Wimbledon. Her perfectly fitting suit was the fashion after next, as became an employee of Avril. Her complexion of the moment was painted in strange hues, deep blue green beneath the slanting, half-shut eyes, and her mouth a line of brick red. Her eye-brows, plucked and carefully arched, mounted under her small hat, and when she spoke she seemed to move no muscle of her face.

She shook hands with Mrs. Swithin quite unaware that she was an object of surprise and worse, saying at the same time to Una:

"When will Jeremy and Anne be back?"

"Not for hours, I'm afraid."

"Help!"

"My grandmother was hoping to see them too,"

said Una in a vain effort to make the conversation general.

Robby for the first time looked at old Mrs. Swithin and her professional instincts at once alert, exclaimed:

"Beautiful! How I should love to dress her, Una."

"And I, young lady," said Mrs. Swithin in a voice of outrage, "should like to dress you, I should indeed."

"Robby means to be complimentary, she does really, grandmother. You see, it is her job and she thinks it would be such a pleasure to make you beautiful gowns."

"You bet your sweet life," said Robby eagerly.

"Indeed? I am afraid I am in need of no assistance of that nature," returned Mrs. Swithin frostily.

"Too bad," said Robby with regret. "Haven't a gasper by any chance, have you, Una?"

"No," said Una, "but I think you'll find some in the little study if you wouldn't mind looking. Tim's in there too. He's better."

"Thanks. Then I'll say good-by, Mrs. Swithin. Don't forget Avril's if you ever want a really posh frock, will you? And I'll see to it myself. I should love to."

"Such a contingency is unlikely to arise. Good afternoon," said grandmother.

ii

"And who may Tim be, if I may be so bold as to ask, Una?" enquired Mrs. Swithin in the tone of an inquisitor.

"Only my dog," said Una smiling. "You know my little terrier? He was hurt and I've been nursing him."

"Is this very extraordinary young woman a friend of your mother's?"

Una felt herself flushing to the roots of her hair.

"She's a friend of all of us," she said defensively. "I know she looks odd, but that is just part of her profession. Robby lost all her money and has to work. She is in one of the very smart dress shops."

If Una hoped a mention of Robby's hard work would appease her grandmother she was mistaken.

"Ah!" said Mrs. Swithin as though her worst suspicions were confirmed, as indeed they were. In her day young ladies who lost their money did not go into shops. They lived on their male relatives as Providence had intended them to do.

"I will leave you, Una, and I rely upon you to give my message about Tuesday to your mother. I shall expect you at ten minutes to seven, remember. for I make it a rule in my house that meals shall be punctual to the minute. One must have order or nothing is done."

"I'll ask mother to send you a note tonight," said Una, accompanying her grandmother downstairs. She didn't see why they should be ordered to come to dinner as though they had no say in the matter,

and this was her way of suggesting as much as
politely as she could; but Mrs. Swithin merely inclined her head as if this were the least that an
erring daughter-in-law could do. She refused Una's
offer to send for a taxi, saying reprovingly that
she had no patience with people who could not walk
a few hundred yards to the Tube. It was sheer
affectation.

Una closed the door upon her with relief and ran
upstairs in search of Robby, wondering why her
grandmother always made her feel so guilty, as
though she had committed a crime.

Robby was walking up and down the little study,
chain-smoking as if her life depended upon it, and
at Una's appearance, she hailed her eagerly.

"Have they taken the car, Una? Look here, it's
horribly urgent. I wanted Anne to drive me somewhere."

"I'm awfully sorry, Robby, but they have."

"Oh, damn!"

"Wouldn't a taxi do?" suggested Una.

"No . . . can't risk it."

Robby put her hand suddenly to her face, and
Una asked:

"Toothache?"

"Eh? . . . no." Robby stared at her, became
aware of the hand and took it away again, lighting
another cigarette and looking to Una's eyes somehow pitiful and strange. Most people said Robby
had no conscience and was always using her friends,
but Una didn't care. The incident with her grandmother had sent her over to Robby's side, and she

said after a moment, though with a regretful glance at Tim rolled up on his chair: .

"Is it very far?"

"Only an hour's run," said Robby, hope springing immediately. "Not much past St. Alban's. . . . I say, have you thought of something?"

"Well, I have my little car and I was going to take Tim for a drive but he oughtn't to be out very long. Could you nurse him on your knee, do you think?"

"I'd nurse an elephant," declared Robby. "Come on . . . quick. Let's get off at once."

She wasted no time on thanks. It did not occur to her. She was conscious of Una only as a means to an end. Life was hell and Avril its presiding devil. You had to fight the devil tooth and nail even for your just commissions; and you went on fighting day after day like an automaton, but only half of you was there. The other half was out beyond St. Alban's, hidden away from the sight of men. And when the other half was in torment you knew it and lied like blazes about someone who might order a trousseau or presentation gown if properly approached, and you ran off and caught a train and walked the two miles from the station. But Avril was a cunning devil and this time all the lies in the world had not availed. Not born yesterday, was what she had said and hinted poisonous things. You'd had to stick the torment for days and now it was Saturday you hadn't dared to use the train. Detectives? She was quite capable of it . . . and what, if anything, had she found out?

"You'll have to show me the way when we get to St. Alban's," said Una as Robby got into the car, and with one hand she tucked the rug round her guest, then very carefully deposited her dog on top of it. Tim sniffed the rug, found it familiar, then raised his head to look at Robby, but he was no grandmother Swithin. As soon as Una entered the car he folded himself down in perfect confidence, for what were blue-green cheeks and brick-red mouths to him? This creature was not offensive and she was comfortable to sit upon.

They drove off, but for the first half hour the going was slow and Robby urged speed in vain. Kilburn, Cricklewood, Hendon, Edgeware, would this string of trams and buses never end? Vans, fruit carts, fools Saturday-marketing and walking in the road, policemen pretending to be gods and putting out their arms, Una putting out hers and dancing to their tune, Robby believing in neither gods nor men, but very certain of a devil and seeing his emissary in every car behind them.

The end of the tram line came at last and then Una let the little car go like the wind. Up a hill and down the other side, country at last, high country, sweet with the lovely scent of trees and grass; the outspread fields beginning to turn yellow with the first buttercups; and then, a narrow village street, a steep run down, and in a moment they were flying along a dappled road, winding in and out and upwards under darkling trees to Bacon's city.

Una was suddenly elated and her troubles dropped away. This wide and spacious country of

gentle slopes and little woods and long, tree-shad-
owed roads, sang to her as a friend, as though
Hertfordshire were in her blood and would not be
denied. And why not? There is a potency in places;
we may come upon one suddenly and in an instant
know ourselves for evermore at home. And who
shall say, of the thousand currents that have gone
to make us, why one runs deeper than the rest?
Beyond St. Alban's Wenlock lay. Two had once
loved it, been happy there and passed; and Una,
troubled, fearful and yet strong, was equally the
child of both.

The little car purred under her hand; Tim, from
the shelter of Robby's protecting arms, sniffed the
sweet air and lifted his nose up, longing to be out
in this rich and rabbity world which should have
been his just inheritance.

Even Robby herself had ceased smoking Jeremy's
cigarettes, purloined from the study, and no longer
called feverishly for greater speed; for the road
behind them was empty now and the journey nearly
done.

Climbing to St. Alban's they turned, at Robby's
direction, to the left, past the Abbey and the gate
house, through sleepy Verulum which was once a
city known to Caesar, and out on to a wide road,
running away into a world of fields and trees. Presently at a cross-road, Robby put out her hand, cast-
ing at the same time a hasty glance behind them.

"This will do, Una, if you'll let me down."

Una stopped the car, gazing about her in surprise.

"But this isn't anywhere."

"I know . . . near enough, though. How long can you give me?"

The clock on the dashboard said it was just after four; they had made a good run in spite of the traffic, and all at once Una realized that Robby had held Tim all the way and, though he was heavy, had never once moved him to ease her cramped limbs.

"Would an hour and a half do? We oughtn't to leave later than half-past five," she said.

"Oh, good-o." This was largesse to Robby and she said in her offhand way: "You drive on round the country a bit then and come back for me here, but mark the place with a cross or something and don't leave me stranded, whatever you do. I'll be here on the tick."

She watched Una start off obediently, and then turned down the cross-road, and in the shelter of a hedge, took a tube of cold cream from her bag and removed the worst of the color from her face. A moment later she was on her way.

iii

It was evident Robby didn't want anyone to know where she was going, but Una did not blame her, and she drove carefully out of view before pulling up to take her bearings and make sure she would know the place again. Telegraph poles told her that this was a main road and she got out her A.A. map, marked it and studied the surrounding country.

So she saw Wenlock. Straight on for a fairish

way, perhaps five miles, a turn to the right, another to the left and she would be there.

She was charmed by this discovery. She had not seen Wenlock for years and years, since she was a small child and had gone there with Anne. She knew indeed little about it; but she remembered hearing her mother say to her father a day or two ago, that the house had been empty for months and the agents advised her to sell rather than spend money on it, rates being high and tenants apparently low, in the agents' opinion.

"All sorts of things want doing to it, it seems," Anne had said. "And I suppose it is merely sentimental to keep it when we never go near the place."

Jeremy had replied: "You must be guided by your own feelings in the matter." And Una had wanted to cry: "Oh, don't sell it," but as usual had said nothing at all.

Actually Wenlock had been to some extent sacrificed to Jeremy's absurd diffidence about his wife's property. Her father's will had decreed that, if Anne decided not to live at Wenlock, the tenants should be allowed to buy in their farms on easy terms over a number of years, for he knew the curse of the absentee landlord. Anne had been married eighteen months when she reached her majority and came into control of her inheritance, and she immediately set about fulfilling this provision, for Jeremy was absorbed in his profession, had no interest in a country life, except for an occasional holiday, and rigidly declined to have anything to do with the handling of her monetary affairs. He went sometimes to Wenlock to please her, but was never at ease there, and after a year or two, when she had an opportunity to let the place just as it stood, she seized it. Her tenants were a pleasant family of Americans, who came for three months and stayed four years, until their country's imminent advent into the War carried them home. They had loved Wenlock and tended it and Anne was sorry to see them go—not without reason. In the bad years that followed hundreds of such estates came into the market every week—they could be had for an old song—and Wenlock's succeeding tenants were people of rising fortunes, who were determined to get their money's worth and thought the titled owner fair game. Anne came to see that her father's provision had been wiser than he could have guessed. Wenlock ceased to be a landed estate, but painlessly, not in the tragic manner of so many greater and older properties, victims of a passing régime.

Of all this Una knew nothing, as she drove her car into Wenlock village that Saturday afternoon. She had to stop to ask the way and was told by the woman she addressed:

"There's no one there, Miss. Simmonses have gone and the hall's been empty these few months."

The Simmonses, she supposed, were the tenants. They didn't matter, but the empty hall had a lonely sound, like something basely deserted; yet she had known it was empty and this had not struck her before.

"Yes, I know," she explained. "I only want to look at it."

"Take the road to the left over the bridge and you'll be at the gates in two minutes," said the woman. "Mrs. Wardell at the lodge will take you over, and glad to do it."

Una looked at her clock and saw it was already a quarter to five. She would have time for only a very brief look and somehow she didn't want any Mrs. Wardell. She could think of nothing but the lonely house.

All at once the picture of it, long forgotten, was in her mind—the tall windows opening straight on to the grass and people in bright colors coming in and out, her mother, men wheeled in long chairs, men on crutches, men without, and presently a crowd of them altogether, herself in the middle, and a man with a camera. Then like a thunder clap a great roar of laughter arose, shout after shout of it, as the camera slipped on the grass, the photographer tried to seize it and slipped too, landing on all fours with the black cloth over his head. Una had laughed too; she had been terribly happy; she could feel the sensation even now. And she knew all about it. They were soldiers; it was the War—the one infinitesimal corner of a great event that had touched her young life.

She knew about the War, of course, had read of it, seen plays about it, had heard the word bandied about, not greatly interested. Every year she had watched London fall into silence for two minutes strangely and dramatically (like a monster holding its breath) to remember the War. And there was the Unknown Soldier in the Abbey, splendid, or

perhaps lonely away from his friends. But none of
that was quite real (it was history, though some of
it stirring, like King Charles riding "by his own
Whitehall"), infinitely less real than the soldiers
laughing as if they were a lot of schoolboys in the
garden at Wenlock. She felt pleased and excited
that she had been there.

They were over the bridge and at the lodge gates
by now, but she did not want to drive in and stir
up Mrs. Wardell. She drew in beneath the garden
wall, lifted Tim out, and very cautiously entered
the drive, walking fast till the lodge was hidden
from view.

There were weeds everywhere, and last year's
leaves had not been carted away. They had drifted
on to the drive and the desolate flower borders
where a few poor plants alone survived. She did not
see that somebody had begun to cut the lawn, for
suddenly the house appeared between the trees and
she stood still in surprise. It had seemed enormous
to her childhood's eyes, as houses do, but now she
saw it was rather small, and shuttered and cold, a
poor little old blind house, forgotten by its friends.

"I haven't forgotten you," said Una pitifully, but
what was the good of that? The house couldn't
hear.

Hugging her dog, she turned and fled back to the
car, almost running and luckily meeting nobody.

It was ten past five, but there was a shorter way
to the main road; some workmen of whom she had
asked directions coming along had pointed it out.
She found the turning and was soon running through

a winding, narrow road, double-hedged and rosy with pink May blossom. The hedges fell away farther along and she saw a solitary little house in an orchard across the field to the left; and in the orchard there was something familiar.

It was Robby . . . Robby and a man.

As if she had been caught spying, she felt her color rise, and her foot pressed the accelerator and sent the little car leaping ahead. Ten minutes later, when Robby came to the meeting place, she found Una waiting sleepily as though she had been there for hours.

iv

Robby looked different and somehow jolly. Why, she had altered her face! Una did not pretend to notice, but lifted Tim off the seat for her to get in, and started off.

Half a mile down the road a small car with a man in it passed them, and Robby said urgently:

"Una, have you seen that car before . . . while you were waiting, I mean?"

"No, I didn't see a soul."

"Oh . . . thought I saw one nosing about down a lane, but it would have come out where you were."

"Might have been me," said Una carefully. "I've been round about and I came back through a lane, lovely it was, hawthorn for miles. I like this country."

She began to whistle; the little car raced like a horse going home to its stable.

"She always knows when we're going home," said

Una, but she knew that Robby was watching her out of the corner of her eye.

"I say, if anyone asks you, you didn't set eyes on me today. Promise."

"Of course . . . but as if anyone would. You are an ass. Still, I haven't, if they do," said Una.

"That's the ticket." Robby, relieved, was silent for a while, but she felt as though some sort of explanation, however lame, was necessary, so she added by and by: "Avril's a swine."

"Why do you stick it, Robby?"

"Hard cash, old dear, iron necessity, a thing you, lucky little devil, know nothing about. You have people to do your worrying for you."

"Nobody has," said Una.

"Oh well, perhaps you're right. Rotten world, isn't it?"

"I'm not sure I think so."

Robby laughed, not in her usual Robot fashion, but as though she were surprised. A rum kid, this, answering a catch phrase so solemnly.

"Well, what did you see in the lane?" Shock tactics were best, thought Robby; suspense was no good and it might be necessary to invent a tale.

"Nothing but hawthorn," said Una, "pink as pink."

Her cheeks were pinker, but she turned the car into Verulum with a steady hand.

"Lies like a good 'un," thought Robby relieved, "and a sticker too. Look at the way she drives."

She knew now it didn't matter what Una had seen, as she lay back in the car thinking of the other half of her in the orchard, talking of apples—he was sure he had invented a new one—and happy as the blackbird shouting overhead.

At Kilburn, where the crowd was safely thick, Robby elected to get out and go on by Tube, and she said to Una:

"Well, thanks for the lift, but don't forget you didn't give me one."

"I haven't seen you for weeks," agreed Una. "Good-by. Curses to Avril."

Why shouldn't Robby go and see a man in an orchard, or dozens if she chose? Una had guessed it was a man from the first; and what was it to Avril? Robby was her own mistress and could do as she liked.

Do as she liked! Tony Corcoran had said he would never be old enough to do that and Una had thought him absurd, but now she saw it was rather like the world—nobody able to do anything, because of somebody else.

She couldn't ask her mother to give her Wenlock, because immediately her father would want to give her some other house, larger probably, that she didn't want at all. And what couldn't Tony do?

Una smiled. She was going to have tea in the studio on Monday, for Kit had sent a note, all proper and correct, by Tony, who always seemed to be in the Gardens whatever time she went out, being ridiculous and asking for his bill. But she said she only sent out her accounts once a year, or that her secretary must have overlooked it. Tony was of opinion the minion must be inefficient and deserved the sack.

On Monday too she would take Tim in for Benyon to have a last look at him. Benyon wouldn't come any more, because he said it would be robbing her father; and when she explained the fees were her affair, he said it would be robbing her, which was ten times worse.

Of course she was paying for Tim. She had her own allowance, two in fact. A year ago her father had arranged to give her one, and a few hours later her mother had doubled it. She didn't know whether her father knew, but that was the kind of thing that always happened.

Discomfort returned to her and, as though out of space, the memory of her grandmother, a person of mysterious anger and ill-will and yet, it seemed to the girl, always so pleased about it. Grandmother would simply love to know that Robby had gone to see a man in an orchard, though it was no concern of hers; and this incident, up till now of no particular importance, became a triumph for Una because her grandmother would never know. "I have no patience with people who can't walk a few hundred yards to the Tube," she had said nastily, and what did she *mean?*

"We walk to the Tube," said Una to herself in high indignation, "but she's old and I thought she might have liked a taxi. I wish I had told her she was old."

She was too tongue-tied in her grandmother's presence ever to compass so perfect a revenge, but at a distance it was easy to be valiant, and as she drove into the garage and put up the car, her mind was gayly demolishing the enemy with a crushing phrase.

It was no good, however, for Jeremy and Anne had just come in when she arrived with Tim, and she joined them, miserably reminded of the wedding dinner.

She gave her grandmother's message carefully and dispassionately to both of them, and Anne exclaimed:

"But oh, dear, we can't, Jeremy. We promised the Spencers."

"Grandmother said it may be the last time," reported Una in an expressionless voice. "She says grandfather is failing fast."

"Good God! Anne, we'll have to go."

"Damn!" said Anne.

Una went despondently upstairs. She knew it. Everything was spoiled, and here it was again. Her mother couldn't do what she liked because of grandmother.

v

The menace of Tuesday's dinner, however, was a little lessened by the anticipation of seeing Tony again tomorrow, or at least the day after. He was always in Kensington Gardens, as far as she could make out, and whenever she suggested he ought to be working, he said he was doing his five mile walk. The Corcorans had to. It was because of the family curse.

He was so absurd that it was the easiest thing in the world to talk to Tony. Una had never felt this with anybody else. Speech was difficult to her, and somehow dangerous, but when she was with Tony it was fun.

He looked so solemn as he felt Tim's pulse, examined his tongue and suggested port wine and jelly, or perhaps a little rat in aspic. . . . "Filleted, of course," he said, "to get his strength up."

That Tim clearly liked these blandishments was an added virtue in Tony, for Tim was by no means an effusive dog. His companionship with Una had been too close.

"You know quite well he saved your life, don't you, Tim?" she said to him, carrying him across the road to the Gardens on Sunday morning. "Still, I dare say he won't be coming out today."

Not being certain made it all the more exciting, and as she put Tim down, debating whether it would be safe to let him go free, she did not turn her head to right or left, lest she should be disappointed.

"Invalid picking up?"

"Oh, hullo! Yes, he's heaps better. As you are here, do you think we might let him off the lead for a little while?"

"Of course he must be let off," said Tony, enchanted by this evidence of her faith in him. "The dog expects it. What do you think he is—a poodle?"

He released Tim, who barked a joyful acknowledgment and ran off on three legs, waiting, however, from time to time, and looking back for his slaves.

"I saw a restaurant the other day old Tim would have liked," said Tony. "It had a notice outside—

'Meals served here all day on all floors.' I went in and asked 'em if the floors were clean and they got quite hot about it."

"What did they say?"

"The haughty young lady behind the counter said, 'What sauce,' so I had a stab at it and guessed tomato. Apparently that was the wrong answer and it should have been Worcester," said Tony mournfully.

"And then what did you do?" Una joyfully encouraged the fairy tale.

"Ran like blazes," confided Tony smiling, charmed by her eager attention and the quality of her voice.

It was not, he thought, just a voice like other voices, but full of wistfulness and a kind of laughing surprise as though she liked his fooling. And she did not, as half the people in the world would do, rush in with a story of her own about a restaurrant, or even tell him he was an ass, after the manner of the other half. An amazing girl!

Tim had come back appealing for notice and Una was throwing a stick for him . . . just a little way.

"Because," she explained seriously to Tony, "we've got to encourage him to use his leg now, Mr. Benyon says, or one of his other paws must be cut to make him, and that would seem so mean after all he has been through."

"Oh, lord, yes, a dirty trick," agreed Tony, with becoming indignation.

His eyes followed her game with Tim, delighting as ever in her grace, though his thoughts were busy now with other pictures of her, imaginary pictures of all the hours when he was not there. He felt suddenly resentful of these hours, full of adventures and delights from which he was left out. He thought forlornly of his own existence, no money, precious little fun, and weeks of this restlessness when it was impossible to work—a feeble business. And she had everything in the world, old Benyon had said, and even Kit had made pointed references to her clothes.

"Another dress?" he said to her accusingly, as she came back with Tim under her arm. "You are an extravagant girl. Have no end of a gay time, don't you?"

"Oh, no, not really," declared Una in surprise, and all at once found herself confiding: "I'm not awfully fond of rushing about, and since Tim was hurt I've skipped everything. It has been lovely. I've got to go to a beastly dinner on Tuesday night though—*family.*"

"No?" said Tony, thinking guiltily of Mrs. Polhampton. "What—aunts and so on?"

"Yes, and worse—a grandmother."

"Don't you be put upon by her," said Tony indignantly, because of the sudden dimming of her face. "What is a grandmother anyway? If she tries to come it over you, just refer her to me."

Under his pleading smile the shadow passed, and she laughed, delighted.

"And who may Tony be if I may make so bold as to ask?" she could hear her grandmother saying

nastily, but she would never give her the chance, the
satisfaction. She thought with a pang of her dance
only ten days off and how, but for the family, she
could have asked Tony and Kit. But that affair was
spoiled already and birthdays filled her with dread.
Presents . . . thanking people and feeling a fool.

"If I could only have an unbirthday party," she
thought, "I'd ask them."

"There is Kit Corcoran, who designed that dress
of yours," she would say to Anne, "and she has a
brother. We might ask them." No fear of insinuating questions from her mother, who would laugh
and say: "What? There really is a Kit Corcoran,
then? Ask them by all means."

Tony would look well in evening dress. He was
so tall and thinnish and his clothes belonged to him.
They were right, but not, she thought, because he
fussed about them, as her father did. And Kit too,
with her curly head, looking jolly in a frock she had
designed herself!

"How's Kit?" she asked Tony, sadly relinquish-
ing the dream.

"Very flourishing."

"I like her," Una found herself saying, unexpectedly.

"Haven't I trained her well?" said Tony with
pride. "Sisters, I've told her, should be seen and not
heard, and not too often seen. Still, they're better
than grandmothers any day. Grandmothers are
the Alsatians of this world . . . always making
trouble."

"Do yours?"

"They would if they hadn't retired from practice," Tony assured her cheerfully. "I've been very clever with my relatives . . . abolished the lot of them, practically."

"I wish I could," said Una with a sigh.

"Aunts," suggested Tony, still endeavoring to place Mrs. Polhampton but afraid to ask outright, "would be snappy Pomeranians, don't you think, or would you say ferrets?"

"Mine are both," said Una with vigor, and wondered why he looked so pleased.

She felt better about the family dinner now, since through Tony she had found the relief of speech, but she did not guess that she had also brought him reassurance. It was so clear that she disliked her relatives, that his spirits rose and he returned to the studio whistling exultantly. Why worry about old Polhampton and her silly statue? Una wouldn't care.

Kit, to whom with great cunning he had taken a cup of tea in bed this morning, had breakfast waiting, and for once made no song about his late appearance. That she was being cunning also did not occur to Tony, though he approved her silence and even found himself approving her. A good sort, Kit, he thought, practical and all that, and not too bad looking for a sister. Una liked her.

CHAPTER VIII

i

THE Swithins' house at Wimbledon was not like any other house that Una knew; it was so dreadfully new and shining. It belonged to an era when maids had been easily come by and poorly paid, a rosy era for the house proud, but now, alas, long past. And if its passing had brought the beauty of simplicity and space into many homes that had known neither before, Mrs. Swithin was not the woman to lower her flag in this weak fashion before the servant problem. Her solid mahogany and bees-waxed linoleum borders needed plenty of elbow grease and got it still, though every registry office for miles knew and dreaded the sound of her voice.

Una had her own reasons for hating her grand-mother's shining floors, because of an episode of her very early youth. She was not much more than five at the time, and had been brought by her nurse to spend a day at Wimbledon, a rite which old Mrs. Swithin periodically demanded. The nurse was at midday dinner in the kitchen and Una, left to her-self for a moment, had wandered off round the drawing-room, seeking adventures in her usual mouselike fashion. All at once, in the shining space between the carpet and the wall, she saw a face look-ing back at her, a face much wider than it was long and altogether entrancing. She bent over to look at it and the face moved too, immediately changing its shape. It was an enthralling game and she could have played it happily for half an hour if grandmother had not caught her at it.

"What are you doing, Una?" said Mrs. Swithin, who had a theory that children should never be left to themselves for a moment. "What is the matter with the floor, child?" And Una, with perfect confidence, leaned over again and joyfully pointed.

"Funny face," she said.

Mrs. Swithin was horrified. Looking at herself in the linoleum . . . such vanity, and at her age! She shook her granddaughter, carried her to a little chair and told her to sit there and not to move again. She was a very vain and wicked little girl. No nice little girl looked at herself either in the mirror or the floor or anything else, or she would grow into a bad and wicked woman, said grandmother. Aunt Fanny came in, was told of the enormity, and Una was talked to, talked over and talked at.

It was terrible and she was utterly bewildered. Such a thing had never before happened to her in a kindly world. She sat without daring to stir, her hands and little bare knees growing colder and colder, and a dreadful feeling inside her as though she were going to be sick.

"It's the force of example," said grandmother, nodding to Aunt Fanny, who nodded back. "I'm sure you never see me looking at myself, Una, or Aunt Fanny either."

Una was too young to see the implication, though she understood it later well enough, too young also to realize that if Aunt Fanny had, with her wispy hair and poor flat features, she would have seen a funny face indeed.

It seemed ages later that her grandfather appeared, and then he had to be told all about it; but he said jovially: "Well, well, it's nothing to what she'll be doing in a few years' time, if I know anything of her sex," and in spite of Mrs. Swithin's indignant protests, he lifted the criminal on to his knee.

"Dear me, who's a frog?" said grandfather, pinching her cheeks and rubbing her cold little knees with his warm hand.

Una loved him from that moment.

She told nobody of the incident. Comprehension and explanation of the dreadful shame that possessed her were equally beyond her then, but for years she never saw her grandmother without feeling guilty and hot all over, and it was torture to enter her house.

Even tonight at the wedding dinner her eyes turned away instinctively from the bright surface of the sideboard which was opposite her place at table, and sought the safety of the cloth instead. Fortunately for Una Mrs. Swithin did not approve of dining at a polished board in the modern manner . . . when had she approved of anything modern? She believed in good plain damask with a runner down the center, and napkins folded into all manner of shapes that meant nothing at all, but had to be handled carefully, as Una knew, lest your bread shoot out on the floor and cover you with ignominy.

From where she sat Una could see her mother on old Mr. Swithin's right, looking, although she had had to let down the Spencers, so gay and pretty in her blue and silver gown. Her father-in-law (who didn't appear in the least to be failing) was clearly delighted to have her there, and was flirting with her gallantly, at which Mrs. Herbert Swithin, half way down the table and over-sequined, pursed her thin lips and looked neglected. She had a brother-in-law on either side of her, but it is true they were little use as entertainment. John Swithin said little at any time and looked cynical always; and Jeremy's attention was engaged by his mother.

Una was on the young side of the table, which of necessity included her Aunt Fanny, two years older than Anne. Seated between the whited sepulchers, Mab and Herbert, Una was conscious that they eyed her furtively and often, and then telegraphed to each other behind her back. Una was wearing a plain little frock of stiff white silk with a red rose on her shoulder. (You had to be so careful what you wore at grandmother's parties, but surely white would be all right.) She was not fond of jewelry and her slender neck and long fingers were bare; but Mab, with a double row of pearls and two rings, was in one of Una's last year's dresses, which made its late owner uncomfortable as it was probably intended to do.

Una did not blame Mab for hating her because

she had to wear her passed-on clothes, but *she* didn't want to pass them on and neither did Anne. It was grandmother. Because Uncle Herbert had been killed in the War, old Mrs. Swithin had ever since demanded Una's clothes for Mab, and how could they refuse her? They sent only the best of them, carefully cleaned and pressed, but Una well knew the spirit in which the charity was received. Herbert and Mab were as meek as mice in their grandmother's presence, saying, "Yes, granny," "No, granny dear" . . . they had lived four years in her house and knew a thing or two, as they put it to Una; for free of her presence they were frank . . . frank and terrible.

ii

"Well, Anne, my dear," said her father-in-law, affectionately, "not a day older than when you were married, I see. How do you manage it?"

"It's a trick," said Anne gayly, "but I don't mind telling you the recipe in strict confidence. You marry into the Swithin family."

"Very nicely put. The age of chivalry is not dead, after all—merely passed on to your sex like everything else. Well, well, it's good to see you, and upon my word, you grow handsomer every day."

"Really, father, I don't know how you can pay Anne such barefaced compliments," protested Fanny, stationed at that end of the table to police her father and sister-in-law.

"If Anne doesn't know she's lovely, my dear, your brother must be a greater fool than I take him for," said Mr. Swithin dryly. "Come, Anne, doesn't he tell you so, as often as ever?"

"He always tries to avoid the obvious," declared Anne with a twinkle in her eye, and the old man laughed, delighted.

"I'm none so sure of the chivalry, after all. It's clear I'll have to keep my wits about me," he said.

Mrs. Herbert Swithin was saying to John in her high, complaining voice:

"All over Italy they've been and wanted me to go too. On my pension. . . . I ask you. It does make me wild the luck some people have."

"Quite," said John.

"You needn't trouble to send that dress to me, because I don't like it," said Mab to Una in a nasty undertone.

"All right," said Una.

"Now then, you young people, what are you talking about so confidentially?" inquired grandmother with her eye on them. "Come, Mab, my dear, let us all hear it."

"We were only talking about Una's dress, granny."

"And I'm sure it's a very nice dress," conceded Mrs. Swithin, "but you are wearing a pretty dress yourself, Mab, and I hope you have thanked Una properly for giving it to you."

"Of course, granny dear."

"I don't think," muttered Herbert in Una's ear.

"And now suppose you show us the wonderful ring we've heard so much about, Una," proceeded grandmother, and held out a hand for it. "Pass it to me, Mab. I'm sure it was very thoughtful of your Aunt Marion to remember Una's birthday on her travels."

Una, looking at her bare fingers, turned hot, then cold.

"I'm sorry, I didn't wear it, grandmother."

Aunt Marion's ring . . . Tony's ring . . . how had they heard of it? Oh, she might have known. They heard of everything. She glanced at her father, who was watching her with a slight frown, and she said, smiling at him apologetically:

"It's rather large. It doesn't fit me very well!"

"I'll have it made smaller for you," said Jeremy.

"Do," commanded grandmother, "and see that she takes care of it. I have no doubt Marion paid a great deal of money for the ring, and I must say I'm sorry Una didn't bring it with her. I should have been glad to see it. However. . . ."

"Una isn't wearing any jewelry at all," said Mab's voice in innocent surprise at this moment.

"No doubt she keeps it for her grander parties," observed Aunt Herbert disagreeably.

"Nonsense!" snapped old Mrs. Swithin to this. "A lot of fallalls and trinkets on young girls are quite out of place, but the ring is a different matter. We should necessarily have liked to see it. Una must try to be more thoughtful in future."

John Swithin, watching his young niece being baited, thought what an obnoxious thing family tyranny may be. He himself had cut away from it long ago . . . luckier than Jeremy, after all. He was the eldest of the Swithins and the cleverest, but had had to play second fiddle all his life to his more brilliant and attractive brother. It amused him to remember that this had once hurt, for now he could sit aloof and watch the family comedy with a dispassionate eye. He understood his mother perfectly . . . her pride in her son's marriage to Lady Anne and her jealous though unconscious determination not to be proud of it, but to find every fault in her daughter-in-law so that the benefit of the alliance should seem to balance on the other side. It was a new peerage, as she frequently pointed out in the family circle (though never beyond it) and who were the Challices after all? Not a whit better than the Swithins, that she would guarantee.

The human game, how little it changed, thought John, talk as they might about all this modernity. The very gusto with which his mother, Fanny, Herbert's wife, the whole boiling of 'em, used Anne's Christian name whenever they spoke to her, as though savoring the privilege, was part of the comedy. And in private among themselves they bewailed the sacrifices they had made to the marriage.

Sacrifices? John smiled cynically. They had had their money's worth, he knew, were drawing dividends at this very hour. What did Anne, sitting light-heartedly beside him, think of it all, he wondered. He and she were not much acquainted, but in the course of his business, knowledge of many people came his way, and he knew there was no whisper against her . . . none at least save the whispers of fools, which could be disregarded. He was aware, however, that this information would be small com-

fort to his mother, who "knew what she knew."
(Don't ask me how, John.)

Once more his eyes turned to the tall grave child
who was the daughter of Jeremy and Anne. Distinc-
tion there, he thought, wherever it came from . . .
and where does it, but from the mind or spirit,
or whatever you choose to call it? She gave nothing
away, that little girl, where most people give a sight
too much.

Anne said to him suddenly, under the cover of
talk, "Is your father really as well as he thinks?"

"Perfectly well, except for an occasional touch of
rheumatism. Why?"

"I'm glad. . . . Jeremy was worried."

"Humph!" said John non-committally. His
mother again, he supposed . . . one of her little
wiles, persuading herself she was forced to invent
a crisis to get Jeremy and Anne here out of their
gay life. "Still, he always was a chap to worry."

"Was he?"

He looked at her, his thin face wrinkled into a
faint smile, knowing that in some shadowy way he
had given her relief. For a moment they were near,
but the moment passed.

Mrs. Herbert leaned across him in the fashion he
detested (the woman looked like a fish in all those
scales) and said stridently to her sister-in-law:

"So Wenlock's empty, I see, Anne? Some friends
drove me out there in their saloon car the other
Sunday, and isn't it in a mess? It would make me
wild to see the place going to rack and ruin like that
if it was mine. My friend's in the estate business and

he said it would fetch next to nothing. Two a penny, places like that, my friend said."

"Really?" inquired Anne, imperturbably. "He may be right."

Una heard her aunt's words, though not her mother's cool reply. Wenlock, poor lonely Wenlock, and Aunt Herbert daring to talk of it like that! She felt resentful and affronted, and for a moment she forgot her father and saw this member of his family as she really was—a dreadful person. She was as little part of the Swithins' world as of her mother's, and yet just because Uncle Herbert had been killed in the War, they hung on to her and were kind. Or were they?

No, thought Una in sudden illumination, it wasn't kindness. She looked at the three men and knew their faces closed against Aunt Herbert. As for grandmother, she snapped at her daughter-in-law and snubbed her in a way she would never have dared to do to the more fortunate Anne, and that was contemptible. Why did Aunt Herbert stand it, why did she come, for it was plain she hated every one of them.

But then, if it came to that, why had any of them come? She looked at her father, who seemed tired and worried, and she knew that she and Anne were there on his account, because he was so absurd about the family, always thinking they despised it. They had come for peace, but it was all wrong; they wouldn't find it here. They were all caught up in this shining crowded room in a sort of family net, none of them really wanting to be there, yet all pre-

tending to each other. And what was the use of it?
Life, thought Una, ought not to be like that, and
yet it was. You were always pretending . . . that
you believed grandfather was failing, for instance,
though you knew it was only a tale, that you had
forgotten to wear Aunt Marion's ring, when you
had really given it to Tony Corcoran; that your
father came first, because he was the odd man out
and you knew he would be hurt and you couldn't
bear it.

Suddenly Jeremy was on his feet, making a little
speech, for this was a wedding dinner and there was
a health to be drunk to these two who had been
bride and bridegroom fifty-two years ago today. He
was saying graceful things to please his mother, and
she was looking complacent, as much as to ask where
but for her would they all be? Six of them at least
not even in the world.

"I should," thought Una. "I should be somebody
else." Wistfully she wondered what it would have
felt like. Being alive at all was such a curious thing.
"I'm myself," said Una over and over in her mind.
Rebelliously she was determined to acknowledge no
obligation to her grandmother.

"Ah, Jeremy, blood is thicker than water," said
Mrs. Swithin in a pleased tone, as though she had
arranged that it should be so, as Jeremy sat down.
She loved stock phrases and used them for her own
ends, and what did this one mean, except, "See what
I've done for you all."

Herbert kicked Una under the table, but she
drew her feet out of his way with distaste. Blood

or no blood, these people were no kin of hers. Then, turning her eyes for a moment to her mother's end of the table, she met the gaze of her Uncle John and found there something that surprised her, so that she was not so sure. It was as though for once her father had looked at her, not jealously, but with humor and understanding.

And now her grandfather was returning thanks, a tall old man, so like yet unlike both his sons, so much softer than the one, so much calmer than the other.

Una suddenly smiled. Her father was a Swithin and all the cleverness in the world could not make her grandmother that.

iii

"Now, you young people, the bagatelle board is set out in the breakfast room," said grandmother, marshaling her daughters-in-law upstairs. "You may come into the drawing-room for coffee later."

"Bagatelle?" muttered Mab contemptuously, as the door was closed upon them by Aunt Fanny. "It's a wonder that granny doesn't buy us a Noah's ark." And she flung herself into the one easy chair.

Herbert, sprawled on the chesterfield, was full of a grievance of his own.

"Dam' rot, not letting me stay with the men. Anyway, I'll have a cig if I die for it. If she smells it I can always say it was my fast cousin Una."

Una, knocking a ball about with the cue, listened in silence, though she knew this was probably no empty threat. They would say anything, these two, and it was useless to argue with them.

"I've got an admirer, Una," said Mab. "Potty about me he is, too. You ought to see."

"Wait till his wife sees," said her brother nastily. "The poor nut."

"A lot I care. He doesn't think I know he's married, but there's not much this child misses, and I'm leading him on for a lark. Next Saturday he's taking me out in his car, and in case you don't know it, Una, I'm spending the day with you, officially, that is. Won't mother and granny be pleased?"

"You are doing nothing of the kind," said Una, indignantly.

"Yes, I am, dearie. You asked me this evening and quite time too. I must have an alibi and you split on me if you dare."

Across the room brother and sister exchanged an understanding grin, and Una looked at them with contempt.

"You shan't drag me into it."

"All right, you little sneak. Go and tell and take the consequences. What about your own mother, if it comes to that?" said Mab. "Her and her Corkran, or whatever his name is. Oh, quite a romance, isn't it, making statues of her and what not? Thought we didn't know, I suppose, but there's not much *we* don't hear. And wouldn't Uncle Jeremy be pleased? Mother's going to let it all out to him and the whole family at your birthday dinner, if Aunt Anne doesn't do something she wants, so you'd better give her a hint to be civil, darling."

"Tell her 'safety first,'" supplemented Herbert.

"Sorry to cramp Aunt Anne's style, but business is business, don't you know."

"Be quiet!" said Una in an awful voice. Her eyes were blazing and her face, which had been scarlet a moment since, was white as death, but her cousins shouted with laughter.

"Now will you tell about Saturday?" cried Mab in triumph.

"You utter cads!"

She did not even look at them, but opened the door and went.

They were suddenly quiet behind her, for this was unexpected and it might be distinctly awkward if Una gave them away. Not that she ever had on past occasions, and they had counted on that . . . her silly attitude of thinking it was low to tell tales. They listened, peered through the keyhole, and finally opened the door and looked out, to find Una flying up the stairs as though a hundred devils were after her.

Shaking from head to foot, she had been standing in the hall, not knowing where to hide herself in this enemy house, when the opening of the door startled her into flight. She could not face them again, for she was in a blind rage such as she had never known before, and she could almost have killed them with her bare hands.

She was at the drawing-room door now, but she could not go in there. It would show . . . it must be written all over her face, the state she was in. The doorway of her grandfather's smoking-room offered her a dark sanctuary, and she stumbled into it, found a chair, and pressing her face to the cool leather, fought for her self-control.

What had they said? She didn't know and she mustn't think . . . not in this awful house at least. Presently she would have to go in for coffee and she must look just as usual. That was the one thing of which she was really conscious.

There was a step on the stairs. It couldn't be . . . oh, surely it wasn't the coffee already? She sat up and smoothed her hair in a panic and sought for a handkerchief to wipe her hot face; but the step came on, the little room was flooded with light and she saw her Uncle John in the doorway.

"Hullo! Hiding away in the dark?" he asked without surprise.

"Yes," said Una eagerly, forcing herself to smile. "I'm hiding from Herbert and Mab." Desperately she hoped he would think it was just a childish game.

"You've come to the right spot then. They won't find you here," said her uncle imperturbably.

"Won't they?"

"Not while I'm about."

He closed the door with a faint chuckle and put her back in the chair from which she had jumped at his coming.

"I've left your father and mine deep in talk and come away to finish my cigar," he said. "I'm not much of a talker."

"No," agreed Una.

"We are birds of a feather, I gather?"

His smile was so kind that she found herself

smiling in return, but easily now. By ignoring her distress, he had helped her to conquer it, and she could even think how queer it was that all her life he had seemed aloof and strange, and now without warning, as it were, he had become a friend.

"You don't mind my cigar?"

"No, I like it."

"But I like a pipe better," added Una confidentially, after a moment.

"Oh, you do?"

"Yes, it looks so comfortable . . . like country clothes."

"Good!"

An odd product this, of a restless and chaotic age, thought John. She was like a throwback to simpler and more peaceful times. And yet, he was not so sure. There had been fight in her face and terror too as he came in, and under his eyes she had taken herself in hand. They had spirit and pluck, these young things, whatever other virtues the world denied them.

He did not ask what Mab and Herbert had been doing to her, but when by and by the other men came upstairs, followed by the coffee and the giggling, whispering pair in question, he shepherded her into the drawing-room and stood by. The young Herberts were afraid of him and he knew it. They dared no more than a furtive glance at their cousin. It was ironic, he thought, that such a good chap as his brother Herbert should have been snapped up by that scheming, overdressed woman, their mother; ironic too that it should be Jeremy's daughter, alone of the family, who could move him to any interest. Sentimentally this was all wrong. Jeremy, favored from childhood, should have made a mess of his marriage, while Herbert's good qualities should have been reproduced in the son and daughter he left behind, to be at once a consolation and a reproach to those who had passed him over. John smiled grimly. Life didn't work out like that; luck held and the scales were always weighted one way or the other.

His mother was once more deep in talk with Jeremy, so it was easy enough to protect Una unobtrusively from any further shafts. They said very little to each other, but presently, when the evening was over, he remarked during the clamor of farewells:

"Come and take me out to lunch some day."

"When may I?" asked Una eagerly.

She knew it was an offer of help and he knew she would never ask it, but like two conspirators they arranged the rendezvous, and he took her out to the car. With every appearance of innocence, he had prevented either Herbert or Mab from saying goodby to her, and she was gratefully certain he had done it on purpose.

"Really, John, you grow very gallant," said Mrs. Herbert, as he returned to the house. "Is it Una or the Lady Anne?"

"Why not both?" inquired John Swithin coolly.

CHAPTER IX

i

THE drive from Wimbledon was a silent one. Even Anne's vitality was at a low ebb, and beyond a reassuring word to Jeremy about his father, which was received with a moody grunt, she said nothing.

Una as a rule loved driving home at night with the shining road unwinding like a bright ribbon before them and ghostly trees and houses hedging them on each side. Even London then became an enchanted country, and when the mists were down and only the road running through a double chain of lights remained, it was like driving to nowhere through an empty world, eerie and wonderful.

But tonight no such solace reached her troubled spirit, as she lay back in her dark corner staring straight ahead yet seeing nothing, her heart heavy with the sense of loss. Her secret friendship was dead, killed by one blow of Mab Swithin's ugly hand.

Tony! There could not be two people called Corcoran making statues, it was impossible; and she had believed that he and Kit were her own private discovery, gloriously removed from the troubled currents of her life at home. But if he were really her mother's friend, then he was just like anybody else and it was all spoiled. He had wanted to make a little statue of her and Tim, but according to Mab he had made statues of her mother. Most romantic, she had called it, in that beastly, insinuating voice of hers.

Una felt herself flushing scarlet in the darkness, for now she realized, with astonishment and distress, that she had been thinking only of her own side of it, and not at all of her mother's and their disgusting hints about her. Once more she could have killed her cousins, for how dared they talk like that of Anne, as if she were one of those idiot women who play round with young men half their age, looking sentimental and too silly for words? The picture was so far from the truth that Una could have laughed at it coming from any other source, but she knew the family. They would love to believe such a tale and talk it over smugly, having always believed the worst. And then there was her father.

"Won't Uncle Jeremy be pleased?" Mab had said, hinting that her mother was going to let it all out at the birthday dinner if Aunt Anne didn't do something or other.

Una was by no means clear about this except that it was a threat and therefore beneath contempt. Let her aunt say it, then, and perhaps her father would see that these awful family gatherings were a mistake. But would he? She tried to look at her father dispassionately, and she knew that he was jealous. Always he had been jealous of her mother's affection for her, jealous even of the gifts she bought her, jealous that they should be much together. It was ridiculous and unnecessary, but that didn't alter the fact. He was jealous for his family, jealous of the newspapers which were forever publishing her mother's photograph, then why not of Tony Corcoran making a statue of her?

Tony! He was back again in the picture and she did not want him there. He had seemed so gloriously outside these problems, an absurd, light-hearted creature; and here he was, dragged on to the center of the family stage, as a lovesick young man being romantic about her mother. It was revolting.

She did not blame Tony for admiring Anne. If all the sculptors in the world fell in love with her mother it was not surprising, since she was so beautiful, but now Una sadly supposed Tony had sought her out simply because she was her mother's daughter. Or wouldn't that make him avoid her, feeling himself a fool? Besides, for the first week he hadn't even known her name . . . she remembered he had actually asked her what it was as they went to tea together in Kensington Gardens. The revelation had not excited him either, as far as she had noticed, and almost immediately after he had asked her to sit for him.

There! Didn't that prove he didn't know her mother and the name meant nothing to him? It was merely a lie invented by the Herbert Swithins. Yet why should they have mentioned the name Corcoran, of all others in the world? Besides, he had said to her afterwards, quite suddenly and in an awkward voice, "You'd better ask your mother about the sittings," and she had thought how funny he was to think you would, in these days.

Then he did know her mother, after all; but why hadn't he said so, and why hadn't she seen the statue or heard of it, and why hadn't she long ago seen or heard of Tony?

The car drew up; they were at home; and Una, her problem still unsolved and heavier than ever, went into the house after her father and mother.

"Good night," she said to them briefly from the bottom of the stairs, and her father looked after her and called in a voice of irritation:

"Bring down your aunt's ring in the morning, Una, and I'll have it made smaller for you."

More troubles . . . oh, hang the ring and hang the family. Una went on upstairs, suddenly furious and hating everybody. She wasn't going to face that now, but she almost wished she had.

Why hadn't she looked them coolly in the eye and said: "Sorry, I can't. I've given the ring to Tony Corcoran."

ii

Jeremy went into the dining-room for a whiskey and soda and Anne followed him to smoke a cigarette. She was tired, but he was clearly out of humor and it was no good making him worse by omitting the little ceremony. She knew he liked her to be there.

"I don't think there is much need for anxiety about your father," she remarked. "I have never seen him in better spirits."

Jeremy glared at his glass but made no reply.

"Look here, Anne," he burst out suddenly, "it's a great pity that Lyne woman should have been here with Una when my mother called on Saturday."

"My dear boy, if your mother will pay us surprise visits, how can we regulate the company to please her?" said Anne reasonably.

"You know perfectly well that I disapprove of Roberta Lyne, and, as my mother says, she is no fit companion for Una."

"I disagree with your mother, but there is no question of Robby's being a companion to Una. You are talking nonsense, Jeremy."

"Walking about the room, painted like a woman of the streets, and cursing and swearing," went on Jeremy furiously. "No wonder my mother was upset."

Anne laughed.

"A woman of the streets would need to be a good deal more careful of her appearance than that," she said. "As for swearing, I do it myself occasionally, and paint too, with a good deal less excuse than poor Robby. You know that perfectly well; so go to bed, my dear, and sleep off this attack. You'll feel better in the morning."

"Calling me by my Christian name, too," continued Jeremy unheeding. "Damned insolence."

"Most of my friends call you by your Christian name. I've always supposed you liked it," said Anne. It was too bad, she supposed, to rub that in when she knew how true it was; so she shook him gently by the arm and added: "You're trying to quarrel with me and I won't have it, so stop scowling like the heavy husband of melodrama and let us go to bed."

"We've got to have this out," said Jeremy stubbornly. "I'm not going to have that Lyne woman at Una's birthday party and that's certain."

"You are too late. The invitations have gone out."

"Then hers will have to be canceled."

"No," said Anne.

"Quite apart from everything else, her presence would be a direct affront to my mother."

"Jeremy, doesn't it occur to you that your whole discussion with Mrs. Swithin this evening was an affront to me?"

"God, Anne, you know it wasn't. That's not fair. Women never are fair, if it comes to that," declared Jeremy miserably.

"Your mother is a woman."

"Yes, I know, but she is old-fashioned and we must make allowances for her."

"Why must we? That is merely sentimental and economically wrong. She belongs to a past age but she is living in this one, and she must adjust herself to it or keep out."

"Well, if you won't cancel the invitation, I shall tell Una to do it," said Jeremy, returning somewhat lamely to the charge.

"That would be unwise."

"I suppose you'll advise her to defy me?"

"If I know Una, she won't consult me," said

Anne dryly. "She is not a baby and she is the most loyal little soul alive, but she is at a critical age, and what will she think of you? Robby Lyne has had to face the most ghastly domestic troubles that were no fault of hers. One doesn't hit a person who is down."

"My darling girl, you are incapable of understanding that type of girl," exclaimed Jeremy. "Every decent woman is, and you really must be guided by me. I'll cancel the invitation myself and that's an end of it."

"You really mean that?"

"Certainly."

"Very well, then I shall go straight upstairs and cancel the invitation to your mother and sisters."

"I'm damned if you will," shouted Jeremy, jumping to his feet.

"Don't wake the household, please," requested Anne, "and just try to remember we are not living in the stone age. I mean what I say. I have stood all I am going to stand from you on the subject of your family, Jeremy, and you may as well hear what I think about it once and for all. Year after year you grow more touchy and more unreasonable until it has become a positive obsession with you, and if I hadn't been a fool I should have put a stop to it long ago. These family parties are a misery to all three of us, and yet for some mysterious reason you insist upon them as if they were a sacred rite. It is natural that you should be fond of your mother, but the fact that she brought you into the world doesn't give her a divine right to interfere with my

friends, and my daughter, and I shall put up with
no more of it."

"She's my daughter too, isn't she?" said Jeremy
jealously at once.

Anne was almost tempted to ask if his mother
had suggested otherwise, but she could be generous
even in anger and she pushed the flippancy aside.

"Well, your daughter, if you prefer it that way.
Are you so incapable of looking after Una, and am
I, that we should be scolded and called over the
coals by outsiders?"

"A grandmother is hardly an outsider, Anne."

"Of course she is. What, after all, has she ever
done for Una? Has she had to support and educate
and clothe her or have we? Your mother is simply
an old lady like any other old lady, who does not
know the world we live in or one of the people she
criticizes."

"It's not her fault or mine that we belong to a
different world from yours," cried Jeremy at once.

"Oh, my dear, don't be so foolish. My world is
yours and you know it," said Anne impatiently.

"You don't understand."

"No, there you are right. I don't understand you
in the least, though I do understand your mother.
She is a managing woman and there are plenty like
her, but you are a man and leading strings do not
become you."

"Thanks."

"Even mine," added Anne with a little smile.

"Don't try to soften it, please. You've said quite
enough."

"Very well."

She went to the door, waited a moment for him to open it for her, and then as he made no movement, turned the handle.

"I meant what I said about the letter, Jeremy. If you write to Roberta, I shall write to your mother," she said, and was gone.

Jeremy poured out another whiskey and drank it neat.

iii

Sleep came fitfully and seldom to all three of them that night. Una turned her problem over and over until it became unreal and stalked like a nightmare through her half waking dreams, so that she found herself repeating phrases and arguments that were without meaning and yet went on and on.

Once, years after she had gone to bed it seemed, she heard stumbling steps on the stairs, but she was too weary and miserable to wonder what anyone could be doing at that hour of the night.

Anne, however, heard the same sound with a measure of relief. Scenes filled her with distaste and she had always fastidiously avoided them, but tonight she had seen the folly of taking any line of least resistance. It was weak. For years, it seemed to her, a subtle poison had been working in Jeremy, and although she was still blind to its cause, she could see his mother's hand in it and she thought it was just as well that for once they had had the matter out. He would not take up her challenge about Robby the Robot, she was convinced; he was by nature both courteous and kind; and by tomorrow this irritation of his mother's making would have subsided and he would know that he had been absurd.

Anne smiled at the stumbling footsteps. She did not grudge him the comfort of getting mildly drunk, poor darling, and she thought: "After all, we're luckier than most people. It's more than twenty years and we're neither hostile nor indifferent. We still care."

Jeremy was in no state of mind to believe in any such miracle. Leading strings? So that was what she thought of him? He might have known it, for who was he to hold her? All night he tossed restlessly from side to side, rising at last with a raging headache and quite incapable of returning Anne's friendly smile at breakfast. The fact that she could smile seemed only another sign of the difference between them.

He could not eat and, though he opened the newspaper, his throbbing head made it impossible to read, so he closed it again, obstinately refusing to hide behind it like a criminal. Since he could not look at Anne, he turned instead to Una, and recalling her aunt's ring, found relief in speech.

"Now then, Una, where's this ring of yours?"

Una had given up the idea of telling the truth about the ring, so she replied: "I couldn't very well say so last night, but I've lost it."

"Lost it? What do you mean by lost it?" exclaimed her father, as though losing rings were an art utterly new and unknown. "Where . . . how . . . when did you lose it?"

"On Friday . . . probably in Kensington Gardens."

"Good lord, and do you mean to tell me you have done nothing about it? Did you tell the keeper or whatever they call the fellow?"

"No."

"You seem remarkably casual about your valuables, don't you, Una?" said her father sharply. "Why, in heaven's name, didn't you tell me you had lost the ring?"

"Well, it's my loss, father," said Una composedly. "You couldn't help it."

"That remains to be seen. You might have a little more thought for other people with advantage. What do you suppose your aunt will think? She's to be back in England within the next few days."

Una looked at her father in complete amazement as he jumped up from the table and strode angrily into the hall; but Anne said softly: "Headache, don't worry," and followed Jeremy closing the door behind her.

"Written your letter?" she enquired of him lightly.

"No."

"Changed your mind then?"

"I have not and I don't intend to change it," snapped Jeremy, and before he knew quite what had happened, he had slammed the hall door in his wife's face and was running down the steps.

"Mother, was it the ring?"

Anne, at the sound of her daughter's horrified voice, laughed and returned to the dining-room.

"Of course not. He's out of sorts, poor dear, and lost his head in the excitement of being a heavy father. He'll have forgotten you ever had a ring by tonight. No man should be taken seriously at this hour of the morning and not too often at any other hour."

"No, they are difficult, aren't they?" agreed Una seriously.

"That's part of their attraction," said Anne.

Una, though not proof against her mother's charm, was proof against this deception, for the same instinct was deeply embedded in her own nature. When one was in trouble one fought it out alone, telling nobody.

And today above and beyond her own private perplexities about Tony and the statue was the old troubled awareness that something was wrong between her father and mother. It seemed to her that it had been going on and on for years . . . some struggle that she could not understand, and in which she felt herself implicated but impotent, as one who holds his breath in a despairing effort to avoid disaster.

The past week or two of peace which had come so mysteriously on the heels of Tim's injury, seemed heaven to her now they were gone . . . and she knew they were gone without being able to tell why.

After the first moment she had not really supposed it was the ring, though her father had never spoken so sharply to her before that she could remember. Being the heavy father, as Anne called it, was entirely foreign to him.

Una knew secretly that he and she were never really at ease with each other though he sought her so often and in some dumb fashion seemed always to be demanding so much. He was awkward with her and yet appealing and somehow apologetic, and it made her feel uncomfortable, as though he were showing her something he would not want her to see; guilty too, because she felt he wanted to be first with her and she knew he was not.

And now what was the matter? Scolding her about the ring, which was after all her own business, and banging the door in her mother's face! Irritable though he might be, he was always so punctilious in his manners to both of them, much more so than any of the other men she knew in their family life . . . opening doors for them, tucking them into the car, standing when they came into a room, and so careful before the servants or any outsider. Yet everyone in the house must have heard that banging door and some of them no doubt had seen Anne standing inside it.

Una had never heard her father and mother actually quarrel. Anne seemed able to treat light-heartedly even his blackest moods, but what did she think of him really, and did she know what this was all about, or did he?

Una with her problem, wandered restlessly about the house that morning, until Tim's reproachful looks took her into the Gardens at last; but it was safely late by that time and Tony was nowhere to be seen. She was relieved.

She had promised to go out to lunch and was

just getting ready when Brent came to say she was wanted on the telephone.

"Lorenzo the Less speaking," said a voice she knew.

"Oh, hullo," said Una soberly. "Less than what though?"

"Less than nothing, of course," returned Tony. "I thought you would have guessed. Tim had a relapse or anything?"

"No, he's much better and the bandage is off now."

"Good old Tim! But, look here, there's something wrong with Kensington Gardens this morning."

"Really?"

"Yes, you go and have a look."

"I've just been out there, and I didn't see anything."

"Well, didn't that seem wrong?" enquired Tony in an injured voice.

Una smiled into the telephone.

"I was in a bad temper, so I didn't want to see anything," she said.

"Whatever have I done?"

"It isn't you."

"Oh, cheers! You gave me the fright of my life. Lost your lion or something?"

"My what?"

"Your lion. Every Una needs a lion. You read up your Spenser."

"I had to years ago. That's the worst of a name like mine."

"I know . . . gives people an unfair advantage, doesn't it? But never mind, let's go out to lunch."

"I have an engagement and you ought to be working," declared Una.

"It's that model of mine, in fact two of 'em," explained Tony blandly. "You know . . . girl and dog."

"Tim's leg won't be decent enough for at least a week," said Una eagerly, fighting for time.

"Today week then, but I always like to study my subject a bit beforehand, so be kind to the poor old Gardens, won't you? I suppose I couldn't run and buy you another lion?"

"No, thanks."

"So long, then. See you tomorrow," said Tony gaily and hung up the receiver before she could contradict him.

Una, leaving the telephone and smiling in spite of herself, met her mother coming down the stairs, and found herself wondering with a catch at her heart what Tony would have done if by any chance Anne had answered his call. Would he know her voice, or would she know his? She wanted to say, "That was Tony Corcoran ringing up," just to test this thing, but she had a feeling it would be rather mean if it took Anne unawares.

"Going out?" enquired Anne. "Don't forget it's Judy's dance tonight. You ought to come home and rest a little before dinner. By the way, I quite forgot to remind your father. I must ring him up by and by."

"Yes, he's sure to have forgotten," said Una

eagerly, and went off to her luncheon feeling happier.

At dinner, however, Jeremy did not appear and Anne explained composedly that he had a heavy case on hand and was afraid he would be unable to make the party. Una could not remember that such a thing had ever happened before, but she hid her dismay and merely said: "What a shame, because he likes Judy."

"I mean," she added after a moment, "that he doesn't like everybody we know."

"No, darling, but think what a painfully spineless family we should be if we all thought alike," returned her mother with a twinkle.

Anne could guess well enough why Jeremy was avoiding the dance. Judy France's parties were small and intimate affairs and Robby Lyne would certainly be there. It would be impossible for him to take a stand against Robby in Judy's house and anything else would seem to him at the moment a weak surrender. Jeremy was no strategist. He could never see that a weak surrender may sometimes be the strongest move.

CHAPTER X

i

IT CHANCED that on arrival they met the Drews at Judy's shoulder, and Mr. Drew enquired: "Well, Anne, Swithin not here?"

Anne, having that moment delivered Jeremy's excuses to the hostess, carried it off as best she could.

"Of course he is not here," she said in mock indignation, yet with a faint shadow in her eyes. "He's working, as you must know very well. You are a slave-driver."

"Not at all," said the senior partner imperturbably, "these young fellows with pretty wives are ambitious and won't listen to the advice of their elders. That's out of fashion."

"It never was in fashion," said Mrs. Drew, an ungainly woman in a dress too large for her. "The old are bores, Anne, my dear. Never listen to 'em. The very words they speak are dead, killed by repetition. Come along, Richard, and don't make lame excuses which none of us believe. You always were a slave-driver."

They moved away, to Anne's relief, but she did not guess Mrs. Drew's interruption had been designed for no other purpose.

"Is Jeremy *not* working then?" the old woman

asked her husband as soon as they were out of earshot.

"Good God, my dear, how should I know? Swithin's comings and goings are his own affair."

He had little sympathy for Jeremy, who had not after all turned out the self-seeker he had once predicted, and he would long ago have contrived to break the partnership, but for the unexpressed opposition of his wife.

"If he is working too hard, so much the better," he grumbled. "The fool has neglected his opportunities long enough."

"The word may have meant something different to you at that age, Richard," said Mrs. Drew with a faint smile, and turned to watch the dancers.

Among the moving couples, slowly revolving in a maze of silken color under the amber lights, she presently saw her favorite again, immediately recalled to the suspicion which a sixth sense had presented that all was not well with Jeremy and Anne.

Was Jeremy at work or not? Men were such fools, particularly the clever men. "If I could see them together I should know," she thought and set her mind to work, planning to bring this about. If things were going wrong there they must be put right and she felt strong to do it. All her barriers of common sense were broken down where Anne was in question, but she was too wise in the ways of the world to betray the fact, and when at last, between dances, Anne slipped into a vacant chair beside her, she said to her carelessly enough:

"So Jeremy is overworking, is he? Richard too.

These men are all alike, my dear. But I have a little conspiracy in mind if you will help me."

"Of course," agreed Anne.

"I am determined to take Richard down to Warwickshire for Whitsun," went on Mrs. Drew, "but I shall have a struggle to persuade him unless you will lend me your aid and bring Jeremy too. Someone to argue and play golf with, and I shall succeed in getting him into the open air at least. He is far too much in town."

"Jeremy certainly is," said Anne, thinking ahead. Una's party would just be over by then, and it occurred to her grimly that if previous family gatherings were any criterion, the suggested week-end in the country might be rather a godsend to them both. Nor did she wish to refuse. She was held to the Drews by old associations, but even more by the innate business sense which Jeremy would never see in her. He owed much to Mr. Drew and she in turn, as wife of the junior partner, owed him and his every consideration.

"We shall be delighted to come," she said, "if you are sure Jeremy won't make it too much of a business holiday for Mr. Drew."

"For both of them perhaps, my dear," agreed the other, "but that is better than no holiday. I count upon Jeremy's presence to give it the illusion of work. It's good of you to help me."

She beamed upon Anne like any other grateful and scheming old woman who has succeeded in making use of a young one, and Anne suspected nothing else.

"Jeremy must go, of course," she thought. "I must persuade him, in spite of his moods. We can't possibly refuse them."

Mrs. Drew meanwhile had decided: "If Jeremy makes any objection Richard will have to talk to him. Neglecting his opportunities indeed! Which? That is what I want to know and what I intend to find out."

ii

Anne had taken the precaution of being nicer than usual to Robby that night, in case of accidents, and though Una noticed it and was vaguely pleased, she did not see the connection naturally. While she was dancing with Bill France, however, they passed Miss Lyne and her mother together, and Bill remarked: "Robby's surpassed herself. Have a look at the latest face."

"I like her," said Una, moved by some obscure impulse to defend the other girl.

Bill looked surprised. He had been a page at Anne's wedding and had been therefore inclined to look upon Una as a mere child, bearable because she didn't chatter and could dance well, but otherwise beneath his serious consideration. Now he looked at her attentively for some moments before remarking:

"Rum thing, being twins."

"Why?" asked Una.

"I mean the kind of twins Bob and Robby Lyne are—you know, sort of double-banked, same looks, same tastes, same feelings. They have a kind of sixth sense, read each other's thoughts, I believe, and I don't know what."

"I shouldn't like that."

"I don't suppose they like it any too well either sometimes," said Bill, "but there you are. You know, I have a theory about Robby's face. I've never mentioned it to anyone and it may be scientifically wrong. When that woman spoiled poor old Bob's looks, I think Robby, being a twin, got some of the damage, not physically, of course, but it gave her a kink about faces, so that she doesn't care what sort of a sight she makes of hers, in fact rather likes it."

"But I thought Robby did it as a kind of advertisement for Avril's," said Una.

"Yes, that's why she thinks she does it, but hang it all, Una, Robby is really a jolly pretty girl," declared Bill earnestly, "and no pretty girl is going to make herself into a monster for a reason like that. It's against nature. I knew them pretty well . . . was at school with Bob and so forth."

"Really? What was he like?"

"Oh, a nice chap, only too blamed easy-going. Thought life was a huge joke and all that. So did Robby in those days."

"Did you ever see him after it happened, Bill?" asked Una.

"No. Couldn't get near," said Bill savagely. "Can't blame him, I suppose, for being sensitive about it, only I had a feeling something might have been done. But Robby backed him like a young tiger cat. No time for me; no time for anybody.

"That's another thing," added Bill. "It's not natural."

His tone was indignant; he was growing quite hot about it, and it flashed through Una that this had been bottled up in Bill's mind for a long time, and it wasn't really for Bob that he was most concerned. Most of the girls she knew said Bill France was conceited and superior and thought himself too clever for words, and now she saw why. He had no time for them as Robby had no time for him . . . Robby who had once thought life a huge joke, but now considered the world a rotten place. And then there was the man in the orchard! Poor old Bill.

"What became of Bob, do you know?" she asked, because it seemed safer than talking to him about Robby.

"Growing apples or something, so I've heard . . . in Canada very likely. I don't know. You can't mention him to Robby unless you want your head snapped off."

"Oh!"

Una felt suddenly excited, for where did apples grow except in orchards? And she remembered Robby's amazing secrecy about their drive on Saturday, and oddly at this moment something else . . . her face with the paint wiped off it when she came back to the car.

"I like your theory," she said, looking up at Bill with a little smile, "and of course it can't last, can it? She'll get over it after a while."

"Funny you should say that," said Bill eagerly, "because it's what I always think. I mean, it's not natural. Look here, Una, let's get out of this push and have an ice."

iii

Going home that night, Una said to her mother: "Did you ever see Bob Lyne after his injury?"

"Whatever has put him into your head?" asked Anne, startled.

"Oh, I don't know . . . someone mentioned him, that's all. Did you, mother?"

"Yes, once."

"Was it very awful?"

"He had a shade over one side of his face. His left eye had gone, poor lad."

"Couldn't anything be done?"

"It might with plastic surgery perhaps, but it's a costly business. I sometimes think Robby may be saving up for that."

"And so you go on buying frocks?"

"Well, they're very attractive frocks, and I should look ridiculous in a halo, darling; so don't try to fit me out with one."

Anne smiled to herself in the darkness, thinking it was as well she had diverted Jeremy from speaking to Una about Robby Lyne, whatever else he decided to do. She was irresistibly reminded of the incident of Tim two years ago and how confounded they had been, but now she wondered why. They went their own way, these young things, they always had and they always would, no doubt. And why not? Youth is a lonely road.

"Besides," she said in a friendly, chaffing voice

to her daughter, "one collector of lame dogs is enough for any family."

"Tim wasn't lame when I collected him," declared Una, "and besides, look what a bargain he turned out."

"Cheap at the price, you think? Five shillings and a handful of crocodile tears, eh, Una?"

"And your afternoon at golf," supplemented Una.

Her mother could deny it as much as she chose, but she was a sport, and it was jolly driving with her through London at this funny hour, with dawn just beginning to prowl about the sky and put out the stars. Hyde Park Corner looked aloof and proud, and the few late cars ran past it in stealthy haste, as though well aware of the liberty they were taking. Knightsbridge was as still and empty as a picture, and its sign post looked like a very thin policeman waving them on. But Una knew a better road than any it could tell, up the hill to St. Alban's, past an apple orchard, through a winding lane rosy with hawthorn, to an old blind house. She would have loved to race the dawn to Wenlock, but instead they pulled up before a tall house which was watching for them with one yellow eye, reproachfully; and a bird in the square thought it was morning and began to sing.

CHAPTER XI

i

GOING down to breakfast next morning, Una was dismayed to find her father alone. This was surprising, for Anne disliked breakfasting in bed, and having good health and no nerves, usually took late nights in her stride.

Una wished she also had stayed upstairs, until she saw how forlorn her father looked, scowling at his morning paper. What was the matter with him now? Did he suppose her mother was annoyed with him for banging the door, or was he merely embarrassed because he knew he had been ridiculous? The latter seemed the more reasonable explanation, so she said, as though to persuade him she had noticed nothing out of the way: "Isn't mother coming down?"

"No, she's tired," said her father shortly.

"Well, we were rather late."

"Very."

Una flushed, immediately aware from his suspicious look at her that she had said the wrong thing. She had been merely making conversation, not trying to defend her mother, who needed no defense.

"It was a pity you couldn't come to Judy's dance, father," she said, making another effort.

"I don't flatter myself my absence was of much importance," returned Jeremy dryly.

He was like a sulky boy who has refused a treat and is determined to feel injured about it, and Una, trying to use her mother's light touch, replied eagerly: "Oh, but it was. Judy was most upset, and she said to tell you if it occurs again she won't come to you for her divorce."

"Indeed? Perhaps if she knew as much as I do about that subject, she wouldn't use the word so glibly."

Jeremy, having demolished Mrs. France, whom he liked and admired, felt better and departed, quite unconscious of the tumult he left behind in the heart of his young daughter.

Had her father suddenly lost his sense of humor? This was one of his favorite little jokes with Judy . . . that when she grew tired of Peter's fiendish temper, he would take up her case. They invented scenes of comic violence to be produced as evidence, while Peter, the most gentle and amiable of men, sat by making suggestions.

And why, quite suddenly, should he speak in that bitter and meaning way of divorce? Did he imagine that her mother wanted one? . . . Could he be as mad as that? . . . Or could it possibly be that he wanted one himself?

Una grew suddenly cold and pushed away her unfinished breakfast. She tried to remember whether she had ever seen her father pay the smallest attention to any other woman, and she knew she never had; but then, no doubt, he would take care not to let her see. And lots of men were funny, at his age, and women too. She tried to review the various cases of such "funniness" as she had known or heard of, and the evidence mounted at an alarming rate. Domestic infelicity was not only prevalent but almost universal if you were to believe what you heard.

And yet, only two days ago, her father had been jollier and happier than she could remember him for years . . . of that there could be no doubt . . . until the family dinner.

Una saw it all. The family dinner was responsible for everything.

They had said something to her father, hinted something . . . grandmother, of course, or was it Aunt Herbert? Not about Tony and the statue? It couldn't be.

She jumped to her feet and, running upstairs, knocked at her mother's door without waiting to think what she would say; but there was no answer, and Brent coming down the corridor at the moment explained:

"Her ladyship has gone into her bath, Miss."

"Oh!"

The girl turned slowly away and into the little study. After all, it was just as well, for what could she say to her mother? She could not ask her about Tony, or it would look as though she believed their beastly insinuations.

Tim, sitting at her feet unnoticed, took her frock in his mouth and pulled it significantly. After being the king of the castle for a fortnight, he was now being shamefully neglected and it was more than he could bear.

"All right," said Una, looking at him despondently. "We'll go out if you want to."

It was useless, she supposed, to avoid Tony, and besides, she might know by his face.

ii

Tony, hatless and beaming, met them at the gates and conducted them into Kensington Gardens with the air of a host about to display his estate. He took Tim's lead out of Una's hand and released him, and Tim limped off with all his old abandon.

"There's not an Alsatian in sight," said Tony proudly. "I've cleared the course of them. I've also talked very firmly to the keeper and asked him whether the authorities expect us to dress our dogs in full armor or what. I got him so worked up that he's gone to see if he can find anything against Alsatians in the by-laws."

"As I'm in funds today, owing to a little matter of a towel that didn't have to go to the laundry," he continued, with a wary glance at Una's troubled face, "I think we'll treat ourselves to a pair of green chairs under a tree. Hi, Tim! this way, old dog."

Tim rolled over languidly on the grass, then came and sat at their feet. Una summoned a smile.

"What else have you been doing?" she asked.

"I've been going into the lion question," said Tony. "You'd think in a place like London, which is supposed to be the hub of the world, a mere lion would be easy to get, but I've suspected for some time we were going down hill as a nation. If you'll believe me, in the whole London directory there is not one home for lost lions, or even in the Greater London directory."

"Isn't there?" inquired Una, because it seemed unkind not to say something.

"No. I call it scandalous. Then I thought of the zoo and rang up to see if they had a spare lion by any chance, and I was received by a perfect torrent of abuse. They said I evidently wanted the lunatic asylum, but I said no, a home for wild beasts, and was I speaking to one of the inmates."

"You are absurd."

"Not at all. I can't let a friend of mine lose a lion and do nothing about it," declared Tony reasonably. "There's another place I've thought of too. We might try Harrod's. I'd have nipped down there before you came, only I didn't put on a hat this morning, and somehow I thought I'd look a bit conspicuous leading a lion through Knightsbridge without my hat."

She was smiling at last, but to Tony's anxious gaze it seemed such a poor attempt that he dropped his nonsense and said gently: "I say . . . what have I done?"

"You haven't done anything," flashed Una indignantly. "You must have a very guilty conscience. Just because I don't come out every morning. You can't expect it."

He smiled at her angry face.

"I don't really expect it. I only hope," he said. "Every poor devil has to live for some hope or other, so don't grudge me a little thing like that!"

She turned her face away, filled with a terrible and altogether strange desire to cry. He was only talking nonsense, she knew, but it was a different nonsense and his voice was so kind and careful in spite of her bad temper.

"Don't you ever do any work?" she asked gruffly, because she must say something.

"Oh, rather! Night and day, my magnum opus . . . girl and dog," he assured her.

"I can't think why you want to do it."

"Of course you can't. You didn't see what I saw. I want to show you, if I can."

"I don't believe it can possibly be any good . . . as a statue, I mean," said Una doubtfully.

"That's likely enough too, because I'm an incompetent idiot," admitted Tony, "but I can't rest till I've had a shot at it. That's not a pose, really, although I dare say it sounds jolly like it."

"Is it always like that when you work?"

"Oh, lord, no. I plug away and turn out awful bilge and smash it up in a temper generally, but just now and then I do seem to see something. . . ."

"Like the boy in the country?" finished Una.

"I caught the little beggar up in the hills behind Fiesole, singing his head off," confided Tony eagerly, "hid behind a tree and watched him."

"He's perfect."

"I'll give him to you if you like him."

"You won't do anything of the kind," cried Una scandalized. "You can't go giving your masterpieces away like that. Tell me about some of the others you have done."

"All tripe," he said. "I'd hate you to see them."

"Oh, nonsense! I've heard of one person you did a statue of anyway," said Una defiantly, yet in rather a frightened voice.

"My God . . . Mrs. Polhampton," thought Tony.

He had felt uneasy about the old catamaran for a week, because although she might be taken in and flattered by his silly image of her, he knew that anyone with eyes would see that he had been having a joke at her expense. And she might be a favorite relative, or even if not, it would seem pretty bad taste, damned impertinence, lese majesty, anything.

"I knew I'd be found out," he said, and at the sound of his guilty voice, Una gathered up her dog and held him, resting her cheek against his head. "I'm an awful ass at times . . . most times probably . . . and on that occasion I was more blithering than usual, but I hadn't the faintest idea Lady Swithin was a relative of yours. I hadn't, really. I hadn't even met you then."

"It's all right," Una managed to say. "I don't blame you. . . . How could you help it? But look here, Tim, we'll have to go in, old man."

"Oh, I say, you've only just come," pleaded Tony.

"Yes, I know, but Tim isn't well enough to be out very long."

She stood up and fastened his lead with a steady hand, then smiled at Tony as he walked with her to the gate.

"I'm not going in because I'm offended. I'm not,

really. I don't see how you could possibly help it," she said consolingly, thinking of her mother.

"I've been kicking myself about it ever since you told me your name," admitted Tony.

"Well, don't, because I'm not blind and I can quite understand. I'll come and sit for you as soon as I can, though I can't see how you can want me to. I'm not lovely like that."

"*What?*" cried Tony, but she had run off through the waiting traffic.

iii

She had run away from him because it was necessary to think this out alone, not for any other reason, for after all what business was it of hers what he did? and he had looked so abashed and embarrassed that she paused to look back and wave her hand from the other side of the road, casually and gayly, to show him it was all right. Then she turned the corner, but not to go in.

The thought of the house was stifling, and for an hour she walked Tim round the squares and streets, an aimless promenade that surprised and bored him. Even when he held back she hauled him on, and at last, determined to put up with no more of it, he sat firmly down with a sigh of invalid fatigue, as though the next step would be his last. Una looked at him uncomprehendingly, and then, with a rush of remorse, gathered him under her arm.

"Tim! You're worn out."

She held him close in a passion of tenderness and hurried him home; all her emotions, muddled and not half understood, flowed back to Tim. He was her dog, her own, and nobody could possibly take that away. Let them try. Yet she had forgotten him.

At first, after leaving Tony, she had been conscious only of a numb relief, as of one who knows the worst at last. And yet, what did she know . . . except that Tony had been romantic about her mother and made a statue of her? And what was there in that? There would have been nothing at all but for her father's strange behavior and the evil hints of the Herbert Swithins. She loathed the sight of the family. They were vile.

Una, turning into Palace Square at this moment, saw a visitor come out of the house to a waiting taxi, and her heart stood still. Step by step she seemed to be walking into a nightmare, for it was her Aunt Herbert.

Anne, dressed to go out, was just coming downstairs when her daughter let herself into the house. She was frowning, and she walked to the telephone hardly noticing the girl, but Una could bear it no longer and she cried:

"Mother . . . what did she want?"

"You might know she would want something," said Anne, dryly. "Wenlock, my dear, to live in rent free."

"Mother!"

Anne laughed.

"She's modest, isn't she, but don't look so disturbed. I have not the smallest intention of giving it to her."

"But . . . but what did she say . . . what possible reason did she give for asking for it?"

"Oh, she made the usual threatening noises," said Anne carelessly. "Her pension and poverty and other people's luck and so forth. Una, you look tired out this morning. Better take things quietly today, hadn't you?"

"Yes, I will. Are you going out?" asked Una wistfully.

"I must, on business. I shan't be in to lunch, so you'll have a quiet house, but I'll see you later."

Anne took up the receiver and called a number. Una, with Tim still in her arms, crept miserably upstairs into the little study and buried herself in a chair.

Threatening noises! It was just a phrase of the moment meaning nothing, but to Una it took on a terrible significance, for Mab had certainly threatened. "Mother is going to let it all out at your birthday dinner, if Aunt Anne doesn't do something she wants." Blackmail, that's what it was. The Herbert Swithins were capable of anything.

The beastly birthday was only four nights off, and Una could see them all sitting round, and hear her aunt's insinuating voice pretending to chaff her mother, and grandmother crying sharply: "What's this? Let us all hear it."

Very well, let her aunt do it and then she would get up and defy the lot of them and tell them to their faces it was blackmail . . . that Mab had blackmailed her to hide her flirtation with a married man, and Aunt Herbert had blackmailed her

mother to get Wenlock. Then perhaps her father
would see his family for once as it really was.

It was an immense idea, but impossible after all,
at her party before the dance, while they were her
guests. You couldn't have a scene, and besides there
was her father. The old instinct to stand between
her father and mother, warding off some danger
she could not understand, was too strong. Whatever
had happened, whatever was going to happen, the
family could keep out of it. She wasn't going to
have them sitting there, looking so shocked and
pleased as if they had always known.

She sat up and looked at Tim, coiled on her knee.
She picked him up and faced him eagerly, taking
him into her confidence.

"We'll do Aunt Herbert in the eye, Tim. There
won't be any birthday dinner. I'm hanged if there
shall," she said.

iv

Anne faced her brother-in-law across the little
table. She had telephoned him, asking him to give
her lunch, and he had suggested this small restaurant near Lincoln's Inn, instead of one of the
smarter West End places, such as his father or
Jeremy would have assuredly chosen. They would
be quiet for one thing. Jazz bands destroyed life.
They were the index to the uneasy times. And he
thought it would amuse her. . . this ancient, sober
room, looking out on a courtyard where the grass
grew up between the uneven stones and pigeons
strutted lazily.

There was a piquancy in contrasts, and Anne, a shining creature against the paneled walls turned black by the rolling centuries, pleased his fastidious eye. His choice of setting had been right.

"I want some advice and incidentally some information," said Anne with a faint smile, as the oysters were set before them and the waiter moved away. She had watched John Swithin choosing the meal carefully but surely, with an occasional glance for her approval. Men showed their quality, she thought, on these occasions. Some would be ostentatious, some anxious, or knowing and pleased like a child. If you were wise you would take a course of lunches with the various men you knew before marriage, but what nonsense. If wisdom and calculation came into it, where was the adventure? And it was an adventure, even at its worst, said Anne to herself.

John nodded in reply to her appeal. He had not supposed sisterly affection had brought her, though many women, he knew, would have wrapped the errand in some such disguise, and her directness pleased him.

"What have they been doing to you?" he inquired coolly and as one accepting responsibility for the family without surprise.

"I've had a call from Mrs. Herbert, John."

"Oh, you have? Well, refuse the woman, whatever she asked."

Anne laughed.

"I have, but there's more in it than that, apparently. You may have heard her remarks to me about

Wenlock at your mother's dinner, and I imagine she was leading up to it then. She wants me to lend her the house, since it is unlet and not likely to be let in its present condition, she says. She will take care of the place, which will be a service to me, and incidentally she will be saved rent and taxes, for which her pension is inadequate."

"It has never had to be adequate," declared John, imperturbably. "You were quite right to refuse her, and if she troubles you again, just refer her to me."

"No, no. I am not merely telling tales out of school, or even asking for help." Anne went on with her luncheon for a moment, a faint line between her delicate brows. "I couldn't ask your father," she said, facing him again at last. "He is fond of me and he is too much implicated, and I don't want to raise the question with Jeremy, unless there's something in it. I'll try to explain that later. But you are more or less neutral."

He let that pass, for he was interested to know what it was all about, having so far no conception.

"She hinted," went on Anne, "no . . . it was more than a hint . . . that it was unfair her children should be defrauded by Jeremy's marriage to me. She said you had all of you had to suffer for it financially."

"Delicately put," said John with irony.

"Is it true?"

He laughed, but the laughter was chiefly at his own expense, because the various answers he would have made to almost any other woman, leaped into his mind and mocked him. He knew now that he liked and admired her immensely, and of a sudden he was sorry for Jeremy, knowing how little preparation life had ever given him for understanding a mind of just this texture. Clearly, as though for years they had not been alien and divided, he saw his brother regarding this lovely woman he had married as a being from a superior world, oblivious that she had come into his with her eyes open and a twinkle in them. Jeremy must have missed a lot of fun.

"Life's a bit of a circus, Anne," he said, "but if Jeremy has been hiding his disgraceful secrets, you've come to the right place. There's a sort of justice in it. You know, of course, we have never got on?"

"Was that the reason? . . . the money and so on?"

"Certainly not. . . . Merely temperamental differences from the time we were lads. The favored of the gods is never much loved by the other fellows, so see what a chance you offer me. I shall give the old beggar away with the utmost pleasure."

"He's not yours to give. He's mine. So now!"

"Oh, I see, it's like that?" chaffed John, feigning surprise.

"Do you think I'd have come if it had been otherwise, or I would stay if I believed a word you're saying," said Anne with a smile, "or in your hostility either?"

"No. . . . I knew you were an unbeliever. Besides, I've contracted an alliance of sorts with a member of your household. Your young daughter

and I have sworn eternal friendship, not in so many
words, but the fact remains."

"Una?" said Anne, and he knew that she was
pleased.

"I'll buy her from you any time," he offered
handsomely.

"This is certainly a financial conversation, isn't
it? I can never have one with Jeremy. He shies
away from them. He has always had a queer kink
about my money, though I never knew until today it
had gone further than that. He ignores the fact that
I have any, as if it were slightly improper, but I
have a dreadfully commercial spirit, probably inherited from my old grandfather, who made jam.
You've heard of him, haven't you?"

He threw back his head and laughed, seeing nodding heads in the drawing-room at Wimbledon and
hearing complacent whispers of this same vulgarian
she mentioned so calmly.

"You needn't laugh," protested Anne. "You don't
expect me to parade any feudal airs and graces, so
don't pretend. Jeremy is different. He's a romantic,
and I won't spoil his illusions unnecessarily, but if
he has contracted obligations for me, I must know
where I am."

He nodded.

"Obligations is the wrong word," he assured her
seriously. "You must get that out of your head. But
I agree that you have a right, if you wish, to know
the exact position, especially if you are to be sub-
jected to innuendoes from that fool, poor Herbert's
wife. It had never entered my head that you didn't

know. But, joking apart, your estimate of Jeremy is just enough, I think. He is a romantic, and try to realize what it must have meant to a youngster of that type, coming from a somewhat narrow and by no means splendid background, to win a lovely girl, not only very much above him socially, as the world counts such things, but an heiress into the bargain. Standards change, but you must allow us to keep a few of our old prejudices, and a decent chap, whatever else he does, isn't going to live on his wife's money."

"Yes, I'll allow you that one. It's right in theory and very often wrong in practice, but the point is he doesn't even want me to live on it." She laughed, then sobered again. "There are two sides as usual, John. Just think of the girl a little . . . don't you see that she may be glad to bring something to the partnership, other than that of being a mere social ornament? However, that doesn't matter really, and I am deflecting the argument after the manner of my sex. Please go on. Your father gave us the house in Palace Square for a wedding present. That was generous, and Jeremy had his profession after all. Was there more than that?"

"A young barrister makes a poor income in the beginning, my dear. Even with Jeremy's chances, it wouldn't have been adequate, but really the solution was quite simple. My father merely adjusted matters so that Jeremy was given a legacy in advance . . . ten thousand pounds."

"A fair share?" inquired Anne at once, and made a rapid calculation. "There were five of you. No, of course it wasn't fair, so don't talk nonsense. Five thousand possibly, but not ten."

"Just bring that commercial spirit to bear on the argument," suggested John Swithin. "To put it quite bluntly and vulgarly, can't you see that Jeremy's marriage to you brought the Swithins up in the world a step or two? I am not referring to family or lineage, or whatever you choose to call it, or enduing you with those feudal airs and graces you disclaim. The old order is of course passing away, but we're no nearer Plato's ideal State for that. There are optimists who believe that snobbery will vanish from the earth, but not a bit of it. Snobbery comes from below, never from above, and the more democratic we become, the greater snobs we shall be. Very well then. The Swithins were nobody in particular and you were a somebody . . . that is, you knew a great many prominent people and were known, as a sort of household word, to the world in general."

"Yes, I know," mocked Anne, "via the newspapers. You are as bad as Jeremy."

"You listen to me and don't interrupt. We're living in a noisy age . . . what's the atrocious thing? Yes, a saxophone age. I hate the times myself; they are hollow and meretricious, but they are not going to change on my account, and I'm not such a fool that I can't see that a household word is about the biggest asset to any family, things being what they are. Broadly speaking, you have put the Swithins on the market. You must realize that your marriage to Jeremy has been an immense advantage to him professionally, and don't imagine the firm of Swithin and Swithin hasn't come in for some of the thunder. 'Swithin? Oh, yes, you know . . . Lady Anne Swithin. One of that lot,' says the world respectfully. Upon my word, when I think it over, Anne, I'm not sure we haven't treated Jeremy rather shabbily. We should have endowed him for life for being clever enough to catch you."

"You put it so beautifully that I hate to argue with you," said Anne smiling, "but, you see, I'm trying to look at it from Jeremy's point of view. Doing something clever is such a lark and, don't you think, just possibly in his heart of hearts, he may feel he would have liked to have done it off his own bat?"

"What's the matter with Jeremy?" inquired John bluntly, but he was perfectly sure she would not tell him.

"Nothing at all. He's never mentioned the matter to me, but your argument has brought him to the fore, so to speak. He may have intended, or still intend, to return this money, or at least all but his fair share. I'm inclined to think it is an obligation, for in spite of all your charming talk of assets, why should we have more than the rest of you have?"

"My dear, if you are thinking of Herbert's children, believe me, my father allows their mother an ample income, except that no income would be ample to a woman of her kind. The children will be provided for, and as for the rest of us, Marion, as you know, has her own money and my share in the firm is worth considerably more than ten thousand pounds."

"But you worked for that," declared Anne at once.

"Your logic confounds me, and I object to logic in a woman. It's a thing I've not been used to."

"That's a cry of defeat, John."

"Nothing of the sort. It was a cry of anguish at another illusion gone; a cry by the wayside too. Look at this question in a practical manner. If any of us were suffering privations there might be some excuse for you, but we are disgustingly free from financial worries, in spite of Mrs. Herbert and her pension. My father could retire tomorrow, if the prospect didn't bore him. I have no responsibilities and my tastes are simple. What do you suppose I should do if Jeremy made me a present of a sum of money he can ill spare and I don't want? Upon my word, I should punch his head. Money should not lie idle. That is one of the first principles of economics. It should go where it is of most use, and nobody has any right to be sentimental about it."

John Swithin looked out on the little courtyard, but he saw instead his mother's dinner table and a girl in a white frock, immediately aware that his last phrase had been insincere.

"My brother Herbert and I were pretty good friends," he said, "but what will it benefit him now if I sit down and make a will in favor of that young hound, his son, who will throw the money in the gutter? I'd rather leave it to the Chancellor of the Exchequer, though I hate the fellow."

"You may marry," suggested Anne. "Why not?"

"I'm not a domestic animal. I made tracks from Wimbledon for that reason long ago, and I wouldn't change my bachelor quarters for Buckingham Palace . . . or even a house in Palace Square."

"You might like Palace Square better if you saw more of it," suggested Anne mischievously.

"Still, that doesn't alter the fact that I'll buy your daughter," proceeded John unheeding.

Anne's quick mind saw his meaning, and she shook her head at him smiling.

"Give it to the Chancellor of the Exchequer, John," she said. "Don't pile up the obligation. That's unkind."

"Obligations again? Bogeys have gone out. I'm disappointed in you," said her brother-in-law indignantly. "All my eloquence wasted too. What a world!"

"It has not been wasted and I have never met a bogey," she denied. "You have been very good to me, really, for you've told me what I wanted to know, and now I am armed against further surprises from Mrs. Herbert . . . or at least I hope so. The question of obligations was merely a side issue, for after all that is Jeremy's business, and I dislike interference too much myself to practice it on other people; so don't worry. I shall not go home and tell him all is discovered."

Anne spoke lightly and she hoped she had convinced him, but later as she drove home she reviewed those aspects of the situation which it had been quite impossible to mention to John, understanding though he might be. No word had been said of his mother's attitude, or his sister's, and Anne did not believe that Mrs. Herbert was alone in her sense of grievance. She was too much dependent on the Swithins to have ventured upon her cool request unless she had heard Jeremy's indebtedness to his family pretty openly discussed.

Her father-in-law and John could be exonerated, she was sure. They were men of the world, and all those practical considerations which John had outlined so amusingly, had weighed with them to some extent, perhaps, pride a little too, no doubt. Jeremy was making a good marriage and it was both expedient and becoming that they should lend him a hand. But nothing, thought Anne with a smile, would make the Swithin women men of the world. They might make a generous gesture, but they would never be able to forget that they had made it, or fail to feel at once virtuous and injured.

And in the middle of the situation and held in bondage to it was Jeremy. Surely this was the index to his queer, touchy attitude with regard to his family, and his belief that his mother's interference was natural and justified. Consciously or not, he did feel the obligation of what had been done for him and in some inexplicable fashion expected Anne to understand though he had kept her completely in the dark about it.

"Oh, dear, why couldn't he have been frank with me, the idiot," she thought with amused impatience. "It would have been so simple to say, 'They've been good to me, so bear with them for my sake,' instead of talking sentimental nonsense about the rights of a grandmother."

It was natural that she should not understand him. He was possessive to a degree, yet afraid to believe in his possessions. He wanted to appear splendid in her eyes and could not believe that splendor as he saw it meant nothing to her. Money to him was one of the trappings, to her merely something to ease the wheels of life. And he was so amazingly innocent about it in some ways, never suspecting how she supplemented the household allowance, Una's pin money and a hundred and one other expenses out of her own income. After all, she thought, why tell him and spoil his pleasure in the belief that he paid for everything?

The question of his indebtedness to the family, however, went deeper if, as she now suspected, it was even vaguely responsible for such scenes as they had recently gone through. It would be useless to open the question in his present mood, but open it she must when an opportunity arose. Mrs. Herbert had unwittingly given her the key, and there would be no need to betray John. The money, or part of it at least, had better be paid back . . . out of her own funds, if necessary.

CHAPTER XII

i

ANNE, going in search of Una, found her lying on the chesterfield in the study with a rug tucked round her and Tim stretched out luxuriously on the top of it.

"Feeling rested?" she enquired.

"I feel perfectly awful," said Una, and this fairy-tale which she had been carefully preparing for hours past became true in fact. Distress of mind, lack of food . . . for she had been unable to eat her solitary luncheon . . . and little sleep for two nights were having their effect. "Do you think it would matter if I went to bed? I know you have people coming to dinner."

"Only the Spencers and we are going to have a bridge four afterwards. Of course you must go to bed if you feel ill, child. Headache?"

"Yes, and I feel giddy and sick. I don't suppose it's anything," said Una guiltily, at sight of her mother's anxious face. "If father doesn't come home I can easily get up again."

"He is coming home, so that's all right."

"Oh! I thought he might be kept by that case again."

"No, he promised to make a point of coming home, because we disappointed the Spencers on

Tuesday. I was very firm with him," said Anne with a twinkle, because it was impossible to guess how much this dark-eyed young daughter of hers saw of what was going on around her. "I have been lunching with a friend of yours."

"Have you?"

"Yes, your Uncle John."

"Oh," said Una. "Nice, isn't he?" Her voice was husky and she looked so white that Anne began to feel seriously alarmed.

"Go and get into bed, my poor darling, and I'll ask the doctor to come and have a look at you," she said. "You may have caught a chill and it's better to be on the safe side with your dance only a few days off."

"Yes," said Una faintly, and picking up Tim, crept away to her room.

Her mother had gone out to lunch, on business with Uncle John! Now what did that mean?

A new dismay was added to all the rest and when the doctor presently came, his malingering patient was sufficiently agitated in mind to play her part with complete success.

"Sound as a bell," announced the doctor when he had prodded her all over. "Nothing wrong there, Lady Anne. She may have caught a slight chill, but it's far more probable she's been overdoing it like all these young people nowadays. They don't know how to rest—it's a lost art—and no physique can stand the pace. Too many parties, eh, Miss Una?"

"I do feel pretty tired," said Una cautiously.

"Exactly. I can tell that by your pulse. Now you

don't want a breakdown, do you? So I think we must cut out parties for a week or two and keep you quiet until we get you back into condition again."

"Oh, dear," said Anne. "We're having a dance for her next Tuesday, doctor. Don't say we must put it off. Or should we, do you think?"

The doctor was watching his patient, who had turned her head away at mention of the dance, as though completely indifferent, where he had expected an outcry.

"Much better put it off if possible, Lady Anne."

"My poor Una, it's too bad."

"Well, if I felt like this I shouldn't be much use at it," said Una.

"No, of course you wouldn't," approved the doctor. "After all, what is a week or two with all the summer ahead? You make up your mind to rest like a sensible girl." He wrote busily for a moment while Una watched him secretly. This had been almost too easy, and she found it hard to believe he had been taken in.

"We'll give her a sedative," he said to Anne, "and I'll look in again in the morning. Keep visitors away as much as possible, and let her have a thorough rest and no excitement at all. That's the great thing."

Anne went with him out of the room, closing Una's door behind her.

"You're sure there's nothing serious, doctor?"

"Not a sign of any trouble, Lady Anne. It's simply a question of exhausted nerves. After all, she's not much more than a child, and we all live too hard nowadays. It's in the air we breathe. You've taken the thing in plenty of time, so there's no occasion to worry."

"And you think it is absolutely necessary to put off the dance?"

"She's not fit for it and it's no good doing things by halves. All the excitement is only going to knock her up again and prolong matters."

"I suppose you're right," said Anne.

She went back to Una when the doctor had gone.

"I'm so sorry about your party, sweetheart," she said, "but never mind, you shall have one twice as jolly a little later."

"Yes." Una stole a glance at her. "It may be better in some ways," she ventured at last. "If it isn't my birthday, we needn't have the family, need we?"

Anne laughed.

"Don't you like the family?"

"Hate the sight of them," said Una gruffly.

ii

Anne, writing hasty notes to cancel the dance, and thinking of her surprising daughter who had kept her own counsel about the family all these years, knew that the change of plan was not an unmixed evil, for reasons which Una could not suspect. It would save Jeremy's face in the preposterous stand he had taken about Robby Lyne, and the subject could be allowed to drop. She did not think he would reopen it. He must know he had been ridiculous, but it was not in his nature to give in gracefully and laugh as she would have done, though his misery this morning had been plain.

She was dressing for dinner when she heard him come home, and she slipped on a rose pink wrap and opened her door, beckoning him in as he came upstairs.

"Una's ill, Jeremy."

"Good God, what's the matter?"

"Don't look so worried," said Anne. "It's nothing very serious, the doctor says . . . simply a slight breakdown, but we must keep her quiet for a week or two. She's been overdoing it."

"Are you sure the fellow's competent? Oughtn't we to have another opinion? What about a nurse?" began Jeremy anxiously at once.

"No, of course not. A week or so in bed will put her right, and Brent and I can look after her perfectly, but I've had to cancel the birthday dance. I've been writing letters all the afternoon. No excitement and no visitors, by the doctor's orders. Still you are not a visitor, so run along and have a look at her before you begin to dress."

Anne dropped the information about the dance casually, and left it to sink in, but he did not show any relief. He stood looking at her helplessly as she threw off her wrap and sat down before the dressing-table, and at last he burst out: "She has no business to rush about like that until she breaks down."

"I know, but don't tell her so, poor lamb. Be nice with her, Jeremy."

"Nice?" he cried. "Am I ever anything but nice to her?"

"You're perfect, but be pluperfect this time."

Anne threw him a smile over her shoulder, but he went out with an air of defeat. It was all wrong; he couldn't reach her. He had been in hell for two days, but she could still smile. She didn't care. She never had cared.

He went slowly along the corridor towards Una's room. He hadn't meant to blame the child; he had always been decent to her, or tried. His mind went back over the years. Nineteen years ago to the very day, he had been in terror about Anne, and Una was still unborn. He had nearly lost Anne and even at this moment he could feel the anguish of that fear. And then the War, and he came home, and Una was between them, sharing something with Anne. It was all the War. He had never got back. Even in his profession he had not done what he had hoped to do, to outstrip everyone for Anne.

She had said to him the other night that he grew worse and worse year after year. That was how she saw him. She despised him, of course. They both did, Una and she, talked him over and laughed at him, no doubt, for they were friends.

He stood uncertainly outside his daughter's door, and at last, with a nervous knock, opened it and went in.

Two startled dark eyes glanced up at him from the pillows, but he looked so miserable that Una summoned a hasty smile, and moved to let him sit on the edge of her bed.

"Hullo! Sorry you're ill, dear."

"Never mind," said Una kindly.

She felt to him as long ago she had felt to some toy that she didn't care for and yet brought out, lest it should feel neglected if she shut it away. Always there was something about him that distressed her, and tonight she could see he was still odd, as he had been for the last few mornings, and this was so strange that she felt newly afraid. However irritable he might be at breakfast, she had never known it to last like this before, and she wanted to cry: "Whatever is the matter?" but she knew that was no good. He wouldn't tell her.

"You're playing bridge with the Spencers, aren't you?" she said. "Mind you win."

He asked wistfully: "Would you like me to win?"

"Of course . . . you and mother."

"We may not cut like that," said Jeremy in a voice so depressed that she found herself thinking, in a panic: "Doesn't he want to, then? Oh, what is the matter with him? It can't be Tony and the statue."

"What's mother wearing?" she asked with an anxious eye on his face.

"Um? . . . I don't know. I'll go and see," said her father, getting up at once and hurrying away. And it was so silly, as if it had been an important question, which he must answer.

"The pink and gold," he told her, coming back and speaking from the door. "I'll bring you my winnings if there are any, but I must dress now or I shall be late."

He came in and gave her an awkward kiss, as if he had just remembered a duty, and exclaimed:

"Where's Brent? Why aren't they looking after you? They have no business to leave you alone here."

"She'll be here in a moment, father. It's all right."

"Well, if you feel worse, send for me at once. Do you hear? Brent, is that you? Miss Una should not be left, and if she wants anything, come for me, visitors or no visitors."

"It's quiet she wants, sir," said Brent, dourly and with meaning, and Jeremy was obliged to retreat before her.

Brent had been with Anne since before her marriage, and behaved at times as though she owned the house and everybody in it. He felt that there was another of them arrayed against him. Actually Brent was merely one of those prim women who despise men in the mass and love to rout them. They were like a pack of children, she thought, always making a noise at the wrong moment. She tolerated Jeremy because he was Anne's husband, but even so, her expression seemed to say, he needn't think he could come domineering over her.

iii

Brent had at last, at Una's entreaty, turned off the light and taken her sewing away. Her industry was of the aggressive order and probably designed as a reproach to the rest of the world, which she regarded with a good deal of scorn. Her needle raced as if there were not a moment to lose, and Una had watched it till she was dizzy, exclaiming distracted at last: "You're worse than a wall paper with cauliflowers on it."

"I never heard such talk," said Brent indignantly, and took her temperature, suspecting delirium. When the result failed to confirm this suspicion, she was still unconvinced. Thermometers, like everything else, were not what they used to be.

"I think I'll go to sleep," said Una, to get rid of her.

"Humph!" said Brent. "Well, I'll be within call. And now, I suppose you want that Tim."

This was no title of disrespect, as Una knew. Tim, for some inscrutable reason, had taken a fancy to Brent in his youth, and the subtle flattery had not been without effect. She fetched and carried for the dog as if he were one of the family, and in Una's absence guarded him as though she suspected the rest of the household were in league to poison him. So now she whisked him off the hearthrug, where he had been dozing happily, and dumped him on his own little blanket at Una's feet.

"Lie down, you, and don't disturb Miss Una," she said sharply.

Tim wagged his tail, cocked an eye at her, and grinned as though he enjoyed the joke. Then he lifted his injured paw significantly.

"He's asking you to look at his wound, Brent."

"Now don't you put words into his mouth, Miss, as though he was a God-fearing Christian. It's not right," said Brent, but she tucked Tim down with the blanket over him nevertheless, before she departed. He lay there until the door closed behind him; then shook off his covering and strolled up the eiderdown.

An eager hand came out to meet him and he licked it, flinging himself down against her arm with a long sigh of content.

"Darling," whispered Una.

This "illness" was going to be very hard on Tim . . . no lovely runs in the Gardens for days and days. He would have to go out with Brent, and suppose there were Alsatians about and he got into a fight again and was killed? Such terror possessed her at the thought, that she almost determined to get up next morning and abandon her scheme, letting the family do their worst, but she knew in her heart this could not be done. An older loyalty than her love for her dog would hold her to her course. There must be no family dinner; Aunt Herbert must tell no tales, for it was quite clear to her now that if all the sculptors in the world made statues of her mother, her father would not understand.

"I'm afraid you'll have to stay on your lead, Tim," whispered Una confidentially. "Only for a few days, darling. You won't mind, will you? Because there might be Alsatians and Tony Corcoran won't be there to chase 'em off."

Tony! Tony, waiting in the Gardens, looking surprised and indignant when she did not come.

"Do you like him, Tim?" asked Una unnecessarily, and in the darkness saw his soft eyes open drowsily as if he smiled.

The curtains stirred at her open window and the spring night, scented and cool, seemed to slip in, so that, closing her eyes, she could see a starry sky and dark trees marching, and Tony beneath them, swinging along.

How did she know he was like that? He might be dancing now somewhere instead, looking like a faun in evening dress and talking of lions to some other girl.

"Do you think he is, Tim?"

It was an anxious question, and Tim, wrapped in dreams of his own, ignored it.

"No," said Una, with determination. She saw him in the early morning, with the towel round his neck and his hair all wet from his swim, running to help her off the grass; meeting her at the gate this morning and leading her in as though he owned the world; sitting beside her under the trees and saying: "Whatever have I done?" She had snapped his head off and then wanted to cry because he was so kind and careful. He was terribly careful of her and nobody had ever been that before. It was strange. It might be because of the statue, of course. He couldn't rest, he said, until he had had a shot at it. Yes, it must be the statue and, when it was done, he would turn to something else and think he had been a blithering idiot, as he had thought about her mother.

Una saw it all now. He was an artist and like that. He couldn't help it; but still he had saved Tim's life and now he would think she was indignant about her mother and wouldn't come out. How awful! She would have liked to write and explain, but that was too dangerous. Her mother might see the letter, "T. Corcoran, Esq.," or Brent might know. Brent must know a lot of things.

Perhaps he would ring up. . . . Yes, she was sure he would, ready to talk nonsense and entice her out; and they would tell him she was ill and he would understand.

Una sighed with relief. The doctor's sedative was beginning to do its work and she was growing drowsy. The soft stirring of the curtains was like the wind in the trees; she could feel its cool touch on her face, and suddenly she was driving over a high country, through fields of gold, and there was an old house, opening its eyes, as though surprised.

Tim turned over and coiled himself into the curve of her body, but she did not move.

CHAPTER XIII

i

WHEN, on the second morning in succession, his girl and dog did not appear in the Gardens, Tony Corcoran took the Florentine ring out of his pocket and scowled at the image of Lorenzo, who had not after all been magnificent.

"It's all your fault," he said. "Nice sort of sham, aren't you? I'd chuck you away if you hadn't belonged to her."

But for the dam' thing he would never have met Mrs. Polhampton and been tempted to make fun of the pouncing old catamaran. Yet how could he know she would have a perfect niece wandering at large and thinking her lovely? It was an outrage.

"I'll never be as lovely as that," she had said, and left him gasping, and no wonder. Lovely? . . . Mrs. Polhampton? God! the amazing blindness of girls. And about an aunt, of all people. Aunts, in Tony's estimation, had no right to encumber the earth. They were always sticking their pointed noses into something and making trouble. A sensible society would abolish the pests.

And now Una was so indignant with him that for two days she had refused to come out. He had not telephoned yesterday, remembering that she had said he could not expect her every day. She had pitched into him like a good one, sparks in her bonny eyes, but afterwards she had assured him she didn't blame him about the statue, so what could you make of this? Two days . . . it wasn't fair.

Tony had reached this point in his musings when he caught sight of something familiar. . . . Tim, but not with his mistress. He was being hauled along by a maid in a tight fitting black suit and black straw hat, and with a face as hard as her hand on the little dog's lead. Tim was indignant, dragging his feet and simply bursting to be off and about on his own concerns, but his captor marched him relentlessly on.

They passed a shrubbery and it was then that Tony, hidden among the bushes, whistled enticingly. Tim cocked his ears and pulled with all his might, for he knew that sound. It belonged to a friend and heralded games just suited to his mood.

"Come on, sir," said Brent sharply, but her arm was aching and she chose this moment to change the lead from one hand to the other. It was unfortunate. Tim heard the call again, gave one mighty wrench and was off to his friend before Brent had collected her wits.

For a distracted hour she rushed up and down the Gardens, peering short-sightedly at every terrier she met, calling him in a high falsetto, and, her dignity and scorn of the world in tatters, desperately asking help of everybody.

Tim, meanwhile, relieved of the trailing lead, had danced gayly off after his friend to the other side of the Gardens, fronting the Bayswater road. Brent had brought him out on former occasions, but never to treat him like this, and he was bored to death with her. He wanted his mistress and was extremely indignant that he had been whisked out of the house without her. But this man would see to it. He belonged to them like the Garden; he was theirs.

Still slightly lame, but full of life and pleased with it, Tim followed the man on to the Bayswater road in complete confidence, cocking his head at his companion conversationally, and even leading the way, as much as to say: "Come on. We'll find her."

Near Church Street Tony picked him up and carried him, for the traffic was heavy and Tim, a stolen treasure, something of a responsibility. It would give the acid-faced woman a lesson in the treatment of dogs to lose him for a bit, and when Una heard she would see it was dangerous not to bring him into the Gardens with her own hand. She had gone out elsewhere, he supposed, and left Tim to the maid, but what was the matter with the early hours of the morning? Eleven thirty was far too late for decent dogs to have their walk.

"Come on, old sport," said Tony, running up stairs to the studio, and Tim quivered with excitement. He knew this place and she would be there. There wasn't a doubt of it.

The studio, however, was empty except for a large bundle of fur and whiskers which gathered itself into a corner and spat with violence. Tony picked it up and put it out of the window and Tim, in high excitement, pressed his nose to the glass and barked. The bundle put out a savage paw to slap his face, but the window intervened, so it turned away in disgust, still swearing, and sat down in the sun with its back to the company. Tim was called away from the contemplation of this unsportsman-like and ungentlemanly beast by Tony, who produced a lump of sugar.

Having eaten this, the terrier remembered Una again, and began an excited hunt for her. It was very odd. She was nowhere to be found, and the man, hitherto intelligent, was sitting doing something with a lot of white stuff and not attempting to find her. Tim ran to him to point out that they were wasting precious time, but the man couldn't take a hint this morning. Tim circled round, worrying in vain. At last he went and sat before the door, trying to open it with his nose, and whining softly.

"All right, Tim, old dog. No cause to worry."

Tim at this moment barked with joy, for there was a step on the stairs and a hand on the door. She was coming at last.

It was Kit who came in, carrying a basket, and she stopped to greet the visitor, looking surprised and pleased.

"Where's your mistress, Tim? Tony, what have you done with her?"

"Eh?" said Tony, pretending absence of mind.

Kit looked about her suspiciously; then with Tim eager at her heels, glanced into each of the other rooms in turn.

"You don't mean to say Una has lent you her dog?"

"Well, not officially," admitted Tony with a chuckle.

"What do you mean by that?" inquired his sister, sternly. Tony had been for days in one of those moods when he was capable of anything, and he had said so little about Una that sisterly instincts were immediately awake to the cause. "If you mean she doesn't know Tim is here, you're a brute and you'll take him home immediately. The poor child will be mad with anxiety, thinking him killed very likely. You know how fond of him she is."

"Rats!" said Tony, looking innocent, but feeling like a murderer. "Una's out, so she won't be anxious."

"How do you know she's out?" Kit had a terrible habit of coming straight to the point.

"Must be, because Tim was in charge of an old female of about ninety, with a face that would stop a clock. She was hauling the poor chap along on a lead, and when he broke away and came after me, do you suppose I was going to let him down? Certainly not," said Tony, piously. "Do her good to get a bit of a fright. Teach her how to treat a gentleman, won't it, Tim?"

Kit said indignantly: "You don't even know Una's out. There may be a dozen reasons why she sent Tim by a maid, and I'm surprised at you. Go and telephone at once and tell them you have the dog, or I'll let him go and then he *will* be lost and you'll be responsible."

"Well, don't get your hair off."

Tony got up. The suggestion that Una might be

at home after all, and worrying about her dog, was more than he could bear, and though he made a practice of resisting Kit's orders, since sisters must be kept in their places, he threw his dignity to the winds for once, and clattered downstairs to borrow old Benyon's telephone.

"Is Miss Una in?"

"Yes, sir," answered a voice at the other end, "but I'm afraid that you can't speak to her. Just a moment and I'll call the mistress."

Tony hung up the receiver and fled. He wasn't going to speak to any parent, and besides, he knew all he wanted to know. She was in, after all, and he was a brute. He dashed upstairs, seized a hat, Tim, and the lead, and was off before Kit could ask a question, rushing down Church Street and along the Kensington road.

ii

Brent had gone all to pieces and her pride was in the dust. She, of all people, to lose anything, and Tim at that, whom she would have guarded with her life. Why, the dog was fond of her, let those hussies downstairs deny it as they might. And then to run off like that, without so much as a by your leave. It was incredible. After a frantic hour of search in the Gardens, she crept home to break the dreadful tidings to her mistress. She was shaking all over, her hat awry, and her hard face streaked with tears, a form of weakness she had always despised, but she was not even conscious of it now. Something must be done, and that quickly, with

Miss Una ill and everything. It was enough to kill the child.

Brent flung through the basement in search of Anne and poured out her story, wringing her hands.

Anne quieted her at last, gave orders that the news should be kept from Una, and telephoned all the police stations within reach of the Gardens. Then, because it seemed better to give the poor old thing something practical to do, she sent her to interview the Garden authorities and offer a reward to anyone who should return the little dog.

Brent was returning from this errand when Tony reached Palace Square and almost collided with her.

"That's my dog . . . you've got my dog, so don't deny it. How dare you?" cried the woman, overcome with excitement and relief, and she tried to snatch the lead out of his hand.

Tony, however, held her off.

"Pity you don't take proper care of him, isn't it?" he began austerely, but at sight of her face, crumpled with distress, he smiled.

"All right. I'm not going to eat the little chap, but you'd better let me lead him to the door or he'll be off again. Look how you're shaking . . . pull yourself together."

"I'm that upset, sir, I don't know what I'm saying and that's the truth," admitted Brent. "There's nobody more careful than me of the dog and him as attached to me as you'd never think, and yet he just run off. A pretty dance I've had. Ah, you're a bad one, Tim. I wouldn't have believed it of you. Never."

Tim, quite accustomed to Brent's reproachful tones and expecting no other from her, wagged his tail gayly and pattered on. They were going to find his mistress, the man and he, and this was the way. He knew every stone of it, and he dashed up the steps, endeavoring to drag Tony with him, when the door opened and the young man was aware of a large policeman, a maid, and a perfect clatter of tongues.

Tony thrust the lead into Brent's hand and fled, quite unable to face this alien multitude.

It was all wrong. He hadn't intended the dam' silly incident to finish like that. Coming along he had discovered that Tim's collar bore Una's name and address, and he had intended to walk up and ring the bell and ask for her, giving the runaway into her own grateful hand and seeing her smile at him again. Some time in the future, perhaps, he would confess his villainy, but certainly not now with the memory of old Polhampton fresh in her mind. Instead of that the place had been infested with excitement and policemen, and all he had done was to give the little darling an hour's hideous anxiety about her dog, no doubt, and get not a glimpse of her after all. It was just like him. He foozled everything.

He returned to the studio and mooned about it all the afternoon, until Kit's sarcasm drove him forth to seek solace in town. He dined at a noisy restaurant, hating everybody in it, went to a show and left it in the first interval, and walked home to tumble into bed.

Whiskers, coiled on the end of it, sat up, feeling the bedclothes heave about him, then yawned in his master's face.

"That's right," said Tony, indignantly. "Say I'm a bore and be done with it. Who am I?"

iii

Coming into breakfast next morning, he found a copy of the *Times* lying on the window seat, and Kit explained casually that Carstairs had left it behind him the night before.

"Damn it all, why does the silly ass come when I'm out?" inquired Tony, aggrieved but unsuspicious.

"Well, you don't advertise your movements, that I know of," returned Kit, hiding a smile.

"Bit of a plutocrat he's getting, isn't he—chucking the *Times* about? Reads the leading articles, no doubt. . . . Well, what are you looking like that for?"

"We have one cat already," said Kit.

Tony shouted with laughter and, feeling better, picked up the *Times* and proceeded to revel in the Personal column. He read that Lovey still loved Dovey, that Mabel was sick of waiting, please send fiver immediately, that ex-officer wished to meet with £500 free of encumbrances or words to that effect; and that an exceptionally perfect bungalow was to be let at Winkle-by-the-Sea. Then followed a notice full of such exotic verbiage that it could only mean "We have buried the body in the cellar" or "Meet me with the swag at Seven Dials." Tony was satisfied either way, because he was disliking policemen at this moment. They were such large flat brutes, standing in doorways and blocking out the view. Rather nice to think of their being done down by Milly-the-Murderer or Charlie-the-Crook.

He folded the paper and was just about to put it down when his eye caught an advertisement in the next column and he nearly jumped out of his chair.

"£5 Reward. Lost Friday Kensington Gardens, engraved onyx ring set in silver. 017 Palace Square, S. W."

Tony stared at this, scarcely able to believe his eyes. Lorenzo's ring, which she had given him on Friday. It could be no other, but why, if she wanted it back, hadn't she said so, instead of advertising? The blighted ring was bewitched. He had known it from the start, and the whole history of it would sound like sheer lunacy.

Tony, over his breakfast, pondered this latest development and could make nothing of it, unless Mrs. Polhampton had come home and made a song about the ring and this had been done to keep her quiet. It seemed the only possible explanation, and presently, when Kit's back was turned, he tore out the notice and stuffed it in his pocket. He had never shown her the ring, nor told her that Una had given it to him, and when she remarked the torn paper and asked if he had found something interesting, he replied airily:

"Somebody advertising for a grave-digger. I shall apply."

Kit carried his plate into the kitchenette, and exchanged a meaning smile with Whiskers. She knew where a young man's fancy turned in springtime, and a maiden's too, for that matter. Gravedigging was a new name for it.

iv

Tony hovered about the Gardens all the morning, keeping his eye on Palace Square, but this time neither girl nor dog appeared. If he had wasted too many hours already in these Gardens, he consoled himself with the reflection that it was all in the interests of his masterpiece-to-come. It was no good toiling at other things until he had got this out of his system, as he knew by experience. He had a queer and quite unusual confidence in this masterpiece, because no other subject had so much obsessed him, and he did not yet admit to himself that more than his art was concerned. His preoccupations with girls in the past had been few and fleeting, and marriage on a hundred and fifty pounds a year, with an earning capacity likely to be small and precarious for an age to come, was out of the question. There was no need, therefore, for the house in Palace Square to mock him on this May morning. Tony was living for the present only.

It was a golden day. Under the noon sun it took on an air of holiday, as faster and faster the cars raced by, carrying week-end parties out of town. Tony watched them enviously, seeing cool, green woods and fields where the larks rose under a still sky, soaring and singing to some world beyond the clouds.

She loved the country and here was a heaven-sent day for it. He wanted to take her there, and why not? It was a free world and dragons had gone out. Not to ask her, at least, argued a contemptible weakness of spirit.

An elderly lady came down the steps of the house and walked briskly away to Kensington High Street. Her mother, translated Tony in high delight. One obstacle gone. He took out the cutting from the *Times,* blessing Freddy Carstairs, for hadn't this given him just the excuse he needed?

He did not go home to luncheon, but paraded up and down with his pipe until it seemed reasonable to suppose Palace Square would have finished its midday meal. Then, with all the confidence he could muster, he strolled across the road, up the steps of 017 and rang the bell. He was not going to give any name, for there was no knowing what old Polhampton had said about him and they might show him the door. Besides, dragons or no dragons, parents in Palace Square would perhaps suspect young men whom their daughters met by accident in Kensington Gardens. This idea had never occurred to Tony before, and it gave him the fright of his life. They might have forbidden her to speak to him and that would explain her desertion . . . temporarily. You had no doubt to be tactful with parents who put their foot down. However, it was too late to retreat now, for the door was opening.

"I want to see the young lady who lost a ring in Kensington Gardens," he said firmly to the maid. "Will you say I've come about her advertisement?"

"Yes, sir, will you come in?" said Turner.

She hesitated a moment, then seeing that the visitor had a certain air, ushered him into the drawing-room and left him.

Two minutes later Tony, hearing a light step on the stairs, rose with a beaming smile, to find himself confronted by a complete stranger.

"Good afternoon," said Anne inquiringly. "I think the maid said you had called about an advertisement?"

She must be a sister, thought Tony, his smile fading, and by Jove, what a good-looking family. Sisters, however, were no good to him.

"I'm frightfully sorry," he said, "but you're not the young lady I meant."

"No," said Anne, smiling faintly. "My daughter is ill, but can't I do anything? What is it exactly?"

"Oh, she couldn't possibly be your daughter," protested Tony to this. "It wasn't a little girl."

"My daughter is grown up."

"Really?" His confusion was plain, but it was more than confusion. He was not going to give up the ring to any parent, that was certain. Whatever would Una think of him if he did? Still, it was necessary to get out of this, so he summoned his wits and said brightly: "Is she a tall, very fair young lady?"

"No, dark."

"Then it's a mistake. I thought it must be. This one was so fair she was almost whitish, if you know what I mean."

Anne looked at him with a puzzled face.

"We seem to be talking at cross purposes," she observed. "It isn't a daughter we've lost, but a ring."

There was a twinkle in her eye and Tony caught it and laughed.

"I know . . . you must think me completely mad, but really it's quite simple. I saw this fair girl in the Gardens and noticed her ring. She was sitting quite near me and later I found the ring in the grass. I've been looking out for her to return it, and when I saw this advertisement in the *Times* I supposed it was the same ring."

He handed her the slip of paper and proceeded to search in his pockets for the ring he had no intention of finding.

"It was a round pink stone, set in a silver band," he embroidered. "Don't say I've left it in my other coat after all."

"But this is an onyx intaglio," explained Anne. "Not a round pink stone."

"I don't know much about gems," confessed Tony, "so onyx conveyed little to me, but I know an intaglio, of course, and this was nothing like that. To be quite frank, it looked a cheap little trifle, and I had a feeling directly I entered the house there must be some mistake. I'm so sorry to have troubled you. I ought to have given the thing to the police if I hadn't been lazy."

He smiled his apologies and Anne smiled too, as she rang for Turner to show him out.

"It was very good of you to come," she said. "I hope you will find the right owner."

"Thanks awfully. I . . . I hope your daughter isn't seriously ill?" stumbled Tony.

"Not at all, thank you. Good-by."

Anne stood in the middle of the drawing-room when he had gone, half puzzled, half amused. He had looked a nice lad, but she supposed he had been hoping to find this mysterious fair girl who owned the pink ring. A romance nipped in the bud. It was too bad.

At this moment Turner came back full of importance.

"If you please, my lady, that was the same young gentleman who brought back Tim yesterday."

"Oh, nonsense, Turner!"

"Yes, my lady, I could swear to it. I thought his face looked familiar when I opened the door to him, and just now it came over me where I had seen him before. I was letting the officer out and saw him quite plain."

"Oh, well, it may be so," said Anne, dismissing her; but when the girl had gone, she sat down and suddenly laughed.

Recalling their conversation, she began to doubt the existence of the tall fair girl with the pink ring or any ring at all, for why had he failed to produce the lost article when it came to the point? Turner had sharp eyes, too, and an unfailing memory for faces. No, this bright youth was evidently some friend of Una's, probably a rather new friend, seizing any ridiculous occasion to see her because he was too shy or had no excuse to call in the ordinary way. He had been disconcerted when she appeared, Anne was sure. Presumably he did not even know her by sight, a new and amusing thought. And then there had been his stammering inquiry about Una's illness. Anne saw it all and was much diverted. He was a plausible rascal and she rather liked him. She wondered what his next move in the game would be.

The telephone rang and she went out into the hall to answer it.

"Is that Mr. Swithin's house? How is Miss Una today?" asked a voice which she instantly recognized.

"Much better, thank you. Who is speaking?" inquired Anne.

"Oh, splendid!" The voice had changed and she knew he had been expecting his call to be answered by one of the servants. "That is topping, isn't it? Do the doctors say what is the matter?"

"She has been overdoing it a little and needs a rest. That's all. Who is it, though? I don't seem to recognize your voice," said Anne wickedly.

"Rather! I *am* glad. Well, give her my love, won't you, Mrs. Swithin."

He rang off and Anne hung up the receiver, convulsed with laughter, for now he had given himself completely away. Mrs. Swithin! Who could he be, the scamp?

She glanced up in the direction of Una's room, but Jeremy was there, she knew, and this was not the kind of incident she could retail before him, in his present mood. Anne sighed. He had refused to play golf this afternoon, returning home instead to sit jealously with his daughter though it would have been so much better for him out of doors—better for his health and his temper, and hers. Anne was going through a trying time. To add to Jeremy's gloom and the worry of Una's illness, with the consequent upsetting of her plans, she had this morning a long and dictatorial visit from her mother-in-law, who was sure the doctor, whom she had never seen, was incompetent, and greatly incensed that she should be kept from the patient at his instigation. She had no patience with all this modern stuff and nonsense about nerves and rest cures, and she would guarantee to cure her granddaughter, in spite of the doctors, who were all alike, piling up bills and talking twaddle.

Anne had been firm, at some cost to her temper, but the mention of the bills, which Mrs. Swithin had talked about as though they were a personal grievance, had recalled the question she had discussed with John a day or two ago. Debt or no debt—and she could not see it as a debt herself—as soon as present anxieties were dispersed, she must talk to Jeremy and persuade him to pay the money back.

She must purchase her freedom from interference, if she could get it no other way, even it it meant selling Wenlock. Anne at this point had thought rather wistfully of her father who, though of Mrs. Swithin's generation, had been to his daughter both a parent and a friend. She did not believe that one generation was naturally hostile to another. Clever people were far too fond, she thought, of dividing the world into groups to explain the shortcomings of individuals, when the fact was they were just plain nasty. When old people were obnoxious, it was argued that the world was changing and they could not understand; and when young people went over the rails, it was argued that the world was changing and they were misunderstood. Rubbish! The world and the people in it had been changing and behaving in precisely the same way, since the days of Homer and before.

Anne, standing at the foot of the stairs, and thinking of her recent surprising visitor, knew exactly how scandalized and catechizing Mrs. Swithin would have been in her place; but she was no spoil sport, and she had no intention of extracting information from her daughter. The girl could be trusted. She would, however, when Jeremy was out of the way, tell her the tale, comedy fashion, of the tall fair girl and the pink ring, and possibly also of the telephone call. He was a nice lad and he deserved to have his faithful efforts reported.

v

Kit returned to the studio late that afternoon, to find Tony hard at work, and loath to disturb such a pleasant change of mood, she left him and began to prepare their dinner.

Tony, indeed, was relieved by his afternoon adventure. Una, instead of avoiding him, was ill, but not seriously, and although he had got himself into a tight corner with her mother concerning the ring, he had managed to slip out of it without arousing the least suspicion. Even on the telephone he had been very cunning, disguising his voice as soon as he recognized hers. A most successful afternoon!

Hearing the clatter of plates and feeling ravenous, he put his work away, had a bath, and changed into a dinner coat, arriving at the kitchen door with amiable offers to assist the cook.

"Are you ill?" was Kit's caustic retort to this.

"No . . . but I say, Kit, Una is."

"I know. There's a paper in there. Better have a look at it."

Kit was rather sorry for him and had meant to keep her shock till after dinner; for it would be a shock, she supposed, to find that Una was a daughter of the beautiful Lady Anne Swithin. Kit, who had designed frocks for this celebrity through Robby the Robot, had never connected her with the girl and the dog, but this did put poor old Tony out of the running, she was afraid. At all events, it was just as well he should know where he was.

She found him with his elbows on the dinnertable, staring at a photograph of Anne, beneath which was the usual society gush about Una's illness and the postponement of her mother's dance for her.

"Tuesday must be her birthday, then. I know it's some time this month," exclaimed Tony.

"Giving her a diamond tiara?"

Kit was being unkind with the best intentions, but for once Tony was not to be drawn.

"Did you know her mother was the famous Lady Anne?" proceeded Kit.

"Famous for what?"

"The famous beauty, of course. Do you never read the newspapers?"

"Not the tripe section. Good lord, they're bristling with titles then. That old Polhampton woman in Florence was a Lady Swithin. We *are* getting in with the nobs," said Tony despondently.

Kit went on with her dinner for a while in silence; then she remarked casually: "Perhaps if it came to a question of marriage, the governor would buy us off for a lump sum."

"Who's talking of marriage?" inquired her brother, looking startled.

"I am, for one. You didn't really think that Freddy came here for love of your bright eyes, did you?"

He dropped his fork and stared at her, as one bewitched.

"Freddy? You don't mean to say you've snaffled old Carstairs? You clever little devil!"

"I saw rather a lot of him while you were away," said Kit with calm. "On the whole, I think I'll tackle the governor fairly soon, because if he only gave us five thousand, it would not be so bad. Then you, as the supporter-sex could have four and I as a mere supportee the rest."

Tony did not all at once appreciate this handsome suggestion, because he was transfixed by her effrontery.

"My poor child, you're mad," he said, "the governor would never bite."

"Why not? We've cost him nothing for the past two years, and he can well afford it," retorted Kit.

"Yes, but hang it, we cleared out to please ourselves, after all."

"That is no reason why he shouldn't give us a start in life according to his means."

"But if you've never troubled to go near him since you've left home. . . . After all, you didn't quarrel with the governor . . . or did you?" asked Tony, suddenly suspicious.

"Certainly not. I said I was going and he said I wasn't and I went. He knows my address if he wants to see me."

"My God, girls are hard, for you can't deny the old boy was fond of you, Kit."

"Better be hard than sloppy anyway," said Kit, getting up to clear away. "Father indulged me and favored me right and left from the time I was born, because it pleased his vanity that I was rather like him."

She carried the plates into the kitchenette and almost flung them down in her scorn.

"It didn't flatter my vanity," she went on, returning. "I hate tyranny. . . . Well, what are you looking like that for? It wasn't on your account, so you needn't think it. It was simply a matter of principle."

"Oh, rather," said Tony.

He watched her helplessly for a moment, then feigning nonchalance, strolled out of the room and ran downstairs and into the street where the lights were waking, one by one, in the kindly dusk.

Kit could deny it as much as she chose, but he knew now why she had left home and he was touched and grateful and terribly abashed. Hard, he had called her, but now he saw that quality in a new light, remembering how often in the hateful past this very hardness in a mere girl had kept his own precarious courage up. He wondered if she knew.

Tony strolled up and down in a world that suddenly seemed kinder than he had ever known it. Even his bitterness against his father, which had been all the deeper because unspoken, slipped away, for Kit had squared the account. He would have liked to rush up and tell her so, but the barriers of intimacy stood between them, and he even felt an absurd embarrassment about going back to the studio until he remembered old Carstairs.

At that he sprinted towards the High Street appearing a few moments later before Kit with a parcel under his arm.

"What on earth have you got there?" demanded Kit suspiciously.

Rather guiltily he unwrapped a bottle of champagne.

"I suppose that kidnapper will be coming round," he said in an aggressive tone. "I've a good mind to knock his head off with it."

"Nice of you," was Kit's somewhat ambiguous reply to this.

CHAPTER XIV

i

NOT till Monday morning when Jeremy had gone to his chambers did Anne find an opportunity to tell Una her little story.

The girl lay in bed with the sunlight streaming in through the open window, and her longing gaze fixed on the little space of sky. This illness was a dreadful and boring business, and it seemed to her that she had been lying there for months. Now that the party was safely canceled, wouldn't it be safe to recover completely, she wondered? She was still troubled and uneasy about her father, who had been hovering about her for two days, wrapped in gloom; and one difficulty she had not foreseen in planning this breakdown, was that she could not be downstairs for meals, to see with her own eyes how things were between him and her mother.

For several days now Anne had taken Tim out for his run, instead of leaving Brent to do it, and Una, who had been told nothing of Tim's temporary loss, was amazed and grateful at this attention to her dog, until she remembered Tony's habit of lying in wait out there. Suppose they met!

She could not think what might happen then, but every morning she searched her mother's face when she and Tim returned, and drew a breath of relief when Anne looked serene as usual.

"Was he any trouble?" she inquired, when Tim was brought to her this morning.

"Not in the least. Tim is a dignified gentleman and the admired of all beholders," returned Anne. "Feeling better this morning?"

"Perfectly. I should like to get up."

Anne brought her dressing-gown out of the wardrobe, found her slippers and carried the eiderdown to an easy chair by the window.

"Come along then, just for a little while. It can't do you any harm."

The invalid hopped out with every appearance of bounding health.

"Tomorrow I shall be quite well, don't you think?" she inquired anxiously.

"Unofficially, perhaps . . . as far as the study . . . and I might smuggle in a few visitors, as it is your birthday, but carefully censored, of course. By the way, Bill France rang up to ask for you. I didn't know he was a particular friend of yours."

"Oh, rather!"

"Which reminds me," said Anne, sitting down on Una's bed, "did you know Jeremy had advertised for your ring?"

"Mother! How silly of him, with Aunt Marion coming home."

"I know, but I suppose the poor darling never thought of that. And the advertisement brought me a most amusing visitor on Saturday."

"Who?" Una's glance was cautious, but her voice eager and Anne smiled inwardly.

"An absurd young man who asked for the girl

who lost a ring in the Gardens and looked dreadfully disconcerted when I appeared instead."

"Was he a stranger . . . hadn't you ever seen him before?" This time all the effort in the world could not keep the anxiety out of Una's face.

"Never. It seems he saw this girl wearing the ring, and then found it in the grass when she had gone, and I believe he had lost his heart, or thought he had, and was hoping to find the girl had it. The beauty of it was, he felt in all his pockets and said I would think he was quite mad, but it must be in his other coat. And then it came out it was a bright pink ring and the girl was fair . . . almost whitish. Wrong house, wrong ring, wrong girl," finished Anne dramatically.

"What an absurd idiot! What was he like?"

"Tall . . . six feet, I should think, with a thin face and wicked, dark blue eyes. Much too nice a rascal to be picking up fair young hussies in the park, but I didn't like to tell him so, of course.

"Then," proceeded Anne, "a mysterious friend of yours rang up, also slightly mad, I should think. When I asked his name he said 'Rather! Give her my love, won't you, Mrs. Swithin,' and rang off."

"Mother!"

Anne laughed and rose to her feet.

"Yes, you may well say 'Mother.' Mrs. Swithin indeed! There's fame for you. And what do you mean by keeping me dark?"

"Oh, I didn't . . . I wouldn't . . . what did he sound like?" cried Una.

"Rather like the other lunatic, I thought at first,

but that was a mistake. A much deeper voice . . .
very gruff," said Anne in a bass tone and on this
note of comedy departed.

ii

Tony! Who else could it have been? It was so
like him, inventing the fair girl and the pink ring
on the spur of the moment, and then pretending he
had left the ring behind him after all. A tall, thin
young man with wicked dark blue eyes . . . "Too
nice a rascal to pick up fair young hussies in the
park."

Una recalled her mother's words with a chuckle
of delight, which faded, however, into a feeling of
disappointment and confusion, for Anne had never
seen him before, and Tony had admitted the statue.

Brent came in and full of her importance as nurse
to the invalid was duly incensed to find her out of
bed.

"I never heard the like, Miss Una. Such goings
on. Bed was what the doctor ordered and bed it
ought to be."

"Doctors don't know everything."

"None of us knows everything, Miss. We know
what the Lord intends us to know and no more and
no less."

Brent's Deity was responsible for everything, a
perfect catspaw, Una thought. Even when one
dreadful morning when Brent had scorched some
priceless lace, she had put it on to the Lord and considered that the final argument.

The picture of Brent's Deity, sitting on a cloud

and giving orders to one of His angels that a piece of lace was to be scorched in Palace Square, London, S. W., diverted Una momentarily, for if you could believe a tale like that, what was the good of anything? You were just pawns and life was terrible and dangerous; all sorts of horrors might be waiting for you round the corner. And weren't they? Blackmailing cousins and aunts, saying things about your mother and demanding Wenlock; people throwing vitriol in the face of your twin brother like poor old Robby. Were these things arranged, then? It was a revolting notion. What was life, really? What was it for and where did it go? People were always inventing answers to this, but nobody really knew and yet there must be some explanation or why have a world? Una suddenly saw the world with millions of people on it like ants, not knowing why they were there yet hoping for the best. She was one of the ants . . . very small, it felt . . . and Tony was another, talking about fair girls and pink rings, and changing his voice on the telephone and making it sound gruff to deceive Anne.

But he had made a statue of her, and why had he called her Mrs. Swithin? "Lady" Swithin he had said the other day, and though that was wrong too, people were often not quite clear about titles. He had just been flurried, perhaps, but that didn't explain the fact that her mother had never seen him in her life before.

Enlightenment came in a flash. He had made the statue and she didn't know. Why should she? All the world knew and admired her mother, and Una remembered Tony and his singing boy. He had hidden behind a tree and watched him. What could be simpler? Tony had made his statue of Anne, then, without knowing her at all, and the Herbert Swithins had somehow heard of it and just invented the rest out of their evil minds.

All was well: Tony was back in his place as her secret friend; and she had wasted days and days in bed for a tissue of lies. Still she did not really mind this, since she had routed the family. They made trouble whenever they came, and there was still the question of her father and what hints they might have given him.

All day Una planned what she could do to find out, and that evening when Jeremy sat beside her talking of her birthday on the morrow and trying to discover what she wanted and whether she would like the present he had brought her, she gathered her courage together and asked in a voice as casual as she could make it:

"Do you know any sculptors, father?"

"Sculptors? No, I don't think I do," said Jeremy anxiously. "Why?"

"Oh, I don't know. It's rather a wonder, don't you think? You know . . . artists are always wanting to paint mother, so it's surprising some sculptors haven't come along, wanting to make statues of her."

Jeremy looked crestfallen, for he had bought her a little watch set in diamonds and perhaps she would not care for it at all.

"Did you want me to get you a statue of your mother?" he asked doubtfully.

"Oh, good gracious, no. I wasn't talking of birthdays. . . . I wasn't really talking of anything," she assured him eagerly. "We don't want a statue of her because we've got her alive, haven't we?"

"Yes. . . . I suppose we have."

"If anyone brought me a statue," proceeded Una, uttering blasphemy lest he should rush out and buy her statues forthwith, "I should brain them with the silly thing. What's the time, father? My watch has stopped again."

Jeremy told her the time, looking all at once as though someone had given him a gift of price, and presently straightened his shoulders and departed.

"He doesn't know anything about it, evidently," thought Una. "And I do believe he's cheering up."

iii

Next morning, lying among the medley of birthday parcels which had been arriving at the house for several days, the blasphemy returned upon her in a wholly delightful and unexpected fashion. The new watch ticked gayly on her wrist, brought in by Jeremy in person, and she had succeeded in making him believe it was the one thing she had wanted in the world. He had gone down to breakfast happy in the knowledge that Anne's present of a new rug for the car was a small thing in comparison.

There was less terror than usual in the other presents, since she could open them alone, without having to parcel out her appreciation in just and insincere quantities, because his eyes were upon her. For the first time in years she thought birthdays were rather fun, and she began to sort out her loot, separating the handwriting she knew from the unfamiliar superscriptions, and keeping obviously best ones for the last.

Grandmother! This would be a work-basket. Una unpacked it frowning, and after it Aunt Fanny's offering, a camisole, beautifully embroidered, which the recipient regarded with awe.

"How funny of her! Does she think people actually wear them?" wondered Una. "If she'd only made some legs it would do for pyjamas."

Poor Aunt Fanny! The picture of her, embroidering legs under grandmother's nose, made Una so sorry for her that she put aside the camisole kindly, away from the contamination of the work-basket.

Her grandfather had sent a fountain pen, and very nice too; and the Herberts some purple stationery, which Una, who regarded white note paper as necessary as a daily bath, would have returned if she had dared.

Thus complete, the family presents were set out for her father to see, in case he should come back and think she was neglecting them.

She was not expecting anything from Uncle John, who was not likely to know it was her birthday, and had never inflicted her in the past, but presently, when she had just tenderly unwrapped a gorgeous box of silk stockings from Judy France, she saw a letter and tore it open.

"Dear Una," she read,

"Here's a secret for your birthday. Tell no one, put it in the bank, and when you want something you can't afford, go and buy it from

"Your Uncle John."

Inside was a check for a hundred pounds.

"I don't know how he ever came to get into that family," thought Una, glowing all over. "Or father either," she added as a polite after-thought.

The gifts, little and big, came forth until her bed looked like a bazaar. Then from the unknowns she drew a new surprise. It was a box of violets, inscribed, "A few flowers from Bill. Here's luck, partner."

Bill! And then they said he was superior! Una put Robby's postcard of good wishes into the little box for company.

One unknown parcel remained and she looked at it dubiously, for it bore no stamp and was large, and she had a suspicious feeling that this was going to be a white elephant.

When at last she cut the string, however, she found quite another beast, and in a moment she was calling excitedly to her dog.

"Tim . . . oh, Tim darling, it's you. Come and look at yourself."

Out of the wrappings peered Tony's gift, Tim in miniature, Tim to the very last hair, and the original, bounding on to the bed and knocking things right and left, sniffed it, ready to growl indignantly, and then drew back, looking surprised. Wasn't the thing alive?

Una lifted the new Tim out and introduced him, and then, to the other Tim's relief, hid him under the eiderdown, because she heard a step on the stairs. She could not show this to her father, after their talk of statues the night before, and besides. . . .

There wasn't a message or word in the parcel to say where it came from, and how had he known about the birthday? It was marvelous and he had given her the most perfect gift of them all.

Una lay back with starry eyes, and Tim stretched himself beside her, keeping a wary look out for this other dog. When her father came in to say goodby she was even able to admire the work-basket to give him pleasure, and Aunt Fanny's garment which hadn't any legs.

Birthdays were heavenly, presents a lark, Una was happy.

It was more difficult to keep the new Tim from her mother, who had been such a sport about the fair girl and the pink ring; and so when Anne came in to put Bill's flowers in water and tidy the chaos of presents, Una found herself asking:

"Did anybody ever make a statue of you?"

"Never," said Anne. "Of course I'm a heroine, but not a dead one, which makes all the difference. Still, I live in hope. Where do you think they should put it up? Hyde Park Corner or the top of the Albert Hall?"

"I don't mean that kind of statue," declared Una grinning. "I mean an art-y one. You know . . . haven't you ever been sculped, mother?"

"Never. I feel it very much."

Una smiled.

"Tim has," she said, and produced her treasure, standing him on the eiderdown.

"Why, it might be Tim himself," said Anne, amused at the little figure.

"It *is* Tim. It's a statue of him."

"So it is. Who made him for you? He's beautiful."

"I've never seen the writing before and there wasn't a word inside," said Una, disarming and innocent.

Anne laughed at her daughter's glowing face; then, putting a last touch to the violets, made for the door.

"Well, give him my love when you write, and do beg him not to call me Mrs. Swithin, won't you? It's so tactless."

She went out and Tim bustled after her, inviting her to walk in the park. Una addressed his understudy.

"Rather a peach, isn't she?" she said. "You'll like her."

iv

Una was writing letters of thanks the next afternoon in the study, when Turner came to tell her that Miss Marion Swithin was downstairs. The doctor had agreed that she might get up at midday, but had forbidden excitement and visitors for some time to come; and Turner had been dubious but Miss Swithin persistent. Anne was out and Una, guilty about the ring, felt she had better see her aunt and get it over. She hoped her father's advertisement might have escaped the family's notice, but no doubt that was too much to expect.

Miss Swithin, very smartly gowned and hatted, entered the room with all the majesty of old Mrs. Swithin, but affably rather than in any spirit of criticism. As a woman of the world, she knew Anne's house was elegant and rightly so; she approved of it. She flattered herself she was elegant too. In fact she was fond of the word, whereas Anne had probably never used it in her life. She bore Anne no grudge, even in secret, for having a title. Lady Anne Swithin sounded so well, like one of the old noblesse. "Dear Anne," she would say to acquaintances met about Eurpoe, *"très charmante,* isn't she? We are all devoted to her." She really believed so, being one of those wise people who skim the surface of life and avoid the uncomfortable depths. There was a reason for this, hidden away in the beginning of the century, but she had resolutely forgotten it. Her mother, with a bitter memory, was rather afraid of Marion.

"Dear Una," said Miss Swithin, kissing her niece, with what Tony would have called a pounce. "They tried to keep me from you, but it could not be done. I'm too old a bird of passage to be stopped by any servant. One learns how to handle them wandering about the world, *n'est-ce-pas?"*

She looked so pleased about it that Una did not like to argue, so she said: "Oh, rather, and we'll pretend you aren't a visitor as I'm not supposed to have any." ("For otherwise," she thought, "the whole family will be rushing out.") "Are you glad to be back in England, Aunt Marion?"

"No, dear, *entre nous*, I am not, *pas de tout*, and I shall flit away again very soon. I am, I am afraid, a sad cosmopolitan, but then a wise man's country is the world, as Shakespeare said, or somebody. One forgets. Frankly, Una, I have few attachments in England nowadays except your dear mother, to whom as you know I am devoted. Wimbledon would kill me, though I regard it as a duty to run over and see them all occasionally. But poor Fanny, and that dreadful wife of your Uncle Herbert! As I said to your grandfather only this morning, the woman's a charlatan, pure and simple. Abroad she would deceive no one."

"What did he say?" inquired Una in genuine admiration.

"Oh, la, la," cried her aunt, dropping the matter of Mrs. Herbert and pouncing upon Tony's Tim. "The *petit chien. Comme il est gentil. Molto buono!* A birthday present, *hein?*"

Una, rather giddy from this flow of cosmopolitanese, answered in vulgar English: "He's my dog," then lifted the original off the hearth-rug to exhibit him.

"Ah, *le pauvre!*" Miss Swithin's tone was tender but her glance cursory. She did not really care for dogs in the raw. The image of Tim she put down however with her on one side, with a reminiscent smile.

"*Alors.* It might be the *petit chien* himself."

"It is . . . it's a statue of him, Aunt Marion," with eager pride.

Miss Swithin took off her gloves as Turner appeared with tea, the smile growing dreamy.

"And I, Una, have had a little statue made of me. What do you think of that? Your old bachelor aunt . . . ah, *bella Firenze!*"

"Really?"

Una wondered who Bella was and how many more statues she was going to hear of. They seemed to be in the air.

"*Si, si,* oh, most romantic, I assure you and, by the by, Una, you are concerned in this. Your ring. . . ."

"It was a lovely ring," stammered Una, and put down the tea-pot, which suddenly threatened to jump out of her hand.

Miss Swithin beamed, but absently.

"Dear child, I'm glad."

She took her tea and helped herself to a scone, which she nibbled, it seemed to Una, with a kind of pleased excitement like a gigantic mouse who has evaded the cat. Having finished it, she dusted her fingers and shook a waggish head at her niece.

"So you liked the ring? Ah, but what a fight I had to get it for you. There was this young man determined to get it . . . oh, quite determined. *Si, si.* Practically snatched it, but with a little finesse and of course a thorough knowledge of the language, I outwitted him. It wasn't merely a question of *place aux dames,* as I told him quite kindly afterwards, but I had been considering the ring for at least fifteen minutes. Well, there it was, and I must say he turned out more gallant than I had expected. I made, it seems, a tremendous impression on him and a few days later he called at my hotel and presented me with this perfect little statue."

"W . . . what did he say?" inquired Una in a voice which sounded to her own ears small and very far away.

"*Je ne sais* . . . stammered, poor lad, looked shy and embarrassed and finally rushed off before I had recovered from my astonishment. These young artists . . . and then Firenze, the very home of romance. . . ."

Miss Swithin smiled and sighed.

"An amusing episode," she said. "I often laugh over it."

"But what happened then? Didn't you even know his name?" Una managed to ask as she poured her aunt another cup of tea.

"His name? Oh yes, Corkran or something of the kind, but I moved on, my dear, and that was an end of it."

"Perhaps he felt he had been rude and it was a kind of apology?" Una suggested after a silence, rather suddenly.

"*Si, si, peut être!*" Miss Swithin's tone was indulgent as of one remembering the innocence of youth, but it was clear she did not believe so naïve an explanation, and Una's eyes grew dark. "But tell me about yourself, child. You have been going to too many parties, I hear, and what about the young men? Any favorites?"

"I hate the lot of them," said Una violently. "I'll never marry."

She was utterly astonished at herself. The words and the sentiments seemed to have been shaken out of her without her own volition, and she had never seriously considered either subject before. She was covered with the shame of a shy person who sees herself exposed to a hostile gaze, but Miss Swithin noticed nothing.

"A thoroughly modern girl, *n'est-ce-pas?*" she said jovially. "Good! We wouldn't have you otherwise. And if you don't change your mind, you shall come and wander the world with your bachelor aunt. *Alors.* . . ."

v

At last she had gone, complacent, affectionate, and blind to the hatred and scorn she had left behind. Both were unjust, for she would have been a slightly pathetic figure to dispassionate eyes . . . one of the great band of spinster women to whom self-dramatization is the only emotional outlet left.

But Una could see her only in relation to Tony and she was revolted. The past weeks of alternate excitement and agitation and the days of inaction in bed were having their way with the girl and it was inevitable that she should see the incident out of all proportion. Since the night of the wedding dinner all her secret fears and bewilderments had been focused upon her father's family and that Tony should be implicated after all seemed to her the last straw. The hints of Mab and Herbert; their

mother's "threatening noises" to Anne; whatever it
was her grandmother had said to upset her father
and make him talk darkly of divorce, these things
had become unimportant when she had found her
mother actually did not know Tony Corcoran by
sight. And now here was Aunt Marion with her
silly tale! The family seemed to have Tony on the
brain, thought Una indignantly, and as far as she
was concerned they could keep him there. She
wanted no friend of theirs.

Brent coming in to hunt her patient off to bed,
found her unexpectedly docile. Una called Tim list-
lessly but she left the little statue where it stood.
She felt she did not want to hear the word statue
again as long as she lived.

On the couch her aunt had left an evening paper
and she took this up to her room, determined that
she would not even think of Tony. That he should
have been romantic about her mother was easy to
understand, but Aunt Marion! It was an outrage
and he must be blind and weak-minded. Why should
he pick on her family? He would be getting romantic and making statues of her grandmother next.

Una tumbled into bed and opened the paper, but
for a time what she read made little sense, and she
turned over the pages, staring dully at the headlines.

MASKED MAN IN MAYFAIR
BURGLAR RANSACKS DRESS SHOP

Una, not greatly interested, read on and in a
moment she was sitting up, the sheet clutched in her
hand.

"At ten o'clock this morning a masked man entered the show-room of Avril's Robes, 18, Turton St. W.1, threatened Madame Avril and proceeded to ransack the place. Only one assistant, Miss Roberta Lyne, was on duty with the proprietor at that hour, the other employees being engaged in the workrooms to the rear. One of the young ladies, coming in search of Madame Avril at 10.20, found the show-room in disorder and her employer lying unconscious on the floor. Miss Lyne had disappeared.

"Madame Avril was taken to her home in a state of collapse and has been able to give little account of her assailant, except that he was violent and wearing a black mask. Nothing more has been seen or heard of Miss Lyne.

"A curious feature of the affair is that neither the neighbors nor the work-girls heard any commotion, but Mrs. Rose Quill, who manages a massage establishment nearby, noticed a man and woman come out of Avril's soon after 10 o'clock and enter a waiting taxi. The woman she believes to have been Miss Lyne whom she knew by sight and considered somewhat eccentric. The man was tall and dressed in a blue lounge suit and grey felt hat. She did not notice him particularly and was unable to state whether he wore a mask.

"The amount of Madame Avril's loss has not yet been ascertained. The police have the matter in hand."

CHAPTER XV

i

IT was a tempting morsel for an evening edition, but the real tale of the Masked Man in Mayfair, which most of the world never heard, was something quite different.

Robby the Robot, rubbing off her paint and so carefully concealing her private hell when she went to see the man in the orchard, overlooked one salient point. If she could feel his torment in every nerve of her, was it credible that he, considering the curious alliance between them, should not sense something of hers? A lad of twenty, thinking the world a joke, then seeing it smashed before his eyes, may go under for a time; but youth is resilient, and there could be nothing craven in the counterpart of Robby Lyne.

With work to do which in the beginning had merely exercised his body, but at last had come to absorb and interest his mind, he was often now quite happy, but he was aware that, in spite of her lively tales, Robby was not. Her comings and goings of late had become so mysterious, for one thing . . . always by a different route, getting a train or bus to some point and then another across country. His own early terror that someone would discover his retreat had been lulled to rest by this time, for he was supposed to be abroad, and he and his disaster had long ago passed from the public mind. Robby's tactics therefore seemed unnecessary unless there were something else behind them. Finally on the Sunday when Una lay "ill," he tackled Robby and would not be put off.

She laughed, pretended it was a huge joke and told her tale suitably disguised. Poor old Avril was a silly rabbit and had got it into her head that Robby was carrying on with some man, probably married. Respectability being her fetish, and the tone of her establishment her god, she had set detectives to watch Miss Lyne.

"I'm like the persecuted heroine," said Robby gayly, "and I wouldn't miss it for the world. Sport? Every time I dodge 'em, I demand a rise and Avril, who's afraid of losing me, has to shell out. Of course if she discovered anything she thinks she'd have me in the hollow of her hand. Poor lamb, she little knows the dance I'm leading her."

He listened, said nothing and pondered the story for two days, but it was too thin. What did it matter to Avril if Robby carried on? The woman was clearly a hell-cat and it was high time something was done about it. Robby had had enough to bear.

On Wednesday morning therefore, Bob Lyne, feeling strangely like a man returned from the dead, walked calmly into Avril's show-room, told her in the plainest terms what he thought of her, and whisked Robby, almost paralyzed with astonishment, away for good.

It was Avril herself who threw the goods about

and composed herself in a faint on the floor. In terror for the reputation of her business she saw the wisdom of getting in the first blow. Roberta Lyne, who had been a gold mine to Avril's, was lost to her, but she should not ruin her without a struggle. Miss Lyne had powerful friends and it did not enter Avril's head that any young woman possessing these assets would be such a fool as not to use them. The cunning old foreigner who had for two painful years been Robby's presiding devil, played at one stroke for revenge and a thumping advertisement for her shop.

Of all Robby's circle one person only had a clue to what had really occurred, Una Swithin, sitting up in bed with her eyes glued to the newspaper, but her thoughts busy with a man in an orchard, the rumness of being twins, and at last, something her mother had said.

MASKED MAN IN MAYFAIR

The paper was flung away, and Una was out of bed, into dressing-gown and slippers, and flying downstairs to the telephone.

"I want Mr. France . . . no, no, Mr. Bill France . . . Bill, is that you? Una speaking . . . Bill, have you seen the papers?"

The violence of Bill's reply was a clear index to his agitation.

"Yes, I know, but listen," said Una eagerly. "Are you certain Bob Lyne is not in England?"

"No . . . haven't the foggiest notion where he is. I say, Una, do you know anything?"

"Not really, but I have thought of an idea. Wouldn't a man with a shade over one side of his face look like a masked man? Because Bob did wear one. Mother told me the other night."

"Ye gods, I believe you've hit it, you little Briton. Look here, Una, I'm going off to the police. I'll shut up that she-devil if it costs me a fortune," cried Bill in the utmost excitement.

"Yes, do," encouraged Una, then laughed, because she knew she spoke to an empty wire. Bill was losing no time.

At the same moment a sound of a key in the front door sent Una running along the hall and up the back stairs. From the landing above she recognized her father's voice and was just creeping past the study towards her room when she saw the little statue of Tim and knew she must retrieve it before it caught his eye. Tucking it under her dressing-gown she came back to the door and peered out, but seeing her father and mother half way up the stairs, retreated again. Her father would be sure to make a fuss if he caught her like this; he took her illness so seriously; and Una felt she had had all she could bear this afternoon. Therefore, when she saw them actually turn towards the study, panic seized her, and she slipped down behind the chesterfield and sat there against the wall, rather shaken, and hoping they had only come in for a cigarette and would then go.

ii

Jeremy and Anne had arrived home at the same moment by accident. Anne had been calling in the neighborhood and had as yet heard nothing of Robby and the Masked Man. Jeremy's mind was full of it, for it would prove to her that he had been right, the one consolation of a more than usually trying day.

Mr. Drew, prompted by his wife and taking advantage of his years and their long association, had been indulging in a straight talk with the younger man, who needed in his elder's eyes to pull himself together. With his talents and his chances Swithin should have been wearing silk by now and would undoubtedly do so yet if he put his mind to it.

"You're despondent, my boy, a dam' bad thing for any man to be, and you can take it from me, a fatal thing in this profession. And what's the reason of it? You have a charming home, a beautiful and devoted wife and a fine girl. You have, I take it, no financial worries or you would have appealed to me unless you are a bigger fool than I take you for."

No, there were no financial worries, but how could Jeremy explain? The other man's words were kind enough but his fatherly tone was denied by the cold eyes. That Mr. Drew considered him a disappointing investment he had known for some time, and he had had a moment's actual and humiliating terror at the outset of this talk lest it should herald some change.

"Liver perhaps?" presently suggested Drew.

"You should get out of town more. Take a little place in the country."

Jeremy had no interest in the country.

"I'll convert you over Whitsun. It's no good telling me that girl of yours is too ill to be left because my wife has been in communication with Anne and it is all arranged," declared the old man. "She drives down to Warwickshire on Friday morning and you come down with me by an afternoon train."

They had left it at that, Jeremy indeed, relieved that it was no worse, accepting almost gratefully, but going home he felt heavy with defeat. It was all true; he was a failure, but it made it no easier to hear it put into cold words and to be called over the coals like a schoolboy in disgrace. And then he saw Anne just ahead of him, more lovely and more desirable than ever, yet happy in spite of the estrangement of the past week, and his desolation seemed more than he could bear.

She spoke to him and he answered mechanically, not knowing what he said. They went upstairs and when she turned into the study he followed her, throwing himself wearily into a chair.

"I must go and have a look at the poor invalid," remarked Anne. "She has been alone all the afternoon."

"It is always Una now, isn't it, Anne?" said Jeremy sadly, voicing his trouble at last. "I'm only second best . . . always have been, since she came."

Behind the couch his daughter's face turned scarlet and her heart pounded. He'd found out . . . oh, he'd found out.

"Jeremy!" Anne sat down on the arm of his chair and gathered his head to her breast. Una could not see her, but she heard Anne's voice and to her ears it sounded new and strange. "My darling dear, my poor boy, you don't really think that . . . that you are second to anybody in the world?"

"I've always thought so. I've been so damned jealous . . . oh, don't think I haven't fought it and known it was contemptible, but ever since the War she's been there between us, Anne."

He hardly knew how he came to be saying it, and did not hope for her denial, his misery was too profound. He had often voiced this trouble in imagination, but then it had been as a complaint and he had found a forlorn comfort in that. There was no comfort now speech had come, merely a dull conviction, and at first he was not even aware of the amazement in his wife's voice, as she said: "Nonsense! Nobody in the world is between us, no one could be, even Una, much as I love her. She's our own, yours and mine . . . part of us both. It's different."

"Is it?"

"You know it's different."

Una's hands went suddenly to her ears and her mind said over and over: "Oh, please go away . . . go away quickly." But there was silence for a little while, not even a movement and that was more dreadful still, for how long could she bear it? Her limbs were cramped and the confined space seemed to become a tunnel in a nightmare, so that she wanted to cry out. "I mustn't," she thought in a panic, and the sheer physical agony of enforced self-restraint shut out every other problem and every coherent thought.

Was it different? With Anne's arms about him and her cheek pressed to his, Jeremy was almost convinced. Then, ashamed of his weakness, he drew himself away and sat hunched forward, with his hands over his face. She was just being kind, humoring his mood. She did not understand his misery or care as he cared. How could he expect it?

"I have been a blind idiot, haven't I?" said Anne. "I have never even guessed what was the matter, and you have been another, worrying over something that does not exist. You know it doesn't really, in your heart, now don't you?"

Jeremy said dispiritedly: "Oh, of course I'm a fool but I can't forget she nearly killed you when she came. I knew then if you grew to care for her more than me I should be done."

"But she couldn't help it, poor baby, and I've always imagined you adored her, Jeremy."

He got up awkwardly as though he could not look at her and poked the fire into a blaze.

"I am fond of her. I've tried to make it up to her, God knows, but I haven't room for more than one love. You fill my life and my mind."

It was the voice of the boy she had married, so assured with the rest of the world, so diffident and awkward in her presence, and for a moment time rolled back for Anne and the glow of that old love returned. She jumped up and went to him impulsively.

"My dearest, why, we are just like a honeymoon couple, you and I . . . really, underneath. In love with each other after twenty years and in these days! I'm not sure it isn't almost scandalous," she declared resting her cheek against his coat.

Jeremy turned and caught her in his arms.

"I'm a failure, Anne," he said at last.

"Nonsense!"

"Yes, Drew thinks so. He'll tell you."

"He'd better dare. I'll inform the old wretch I don't want a piece of parchment for a husband. So there!"

"I thought I could have conquered the world for you."

"You are my world," said Anne.

iii

Una did not know how long she sat with her hands over her burning ears and her heart pounding as though they must surely hear it. She could not tell how she crept back to bed unseen, or ate her dinner and talked to them just as usual, saying she was better and Aunt Marion had come to tea, as though this were the same world she had always known.

But now they had gone and it was dark and she knew it was a different world—a world where she walked alone.

It was not her father after all who was the odd man out, but she, herself. She always had been.

It was very strange. She felt frightened and strange at first, but that was no good, and hastily she caught up her terrors and locked them away. And then she felt strong and almost exalted but she did not know why. Always she had known there was something the matter with her father and tried desperately to ward the trouble off, and all the time it had been herself.

"Ever since the War she has been there between us, Anne."

She did not count the pity and anguish she had wasted all down the years on this mistaken cause. It was doubtful if she ever would. She had never been very conscious of herself, and as in her childhood, when Jeremy and Anne had gone away and left her disappointingly behind, it had never entered her head to protest, so now she did not think of protesting because she was the odd one out.

But it was very surprising. Even with her mother she did not come first . . . disappointing this, because she had been so sure she did, but now she wondered why. There wasn't any reason why she should be first, and nothing there was really changed. Her mother was lovely and perfect still, even from this strange world where her daughter stood alone.

And she could smile at her as much as she chose now, for her father couldn't mind, as he didn't after all want to be first with her as she had always supposed. Suddenly, as though an immense weight had been lifted from her, she knew a sense of release. The old mysterious responsibility to her father was swept away and she saw that she was free.

A ray of light crept through the blinds from the full moon riding high, and Una thought of shining roads running away through the world . . . the roads to Wenlock.

She could ask her mother to give her Wenlock now. It would be quite easy, and then her secret dream . . . dogs in the country. They didn't need her here.

The moonlight caught the little white head of Tony's Tim, standing beside her bed, and with a pang she turned her back on it, lying very still for a long moment, and trying not to think of Tony. Then she turned round and smiled at it apologetically.

"It's all right," she said. "It isn't your fault."

CHAPTER XVI

i

JEREMY had not after all mentioned Robby and
her Masked Man to Anne. In his happiness he
saw his attitude to Miss Lyne as just part of his own
unendurable misery, enhanced by his mother's
prejudices, and he was even sorry that he and his
mother should inadvertently have been right, because Robby was a friend of Anne's. When on
Thursday morning the affair was practically con-
tradicted by the newspapers, he thanked heaven he
had kept silence.

There were no headlines on this occasion, and
Anne, skimming the news rather hurriedly, missed
the small paragraph hidden away in one of those
obscure corners, where the press corrects its mistakes. During the morning someone did ring up
eager to discuss the scandal, but by that time Anne
was being led to Elysium by Tim, so here again the
news miscarried.

Una, immersed in her own problems, was only
recalled to Robby's when her mother had gone out.
She immediately dressed and ran downstairs for the
newspaper, finding after a long search the following
item:

"A rumor which gained currency yesterday that a fash-
ionable dress shop in the West End had been raided by a

masked man who ransacked the place and departed with one of the young lady assistants, proved to be greatly exaggerated. The premises of Madame Avril, 15, Turton St. W. were entered about ten A.M. by a somewhat eccentric customer, who alarmed the proprietor to such an extent that she fainted and had to be taken to her home. She informs us, however, that the stranger took nothing away, and that Miss Lyne, the assistant mentioned by some of the evening papers, has in fact left the firm, and is visiting friends in the country."

Una was delighted. Bill had done his work well, though she could not imagine how, and it looked as though their random explanation had been right.

She wanted to know more . . . what people were saying, for instance, and whether anyone else had guessed the truth. Perhaps her mother would mention it.

She went to one of the drawing-room windows and looked wistfully out, but the Gardens were lost to her and she thought she would never want to go into them any more. She would like to get right away and she meant to do it too.

The telephone rang so that she jumped, and when Turner came to say that she was wanted, she exclaimed in an agitated voice:

"No, no. Say I'm not up."

"It's Mr. France, Miss, wanting you particular."

"Oh!" cried Una running eagerly to the telephone. She had imagined it was somebody else, who would talk about lions and rings and she didn't want to hear him ever.

"Hullo, Una. Did you see I'd put that old cat's pot on?"

"Yes, rather! But how on earth did you do it, Bill?"

"Threatened blue murder in various forms until she was ready to eat out of my hand. I stood over her and made her write that stuff for the press. She thought I came from Robby."

"Was it Bob, do you think?"

"God knows, but it looks like it. Anyhow, Avril's conscience isn't clear. I haven't a suspicion where Robby is though."

"No." Una was silent for a moment and then she said in a careful voice: "If I hear anything I'll let you know."

"Good old partner. Your tip simply saved the day. Oh, and by the way, mum's the word."

"Yes, rather!"

ii

When Anne came in with Tim she found her daughter standing in the drawing-room doorway, smiling eagerly, and she was surprised.

"Up already?"

"I'm quite well," said Una in a determined voice. "Are you going out today?"

"I've promised to lunch quietly with Judy because we have to talk over the History Ball."

"I think I'll come with you," said Una unexpectedly and with great calm.

Anne did not show her astonishment, though she could not remember that Una had ever made such a suggestion before. It was dull for the child seeing nobody day after day, she supposed, and she

certainly was better. A quiet outing could do her no
harm.

"Come along then and we'll defy the doctor," she
cried encouragingly. "After all, he can't call lunch
with Judy and me an excitement."

Una smiled and looked at her mother secretly as
they went upstairs, side by side. Doctors didn't know
everything. And presently she was dressing herself
with the greatest care, for in a way this was an occasion. She was going out with her mother self-invited
and she was going to smile at her and admire her as
much as she chose.

And people who wanted to talk to her on the
telephone about lions could ring and ring until they
were blue in the face.

"What splendor," said Anne admiring the cream
suit and smart new hat waiting for her when she
went down. "And all for Judy and me."

"The stockings are for Judy," returned Una.
"Some of her birthday ones." (She'd pay her mother
compliments too, if she wanted to.)

"I'm rather sorry we're going off for Whitsun
to leave you alone, now you are able to be up, child,"
said Anne, as they drove away. "But one has to pay
some attention to the Drews for Jeremy's sake.
They're fond of him."

"Mother, of course you must go," protested
Una at once. "It's all right because there are dozens
of people I can go to see if I feel like it."

"Well, I shouldn't go out at night, darling."

"No, I don't intend to go out at night," said Una
firmly. She didn't intend to go to see dozens of

people either; she had other plans in mind. "Besides, it will do you good, and you like the country, don't you?"

"Love it. I wish your father did."

"Never mind!" Her daughter's voice was eager, her dark eyes full of excitement, and Anne thought: "What's happened to her? I suppose it's the fun of being nineteen."

iii

"Well, what do you think of Robby's latest?" inquired Judy France, who was small and blue-eyed and rather like a frisky kitten. "You haven't *heard?* My lovely one, are you blind and deaf? The whole of London has been ringing with it . . . and on my telephone too."

Judy proceeded to outline the story and its pseudo-contradiction, adding a complete list of all the people with whom she had discussed it and their theories and opinions. Una, listening eagerly but saying nothing, decided that even Judy had not guessed the truth, and that a great many of Robby's so-called friends were perfect hypocrites.

"I'd have rung you up, Anne," continued Judy, "if Bill hadn't come round and behaved like a bear, raging and fuming all over the house and calling me a chattering cat. As if I *ever* chattered! You know yourself I don't encourage gossip, but how can I help it if people will tell me things? So I said to Bill, 'Well, go and find the girl instead of tearing about my house like a mad bull, and I'll take her under my wing and be a mother to her. Personally I think it rather chic of her to walk out of Avril's with a masked man instead of a plain one, and I can't see what you're making all the fuss about.' And all the thanks I got for that from the ungrateful young hound was a snort," ended Judy in indignant surprise.

"I was afraid Bill had never got over that affair," said Anne. "He's very faithful."

"Yes, I know, darling, but what's the good of that? Why didn't he think of this masked man stunt himself and carry her off by force? Sitting down and being faithful is so dull-witted. Any donkey can do it."

"He hasn't found her, I suppose?"

"Found her? Of course not. She's in Paris by this time no doubt, and it's no use Bill's baying the moon, as I told the poor angel."

"But why Paris?" said a serious, inquiring voice.

At this Judy turned joyfully to gaze at her young guest.

"Isn't she too sweet?"

"No, I'm not," denied Una indignantly. "Of course I know you mean she's eloped, but why Paris? And, anyway, I don't believe it."

"And what do you believe, oh wise young judge?" said her mother.

Una gathered herself together.

"Oh, I don't know," she said feigning indifference, "but not in masked men anyway. It's . . . it's positively Victorian."

"Anne," wailed Judy. "The little wretch thinks we're quite old."

iv

The subject was safely changed when luncheon began and Judy and Anne were soon deep in the question of frocks and committees for the forthcoming ball. Una sat silent as though it were the most important discussion in the world, and watching her mother's face.

At length the business was finished, farewells had been said and Anne and her daughter were out in Grosvenor Place, but Una did not intend to go home yet if she could help it.

"Mother, let's shop."

"Child of my heart and prop of my declining years, you are very sudden today. What do you want to buy?" asked Anne amused.

"There must be something you need. A hat for the country. I'll choose it."

"Come along then, though I haven't a doubt the doctor will double his bill with rage when he hears how we have defied him."

"I don't care. It's a celebration . . . my birthday celebration," declared Una, pleased to have found so plausible a name for her mood.

They walked to Bond Street, where Una proved unexpectedly critical of all the hats produced for her inspection, and finally suggested tea.

She wanted to watch the turning heads as her mother passed, and she did. "She's much better looking than anybody else," thought Una, elated. She felt proud, like one owning a priceless treasure and envied by all the world.

She would not relinquish the hat at Anne's suggestion, but when tea was over, carried her off elsewhere, finding one at last and paying for it herself, while Anne stood by and laughed.

"We'll take it with us, please, and I want a taxi," commanded Una.

She followed the shopman, saw the hat and her mother safely into the cab, then slipped in after them with a sigh for good work done.

"Nobody," said Anne, "has ever taken me out and bought me a hat before. Thank you very much."

"Haven't they?" asked Una and felt she was one up on the world.

As a birthday celebration Anne thought it the oddest thing she had ever heard of, but Una had never been quite like anybody else. It was part of her charm.

Knowing nothing of the little figure crouched behind the chesterfield the night before, she could have no clue to her daughter's mood, or know that this day had been partly a gesture of defiance, partly a farewell to childish things. Una hardly knew it herself.

But when they were at length at home again, she said calmly: "I think I'll go to bed."

The day was over; she had had her fling. Her father would be coming home and it was his turn now. She wouldn't stand between them. Odd one out or not, the old protective instinct remained and the sentry was still at his post, though it was a new sentry and the post was strange. Today's ceremony, after all, had been a changing of the guard.

CHAPTER XVII

i

UNA and Tim in the little car were driving away to Wenlock from one empty house to another.

Jeremy had gone off to his chambers, looking like a boy on holiday, merely calling farewells to his daughter, who was in her bath. He left five pounds for her with Anne, saying she might like to take some of her friends to a matinee, and this gift, the first he had ever made her not jealously bestowed, marked the change in him. Una received it for once without a tremor but as a wage she had earned.

Later the car had come round, the luggage was taken out, and Anne, wearing the new hat, had set off for Warwickshire. The sentry from the steps had watched her for a moment, and then remarking, "I shan't be in to lunch, Turner," had walked out into the world with her dog at her heels. The guard was dismissed.

And now at last, running away through the traffic, she knew desolation, and the past weeks with their agonies and joys, each one mistaken, seemed to run beside her, mocking her. Her childhood was over and she was alone.

The summer day whispered of holiday to her troubled heart but she could not wait to hear it. All in a flash before her eyes, her place in the world had been swept away and she was hurrying off to find another.

Wenlock! Would it do . . . oh, would it? The old house had been lonely and she had run away from it, but now lonely herself she was running back, and how would it receive her?

For years in moments of distress and misery she had dreamt of a dog farm in the country, but it had been only a dream. She had studied the subject because she liked it and wanted occupation . . . rather as one plays a secret game . . . lest in some far distant future the dream might come true. She had not expected the moment to come suddenly like this, and, now it was here, some of the glory had departed and she felt unprepared.

And yet she clutched it. Tim at least would be pleased. Not Kensington Gardens any more, for they were closed to him, but real country . . . woods and fields and rabbits and other dogs. She looked at him riding beside her with his nose raised to the wind and every hair bristling as though with delight, and she smiled. The day took on a brighter hue.

She knew the difficulties before her. Wenlock might be too big or too expensive to run. Even if not they would say she was too young. She must have all her plans shipshape and secure before they voiced that argument, for crocodile tears would not avail her here. Two avenues of help lay open to her, Uncle John on the business side and Benyon upon the technical. She had confided her dream to the old veterinary surgeon, who knew more about dogs than all her books, and he had said: "Fine. Whenever you are ready to start, Missy, you come to me."

Benyon who lived under a studio where she had once had a secret friend!

Una's eyes grew wide and she banished her thoughts away and fixed her attention sternly on the road ahead, dodging the traffic and racing furiously whenever she had a chance. Wenlock had become a sanctuary.

Hertfordshire welcomed her in a blaze of beauty as though high summer had arrived before. Never had she seen such buttercups. Tall among the grasses they marched beside her, and the glowing fields seemed to light up the very air. Beside the river where long ago the monks from the Abbey had come down to fish, over the wall the Romans made rose the bright helmets of this golden army as the little car raced by.

In Robby's lane the hawthorn was nearly over, but what of the orchard across the field? Una knew that she must not turn her eyes to see. But now she was thinking of Robby and all the world talking about her with envy or admiration or scorn or surprise, but nobody attempting to do anything, except Bill who was faithful. And Judy thought it dull-witted of him, and Robby herself thought nothing at all. She wouldn't even know.

"Well, I can't tell her, can I?" said Una to Tim, who turned his loving eyes to her and smiled, then settled down with his nose upon her knee. "I couldn't, could I, Tim?"

She knew that she could not, for on one side Bill had said "Mum's the word," and on the other, Robby had asked her: "Well, what did you see in the lane?" and she had replied, "Only hawthorn, pink as pink."

In her hands only the secret lay, but her hands were tied.

ii

Three Challices slept in Wenlock churchyard, the old jam-maker, Mary his wife, and Gilbert who had died an earl. The square-faced clock in the Norman tower beside them, measuring day in and day out the hours that would trouble them no more, saluted their young descendant driving in with twelve deep strokes that fell into the air and lingered, as though reluctant to depart. Across the green, over the bridge and in at the gates, they played her home, then dropped to silence.

She drove slowly, looking about her and almost holding her breath, it was so very still.

The fallen leaves had been gathered up and carried away, and the old trees interlacing their arms above her head let in the sunlight here and there, so that the green twilight before her was splashed with gold. Then the trees gave way to shrubs and she saw the lawn, shaven and starred with daisies, running up to the house which was blind no longer but had opened its eyes.

Una pulled up and stared at it hardly able to believe her senses, but it was true. The heavy door and two of the long windows were open wide. In a moment she was out of the car and she and Tim were racing across the grass.

Very softly she walked in. She saw a small square hall paneled to the ceiling, and a shallow staircase, black with years, climbing above. A door to the right was open and here was a long narrow graceful room, opening at each end into the garden, its rugs rolled up, its furniture swathed in linen and the sunlight pouring in. This was the drawing-room she remembered now. Its satiny walls were brown in places where pictures had been removed, and she wanted to cover its scars and bring in pictures to make it smile again. She felt the room looked to her as a friend.

Excitement filled the girl as a sense of the house came back to her out of the years. The dining-room was on the left of the hall, she thought, and the library behind it, and that door in the opposite wall should lead into quite a little room, which she and her mother had often used when the soldiers were here. It should have two windows, one opening on the grass and the other into a rose garden at the side of the house.

She tiptoed across the floor, pushed the door open with a beating heart and saw she had remembered well. The floor had been recently washed and both windows were thrown wide and the sweet air blew in. The rose garden was a wilderness but already flowering and in a week or two would be ablaze with blooms.

Una walked into the little room and smiled at it, turning herself slowly round to take it in, and so she met the two pairs of eyes that seemed to be watching her from the wall. Incongruously between a set of hunting prints, the two old portraits hung side by side, probably carried here from some other room because their frames were tarnished and shabby, and their subjects of little interest to the Simmonses and their kind. As paintings they were of no great value, but they had pleased mightily the first Challice of Wenlock and Mary his wife.

Mary with her dark hair built so strangely and her prim hands folded on her wide-flounced, silken dress looked out from dark eyes on this girl of another century, brief-skirted, hands in pockets, who yet with the same eyes, gazed back. But there the resemblance ended. The tilt of Una's head, the strength of her small chin, were in the other portrait. The man in the stock and neat side-whiskers, with cheeks pinker than any male creature she had ever seen in the flesh, and yet looking no soft fool for all that, had given this child of his race, though she did not know it, more than his Mary had.

iii

"Now then, what are you doing here, walkin' into houses that don't belong to you? Sauce!"

Una jumped and Tim, who had been peering longingly into the garden, rushed back to her side and made ready for battle.

A tall thin woman with a sack pinned round her and outrage written all over her face, stood in the door, and Una, restraining Tim, collected her scattered wits and smiled.

"It's all right. This is my mother's house. Are you Mrs. Wardell from the lodge?"

The woman, recalling her manners from another age, curtseyed hurriedly.

"Yes, Miss, I beg pardon, I'm sure, but you're never her ladyship's little daughter? Why, I couldn't have believed it. And such a dirty house to bring you into. I'm ashamed, but it's all I can do to keep it dry and aired with only one pair of hands, though that agent, he won't never believe me. It isn't that I wouldn't work my hands off for her ladyship, but what's the sense with no one to see the place and the dust gathering as soon as swept up? It takes the heart out of you, that it does."

"Never mind," said Una. "I shan't notice the dust and you can't help it. I only came because I thought I'd like to see Wenlock again."

"You wouldn't be coming back, Miss, I suppose?" said Mrs. Wardell longingly. "If the family was to open it up again, that's what we'd like to see. I was born on the place and the way these tenants use it fair makes my blood boil."

"Were you born at Wenlock?"

"That I was, Miss, fifty-two years ago. My dad was head kennelman to old Mr. Challice, and a rare good master he was too. Well I recollect his funeral, poor gentleman, though I was only a bit of a girl at the time. And then there was your grandfather, the Earl, a very fine and handsome gentleman, but much away over the politics, though he was well-liked by all none the less. Well, my old dad passed to rest and I married as silly girls will and moved away, more's the pity. My man was a bad lot and left me and young Tommy at last without so much as a crust to our mouths. It was then I took heart and wrote to her ladyship and out of her kindness she gave me the lodge. Sixteen year ago, that was, and it's in the tenants' lease that I go with the place. The Challices, they look after their people, my dear. There isn't many nowadays as would have done what her ladyship did." Mrs. Wardell was pulling out all the sentimental stops for the owner's daughter.

"I'm glad you wrote to her," said Una shyly. She could see her mother doing it, quite casually without any fuss and never thinking of it again, and she was glad Wenlock had had someone who belonged to it, all these years, if it was only the kennelman's daughter.

She picked up Tim, who was circling round Mrs. Wardell sniffing amiably.

"This is my dog. I think he wants to be friends," she said.

"There now, and isn't he a fine little fellow? I was bred among dogs, Miss, and they always know. My poor dog, I lost him, got in a fight with a great brute of a mastiff and had to be put away. Fair broke my heart it did. But now you're wanting to see the house, and I'll go before, my dear, and open the windows or you'll be that choked with dust. Unless you'll be wanting me to take you round?" finished Mrs. Wardell doubtfully.

"No, I shall be all right, but I would like you to open them please."

"Yes indeed, Miss, and then if you'll excuse me I'll run home and give my Tommy his dinner and be back again in case you want me."

Mrs. Wardell hurried away and Una stood with her dog in her arms under the two old portraits, very still, the strangest feeling flooding her heart, half pain, half happiness.

"Got into a fight and had to be put away."

Tony was back again, brought by the woman's unconscious hand. He had saved Tim's life.

She held her dog close for a moment, then put him down and went out through the open window, looking back just once with an uncertain smile at those two who had been lovers long ago.

She knew now. Wenlock had somehow opened her eyes. It was not after all the home where she was the odd man out from which she was running away, but Tony.

Tim raced off over the daisied grass to the heaven of trees beyond and then came tearing back to tell her about it and hurry her on. She followed him as one in a dream, and it seemed to her that Tony must be waiting there.

She wanted him. The sound of his voice, so kind and careful, making her want to cry, his funny air of owning the world, his nonsense, were suddenly significant and dear. She loved him terribly and so, in anger and disgust, because of his being romantic about impossible people, she had run away. She slipped down under an old tree and laid her head against it, thinking of love and how strange it was, and at once she was back in the little study, hearing with burning cheeks the torment in her father's voice, and her mother, usually so gay and casual, saying in a tone she had never heard before: "It's different."

Yes, it was different. It made you happy and excited and miserable all at the same time. Nothing in all her life had been like this. Love did queer things to everyone. It made Bill superior . . . only he wasn't really . . . and her father jealous. It had made her ungrateful and unkind. Tony had saved Tim's life and she had promised to sit for him and here she was, running away. Was she like her father then? The horror of this thought made her sit up in dismay. No, no, she would not be like that. She remembered her father all down the years, restless, unreasonable, missing the happiness that was within his grasp, and she knew it was all wrong. Love should not be like that. Anyone save her mother would have ceased to care for him long ago, but her mother had always been beyond ordinary standards and no one could reach the pinnacle where her daughter saw her. She was still the fairy princess as of old.

Una knew now that she must go back to Tony. She could not let him down. She did not know whether he cared for her, or whether, if he did, he would soon cease to care and be romantic about somebody else. It was a dreadful thought and she knew that she could not bear it, but at least she was not going to throw her happiness away until she was sure. Perhaps he was merely a friend who liked her, and though even that was sweet, she knew wist-

fully that she would have her dog farm and be faithful like Bill. Tony could not help it.

She got up at last and called Tim, filled with a
new resolution. She was going to find out. That
was the only thing to do, but not until she had seen
the whole of Wenlock and finished her day's job.
There was work ahead.

They left the leafy silence under the trees and
came out on the lawn again, and lo, the old house
had opened all its eyes. Every window was wide to
the summer day and it looked wise and smiling now,
as though it knew all her troubles and would sweep
them away.

She went in again and up the stairs. Mrs. Wardell
had gone off to the lodge and she was quite alone
except for Tim pattering at her heels, but she did
not feel lonely or afraid. The house was friendly
as though the old love that had been kin of hers and
had blossomed within its walls, took her by the hand
and walked with her.

It was not so very large, yet too large certainly
for one person and her dogs, but a wing could be
shut up, and then, she thought, it would not be a
difficult house to run. She was inexperienced, however, and she must find out about that . . . how
many servants you would need for so many rooms.
Perhaps Mrs. Wardell could tell her. The furniture
was shabby and had been badly used. Her mother
she knew had moved the more valuable pieces to
Palace Square long ago. But shabbiness did not
trouble her much. She could make it better by de-
grees. There was a great attic crowded with dusty

broken chairs and tables, with windows on three sides, and as she surveyed it, she found herself saying to her dog: "Can you make statues in the country, Tim?"

The sound of her own voice startled her but Tim wagged his tail, as though he thought you could, and she smiled.

"He mightn't want to, though."

At once a great idea assailed her out of space. She must bring Tony here and show him her house. (Already she called it hers.) Tony and Kit, her friends. Why shouldn't she bring them here over the Whitsun holiday? They couldn't want to work when no one was working and the lovely weather simply called you out. And it would be fun to open up some of the rooms and take off their covers and see them come alive again, and to have a sort of picnic week-end. Meals would be awkward, but perhaps they wouldn't mind, and very likely Mrs. Wardell could be persuaded to cook for them. Or there were hampers that you could buy in town. Her father's five pounds would buy quite a splendid hamper, Una thought, and that would be a better use for it than all the matinees in the world.

She clattered downstairs wondering whether Tommy's dinner would yet be over and saw Mrs. Wardell coming to her across the grass. But she, when consulted, did not think Miss Una and her friends ought to sleep in the house, which might be damp and was certainly dirty, and besides there was no linen and the blankets after being packed away, should have days in the sun to air them. Mrs. Wardell, however, was no obstructionist. She wanted her ladyship's family back in residence and to discourage Una was no way to bring it about she knew. The Lion and Lamb was a small inn but clean and newly decorated and Mrs. Capps, the landlady, would be proud to do her best for Miss Swithin and her friends. If they would sleep at the inn and have one good meal there, Mrs. Wardell said, she would be more easy in her mind like, and would gladly undertake the rest of the preparations.

Una saw the sense of this suggestion and agreed to it eagerly and without a fuss, thereby winning the lodge-keeper, who had been prepared for argument.

"And I could bring out a hamper from town, Mrs. Wardell . . . cold chicken and ham and fruit and any number of things."

An earnest discussion as to what was most required was then begun, and Mrs. Wardell was given money for butter and eggs and milk and bread. This brought about the discovery that the young visitor had entirely forgotten her own lunch this morning in the excitement of seeing Wenlock, and the woman hurried back to the lodge to bring her a cup of tea and an egg and something in the way of a bone and some water for the little dog. It was no luncheon for a young lady and some would turn up their noses at it, thought Mrs. Wardell, but there, it was her own choice, bless her heart. She was a real Challice and it would be a pleasure to see some young life about the place again. The Simmonses had been middle-aged and pompous and fat, demanding much and giving nothing. Mrs. Wardell and her Tommy had suffered much at their hands.

Una wandering out through the back of the house found another lawn and a tennis court, weed-grown and with posts awry, but the kitchen garden and orchard beyond were in fair order, and Tommy himself, back at work here, came bashfully forward at sight of the owner's daughter. He showed her the hothouses where peaches and grapes would ripen later and told her that it was his job when the house was empty to keep the furnace going and look after this section of the property first of all.

"Would it take many gardeners to keep it all in order?" Una asked him eagerly.

"No, Miss, once it was put straight, I could do it easy with a lad to help, if I was let alone. But they Simmonses kept their man hopping all over the place, chauffeur and boots and I don't know what, he was . . . and they was always changing servants. Me they couldn't change, being no servant of theirs and they didn't like that any too well, so I couldn't get my way about the garden or it wouldn't be in the state it is."

Una leaving the young man to his work thought that things were shaping very well. Tommy and a lad for the garden . . . and Tommy was paid already. He went with the place and if she were the tenant, even though she paid no rent, wouldn't it be the same? She had little experience of money matters but she meant to discover the cost of everything and work it all out. There was her uncle's birthday gift to begin with, and since she must be quite an expense to them living at home, perhaps her father would finance her for a little while until the dogs began to pay. There would be wages, a kennel man or maid and presently more of them, but food wouldn't cost much with fruit and vegetables in the garden, and she would want no clothes for an age. Perhaps on the whole a kennel maid would be better, a girl who was fond of dogs and could live with her in the house. Robby Lyne! She had lost her job with Avril and might be glad to come . . . unless she was in Paris with her masked man.

Una, her head full of plans, had just turned into the stable yard, seen the garage, three old loose boxes piled with rubbish and an exciting row of kennels beyond when Mrs. Wardell called that her lunch was ready.

She had uncovered a chair and table in the little room of the portraits and brought in some roses and put them in a bowl out of the drawing-room cabinet. She had brought her best china for the visitor and a dish of rosy apples for dessert. Tim's luncheon was put down for him on the lawn outside and he was soon engaged with it busily.

"You have taken a lot of trouble," exclaimed Una. "Mrs. Wardell, when I've done, could we uncover the drawing-room, do you think?"

"You leave it to me, Miss Una. I couldn't let you spoil all your lovely clothes. I wouldn't think of it."

She was off, closing the door behind her and soon at work. Una could hear her. By and by, when the girl looked in, the long blue rug, faded almost to gray, had been unrolled, and chairs and couches were hiding the more shabby parts of it. Mrs. Wardell had brought down chintz covers too, clean but with their patterns lost in the mists of time and many washing days. Busily she was buttoning them on.

Una went back to the little room and carried in the two portraits to hang here for the present and see their house wake up. She gathered every bowl and jar she could find and filled them with rosebuds and laburnum and honeysuckle; and in spite of Mrs. Wardell's protests, helped her to polish and dust and hang the long curtains which had been packed away. By the time the room was done she loved it for the labor she had given it. It was the most splendid room in the world. But now it was time to be off because she had much to do.

"I'll be back tomorrow," she said to it, though Mrs. Wardell took the speech to herself. "And perhaps there'll be three of us. Thank you for all you've done."

iv

The little car drove off at a great pace as though it knew a momentous errand ahead. Tony, of course, might not come, nor Kit. They might be away or they might not want to come, but Una was going to see. She had always been strong of purpose and love lent her courage now. The day had been kind and hope beat high in her heart. This one week-end surely Fate would give her, whatever might come after that.

In Robby's lane, pink now with fallen blossoms, the car slowed under her hand, and her foot pressed the clutch. She did not look over the field but down at her bright-eyed passenger, as though asking his advice.

Suppose Robby did accuse her of spying, what did it matter? Bill was faithful and she might be glad to know. There was nobody else to tell her. The brake was put on, the engine turned off, and Una and her dog were soon marching over the track to the cottage among the apple trees.

It was quite a small house with no bell, so she knocked and knocked, the sound echoing eerily in that quiet place. There was no answer, however, and she was just beginning to think it must have been Paris after all, when she heard steps on the gravel, and found herself looking into the face of Robby's twin.

"Hullo, Bob," she said. "You don't remember me, I expect. I'm Una Swithin."

"Oh, hullo, are you really? I haven't seen you for an age," returned Bob in surprise.

Una, who had been trembling inwardly, smiled all over her face with relief and she did not know how kind a thing that was to the young man who wore a shade. She was the first girl of his world but Robby whom he had seen for two years, and she had smiled at him as though he were as other men. She had not shrunk away.

"I was looking for Robby really, if she is any-where about," explained Una.

"Oh . . . er . . . excuse me just a moment and

I'll open the door," said Bob as one remembering the rules of hospitality.

He ran round to the back of the house and presently there was a footstep inside and the door was pulled open.

It was Robby herself who looked out, with a carefully made scowl on her face. Una, rather breathless, gazed back.

"Come along then." Robby put out an arm and hauled her in, marching her sternly through the little hall to a kind of den containing a medley of books and pipes but carpetless and bare.

"You know what happens to spies, don't you? Where's your gun, Bob?"

"Do you think I'm going to blow my castle to pieces?" inquired Bob from the background. "Besides, dawn is the proper hour. Look up your book of etiquette."

"Oh, all right."

Robby let her victim go, but thought better of it and caught her by the ear instead.

"I suppose you thought I believed you saw nothing in the lane but hawthorn, you young liar," she said with scorn.

"I haven't told a soul, Robby."

"You haven't? Then what are you doing here, my nosey friend, tell me that?"

"I was just passing. . . ."

"And looked in? Very natural."

Robby sat herself on the table, hands in her blazer pockets, and surveyed her victim.

"Don't you mind her," said Bob to the girl who

had smiled at him. "I think it was jolly nice of you to come."

Robby suddenly laughed.

"Go and put on the kettle and get out the rat poison," she said to her brother. "We must destroy this insect before it informs the police." Then, as Bob left the room, she nodded her head in his direction and remarked: "Meet my masked man."

"I guessed," said Una.

"You're a funny little devil. How did you guess?"

"Oh, I don't know. . . . Bill France did too."

"Good God!" Robby looked at her visitor in the utmost amazement, and Una, pressing her advantage, continued quickly: "It was he who put Avril's pot on, Robby. He frightened her into a fit and made her write that bit for the morning paper. She thought he came from you."

"Clever of him," said Robby, drily. "So the murder's out then?"

"Oh, no, it isn't. Nobody knows but Bill and me. They think you've gone to Paris."

Robby gave a joyful shout.

"Bob, come and listen to this. They think I've gone to Paris with a purple past. How priceless!"

"Silly lot of dam' fools," said Bob, scowling from the doorway. "Who does?"

"Everybody. Except," said Robby in a careless tone, "Bill France, and this rum little owl and her dog."

"I haven't set eyes on Bill for donkey's years," said Bob, looking suddenly pleased. "I'd like to see the old lad again."

"Shall I ring him up when I get home and tell him?" asked Una. "He'd come like a shot. I know he would."

"Oh, I say, thanks, awfully. You really think so?"

Bob turned to look at his sister and she remarked with nonchalance: "Have it your own way. Ask the whole of London out if you like."

She rose from the table and sauntered away to make tea for her guest.

Later when Una had told them about Wenlock and some of her hopes and plans, and had heard of Bob's new apple he hoped to launch upon the world, Robby walked over the field with her to the car.

"And how do you come to know what Bill France thinks, if nobody else does?" inquired Robby sternly.

"I just happened to ring him up and he saw I was a bit worried and he told me," said Una. "But he made me swear not to mention it to a soul." And then at the other's significant smile, she added: "Well, I don't care, he never dreamt I would be seeing you. He had no idea I knew where you were."

"Eh?" Robby walked on for a moment or two with an inscrutable face. Then she grinned. "All right. I'll let you off this time, solemn face, but don't let it occur again." She jerked her head in the direction of the man they had left. "Seems to have done him good," she remarked. "Thanks for coming."

Hands in pockets and whistling softly, she stood in the little lane and watched Bill's messenger drive away.

i

TONY stood at the window critically regarding the little figure in his hands. Whenever Kit was safely out of the way he had been working at it, for although his sister had learned from eloquent experience to be blind when the mood was on him and to leave him undisturbed, he needed complete privacy for his magnum opus. She must not even know. To-day she had been out from ten o'clock until half past five, and now she was safely in the bath. The little figure which his hands had shaped, hidden guiltily away at the sound of her returning steps ten minutes ago, had now come forth again and he saw his girl before him. He had made many studies and destroyed them all, but this time his hands had not betrayed him. The pose of her darling head, her lovely limbs, the sudden young brightness that lit up her face when she smiled, he had caught them all.

For ten days he had not seen the original; for two days past they had said when he telephoned to ask for her that she was better and had gone out, but this time he was undismayed by that. She had not forgotten. The little note written on her birthday morning had told him so.

It was a very short letter and he knew it by heart.

"He's perfect and I do think it was nice of you to make him for me. Tim thought he was alive. But how did you know it was my birthday?

"I've been ill though not really and I shall be out again in a few days. I haven't forgotten about the sittings.

"Una."

A girl of few words this and all of them to the point. Small, firm handwriting . . . round and utterly devoid of frills, a writing you could trust.

Morning after morning, since his call at Palace Square, Tony had watched from a place of hiding Una's mother come into the Gardens with the little dog, and then had promptly melted away. However much she knew or suspected of him, he was running no risks. Uneasily he remembered the bright eyes and mischievous glance of Lady Anne. But today even this deputy had not appeared and for some obscure reason that made him hopeful. Tomorrow all would be as of old.

A knock startled him and he rushed across the studio and hid his treasure behind the screen, wondering who the devil could be calling at this hour and why he hadn't heard the fellow's footsteps.

He opened the door and saw his girl and dog.

"You're not real," exclaimed Tony in a voice of awe. "I know this is only a dream."

She laughed breathlessly.

"It's rather late, but I've only come for a moment," she said.

"A moment?" shouted Tony, outraged at the very idea.

He led her in and over to the window, and then,

very gently, as though she might break, put a hand on each arm and pushed her into an easy chair.

"You *are* real," he said. "I couldn't believe it."

"I'm very dirty. I've been out in the country all day and I never can drive in gloves. The car doesn't like it."

She smiled at him and he wanted to take her in his arms. Instead he sat on the table watching every turn of her head.

"You oughtn't to be driving a car, when you've been ill," he said indignantly. "They had no business to let you, and if you wanted a chauffeur for the day, why didn't you send for me?"

She said, with a little gasp: "I didn't know you could drive."

"Oh, lord, yes. I'm a very handy fellow, drive a car, carry coals, valet the dog, dodge the police, all the fine arts at my finger tips," said Tony. "And I was simply made for the country. Cows come at my call and sheep cluster round me with tears of affection streaming from their eyes. The last time I drove a car, a flock of the little dears formed fours and marched before me for miles and miles . . . a most touching sight. I suppose they recognized a kindred soul."

"Could you work in the country?" inquired a doubtful voice.

"Like a navvy," declared Tony, beaming.

"I mean your real work."

"Oh, I could do that on top of a volcano in full blast."

Una smiled.

"The country wouldn't be in the least like that."

"Ah, but I haven't finished yet . . . or in a desert island or in the middle of a forest, or even in a field full of bulls. Place means nothing to me, except the time the place and the . . ."

He broke off, looking at her apprehensively. He was a blithering idiot and he would be frightening the little dear away, if he didn't keep his head.

"Isn't Kit at home?" asked Una.

"Oh, yes. Kit's wallowing in her bath, washing off the toil and moil of London. She'll be in here directly."

"I was afraid she might have gone away for Whitsun."

"Not she. We're Cinderella, Kit and I, without even a fairy-godmother. Pumpkins are out of season," said Tony mournfully, "and Whiskers has eaten all the mice."

"You see, I wondered whether you and she would come into the country with me over the week-end," explained Una in a rush.

"You don't really mean it?"

"Yes, of course. That's why I came . . . because my people are away and I went out to Wenlock this morning. It is a house my mother has in Hertfordshire, but it's been let for years and now it's empty again. I thought I'd like to have a look at it, and when I got there the country was so lovely I determined to go back for Whitsun if I could get anyone to come with me. We couldn't stay in the house because it might be damp, but there's quite a good little inn; only it would be a sort of picnic, with nothing on earth to do but poke about the woods and gardens, and of course you might be bored."

"Bored?" cried Tony. *"Bored?* Listen to the child. It's the most perfect scheme, but, oh lord, there's Kit." He bounded across the room and called his sister lustily. "Come out of the bath and see your fairy-godmother before she vanishes before my eyes."

Kit, at the sound of voices, had hurried into her clothes and now, clad in a clean blue linen smock, with her hair still damp from the bath, appeared in the studio.

"My dear, how jolly to see you again! Are you better?" she inquired of Una.

"Yes, rather." Una repeated her invitation.

"I want you to be my guests, of course," she finished. "Because father gave me some money for a spree this morning, if I could hunt up some friends, but there won't be anything to do, Kit, except to walk or drive about, and you might think it awfully dull."

Kit, looking at the two pleading faces before her, knew that Tony's chance had come.

"I should simply love to loaf under a tree for days and days," she declared. "Can you wait five minutes while I run downstairs and see if I can arrange to be away?"

"Yes, of course."

So Kit went off to Benyon's telephone to persuade Carstairs that he could live without her for the next few days, a difficult task, but in her view necessary. If Una had been almost any of the other girls she knew, Kit would have suggested Freddy's inclusion in the expedition without a thought, but this situation was too delicate for that. Tony's girl was after all virtually a stranger to them, and a shy stranger. To make a foursome of the party and thereby fling Tony more or less into her arms, would be far too obvious. There were Una's parents to be considered, also, likely to make difficulties enough if the affair came to anything.

Carstairs naturally argued and protested, and cursed young Corky up and down a somewhat handsome vocabulary, but he had to give in at last, and Kit returned to the studio to report that all was well. Benyon would be delighted to entertain Whiskers over the week-end.

She did not admit that there had been any other obstacle, but when his girl and dog had driven away, Tony said to her rather anxiously: "What about old Carstairs?"

"Well, what about him?" retorted Kit. "You don't suppose he's so selfish that he grudges me a few days' real loaf in the country, do you?"

Tony was immensely relieved. Lucky for him, he thought, that Kit and her Freddy were not two of the clinging kind. And it was perfectly true. Kit did need a holiday.

ii

Una, refreshed by a bath and change, went down to her solitary dinner almost breathless with delight. She had seen Tony again, and by his every word and look she knew that he had missed her; he and Kit were coming to Wenlock, and for three whole days they would be together. What more could life hold?

She had nearly finished the meal before she remembered her message for Bill France; in her excitement she had completely forgotten it; and it was nearly nine when she got in touch with him at Judy's, where he was supposed to be playing bridge. Bill, considering her news far too momentous for the telephone, coolly left his sister-in-law in the lurch and ten minutes later arrived at Palace Square.

Una had her map spread out to show him the way to Rob's apple orchard, and the two pored over it together, Bill's questions falling thick and fast. What did Robby say? How did she look? Was old Bob pretty fit? How on earth had Una dug them out? Who had given her the tip that they were in Hertfordshire?

"Well, you see, I don't think anybody knows where they are but us," explained Una, answering the last question first. "I happened to drive Robby out that way once when she was in a hurry . . . dropped her and picked her up again."

"Go on? I suppose she spun you a tale. Where did she say she was off to?"

"I didn't ask her," admitted Una. "Didn't quite like to, but then I happened to see her with a man in the orchard, and, as it was an accident, I pretended I hadn't noticed anything. I thought it was a love affair naturally, until that night you mentioned about twins and said Bob Lyne was growing apples. Then I thought he might be the man."

Bill sat and stared at the eager, serious face of this young arbiter of his destiny, and thought of the night of Judy's party when, bored but dutiful, he had asked Anne's kid to dance. And then all at once because she had defended Robby, he had found himself telling her what he had told nobody else. Fate, for which he had had no civil word for years, had turned into a friend at a touch of this youngster's hand.

"And so you went out there today and hunted them up?" he suggested.

"Oh, no, I didn't really. I was passing and the first time I thought it might seem like spying to go in. And then coming back I decided to risk it, because Robby would probably want to know who shut Avril up. I mean she must have been feeling pretty curious, Bill."

"You told her about that, then? What did she say . . . like my confounded cheek to butt in, I suppose?"

"No, she said it was clever of you."

"Sarcastic, was she?" asked Bill, who was even now afraid to hope too much.

"Not really, because Bob was out of the room when I told her, and as soon as he came back and heard your name, he said he'd like to see you. And if he can read her thoughts, he wouldn't have said that if she were being sarcastic, would he?"

"But didn't she protest or anything?"

"No, she said he could ask all London out if he liked. She didn't mind. Jolly as anything, she was, whistling when I came away. Looked nice, too . . .

hadn't any paint on, except the usual amount. Not pints of it," explained Una.

"You see," said Bill slowly, "the point is she hasn't had any time for me since Bob's affair, but then she hasn't had any time for any other fellow, either. I expect you guessed I've been keen about Robby for a long time."

"I thought you might be," confessed his hostess.

"Before that, when I was about eighteen," continued Bill, grinning broadly, "I was in love with your mother."

"No?"

Una sat up on the table excitedly and it was plain she was delighted.

"Oh, yes, violently . . . up to the neck. But Anne's a sport . . . cured me painlessly and never gave me away. You're very like her, Una."

"Me?" There was no mistaking the dazzled amazement in Una's face.

"Very . . . inside. When I commit a crime and the police are after me I shall come and hide in your house." Bill got up. "I must push off, and I'm awfully obliged for all you've done. I'll do as much for you one of these days."

Una went with him to the door, and he added, smiling down at her: "You're a mascot to me. What about a kiss for luck?"

"All right."

Una raised her face and kissed him cheerfully, calling out after him as he ran down the steps: "I'd get the ring before you go out there if I were you."

"Tempting Providence," laughed Bill.

Brent, who had been lying in wait to hunt her erstwhile patient to bed, and had witnessed the kiss, retreated to the back premises with her eyes nearly starting out of her head.

Such goings on!

When next morning Brent learned that her young mistress was going to Wenlock with friends for the week-end, she almost lost control of herself, and argued and protested, until Una told her to mind her own business and walked out of the house.

Brent immediately put through a trunk call to Anne, but she was out and it was not until the evening that she received the message from Brent in Palace Square and rang up to know what it was all about.

"I can't have it on my conscience not to tell you, my lady," wailed Brent in agitation, "seeing I'm in charge of Miss Una, as you might say. Nothing I could do would stop her."

"What's the matter with Miss Una?" cried Anne sharply. "Pull yourself together, Brent."

"She's gone off for the week-end, my lady, to Wenlock . . . with friends, so she *said*."

"*Wenlock?* Did she say what friends?"

"Never a word, but that young Mr. France was round here last night till close on ten o'clock."

"Well, if she's with the Frances she will be all right. Don't worry, Brent. The little change will do the child good."

"Ah, but that's not all, my lady, and as God is my witness, the responsibility is more than I can bear." Brent lowered her voice to a husky and mysterious whisper. *"I saw him kiss her with my own eyes . . . in the hall . . . and she told him he'd better get the ring."*

i

UNA and her guests sat at luncheon in the shadow of the great cedar, which was the pride of Wenlock, the house with its doors and windows wide before them and a ribbon of smoke drifting from a rear chimney into the golden air. Mrs. Wardell had worked hard. The lower rooms were polished, and bright with flowers by the time the little party arrived, the table was set out in the garden, with salad, cheese and real country cream to add to the stores from Una's hamper. Coffee was waiting ready on the stove, and the lodge-keeper had even produced a niece from the village to be at the beck and call of her young lady.

The three visitors, hungry from their drive, decided to have lunch at once, and to two of them at least nectar and ambrosia were nothing to this feast together under the trees. The third, a tactful soul, conversed with Tim, who would otherwise have been scandalously neglected.

"I am going to ask mother to give me Wenlock for a dog farm," said Una to Tony.

"Oh, but look here, what's going to happen to Kensington Gardens then?"

"Well, you must look after them."

"Not alone," he wailed indignantly. "They'll go

to rack and ruin, and Alsatians will simply over-run the whole place. Besides, you're too young to go to the dogs. Unless," he added hopefully, "you'll take me on as chief-dog-washer or kennelman-in-waiting. . . . You're joking, of course?"

"No, I'm not joking. I mean it, and I want a ken-nelman, but you must be making statues," said Una.

"Give him a job, for heaven's sake, Una," re-quested Kit. "He needs something to occupy him between the bursts of inspiration, and he'll make himself quite useful if you're firm with him."

"All right," agreed Una, "he can have a job."

"Done," cried Tony, believing none of it.

Kit finished her coffee and looked longingly at a hammock which Mrs. Wardell had unearthed from somewhere and hung beneath the trees.

"Would it be a terrible breach of manners if I tumbled into that and went to sleep?" she asked. "The air and the cider have gone to my head."

The two innocents she addressed begged her to sleep by all means, and having settled her with cush-ions and a cigarette, tiptoed away to the waiting house, quite unaware of the smile that followed them.

And now because she was going to show Wenlock her secret friend, Una's heart stood still, for what would it say to him?

"Oh, please like him," her mind said pleadingly to the house.

Tony stepped over the threshold beside her and softly touched her arm.

"Let's start at the top," he begged. "I've been

starting at the bottom for years and years and never getting anywhere. That's life, but this is a dream, and it is only right to start at the top in a dream."

She laughed, and they ran like a pair of children up the stairs to the door of the attic, where Una paused with her hand on the knob and her eyes like stars to say: "I thought this would be a studio for when the inspirations come."

The darling! She was playing to his fancy as though the dream could actually come true. And Tony, following her into his workroom of the future, where the sunlight lay in golden bars over the lumber of years, wished that he might not wake. What should he not do in this heavenly quiet place among the woods and gardens with his girl and her dogs to spur him? But it was all impossible, of course. He hadn't a hope.

He thought of a gift he had hidden in the car to give her, and blessed Kit's sleepy head. Presently, when the tour of the house was over, he would put the little figure into his darling's hands.

They passed to the floor below, spread out in two wings, each room, spacious and well proportioned, calling to his artist's eye. There was no grandeur here, nor had the place been flung together in the modern fashion, but built in a leisurely age with care. The curve of the stairs, the timbered doorways, and deep window spaces charmed him. The house, like the girl beside him, had lovely lines.

"How old is it?" asked Tony, in a whisper, as though it might hear and be shocked.

"I don't know. My great-grandfather Challice bought it. . . . I'll show him to you presently. He made money out of jam."

"And it sweetened his life," said Tony, beaming with satisfaction. "I know. He was a nice old boy. This isn't a haunted house. The ghosts are kind. Can't you feel that?"

"Are they?" She could say no more.

"And friendly," finished Tony. "The ghosts in a house are very important. Always make sure of them before you see if the drains are all right and the roof in repair. Didn't you feel directly we came in that the ghosts were pleased and were smiling at us on every side? Very well, then . . . I say, I haven't frightened you, have I?"

She shook her head with a tremulous smile, as she went downstairs beside him.

"It *is* a friendly house," she said at last, in a small voice.

"I suppose you know it well?"

"Oh, no. I haven't been here till yesterday since I was seven. There were soldiers in it then . . . wounded, you know, from the War, and I can only remember how they laughed and laughed. . . ."

The old incident had taken on significance before her, as though Wenlock had had some mystic responsibility for that laughter, and her voice was eager. Tony watched her as though she might vanish before his eyes.

She led him into the drawing-room and showed him the portraits, nervously, for he was an artist and she knew the paintings were poor. What would he think of them? It was the last and the greatest test.

Tony, however, nodded at the first Challice as one man to another.

"Yes, you're two old dears," he said. "I knew."

Una, finding her happy voice, said: "Someone had stuffed them away behind a door, but I brought them out. Tenants, you know, fat and disagreeable. I wonder the ghosts didn't haunt them."

"They did," said Tony with decision. "But being fat and disagreeable they hadn't any minds, and having no minds they couldn't hear the ghosts. It isn't only ears you need when ghosts are about. And the house hated them, but being fools they thought it was the other way round, so they went off and rented a stucco villa. They never dreamed they were being forcibly ejected. If you're not on good terms with the ghosts in residence, almost anything may happen. You may trip up on the stairs and break your leg, and you blame the stair rod or the heel of your shoe, and never even guess the truth; or they may bore a hole in the roof and let in the damp so that you get rheumatism and have to move to another district. They're ingenious little devils. Why, I've known ghosts to get up in the night and fling the furniture about because the wrong people have got into their house. I have, true as death."

"Perhaps that's how their poor frames got broken. Do you think it would be all right if I bought them new ones? . . . Not really new but old and good?"

He took out his handkerchief and carefully measured the broken frames, making a note of the size in his pocket-book, as though the house were already his own concern, and she was delighted.

"I think I know just where to lay my hands on what you want. You leave it to me," he said. "And now come out to the garage with me for a moment, because I have a portrait too. It's in the car."

His tone was full of mystery, and she followed him smiling, wondering what he meant. She loved him, and already he and Wenlock were friends; his very nonsense had been full of understanding of it, and the whole world sang to her.

She stood watching him as he brought a long box from under the seat of the car and removed the wrapping. She adored his thin face and the way his hair grew, and the look of his hands which were brown and strong, yet so careful and quick in everything they did. He would never break anything, she thought. She hadn't the faintest idea what he was unpacking from his box, and when he turned suddenly and thrust the little figure into her hands, she was speechless for a moment.

"Tony . . . it's wonderful," she cried at last. "You're terribly clever, and without even a sitting." She looked down at the little image of herself and smiled. "I don't know how on earth you did it," she added, handing it back to him.

"No, no . . . it's for you. It isn't in the least wonderful," stammered Tony, looking as though he wanted to run away. "The real one will be very different, but it's just a little study from memory and I wanted you to have it. *Please!*"

Una had turned first white and then red, and she ran to the little box and put the statue down because her hands were shaking and she could not face him. Just like this, shy and stammering, he had given his statue to Aunt Marion and she couldn't bear it. The dream, her lovely dream, was shattered before her eyes, for she was nothing to him after all then, no more than Aunt Marion . . . merely a model he wanted for his work.

"I couldn't let you," she said in a smothered voice. "It's your work and you mustn't give it away."

Mastering herself, she turned back to him with a piteous attempt at a smile.

"I think it's wonderful anyhow," she said, trying to comfort him because he looked so hurt, "but you mustn't give it to me. P . . . put it carefully away in the car again. I couldn't bear it to get broken."

Tony turned without a word and picked up this thing he had made from a handful of lovely memories, knowing miserably that at the first chance he would smash it into a thousand pieces. He would never be able to look at it again.

What had he done to make her look at him like that, so frightened and white? He was a clumsy brute, going too fast, taking too much for granted, and now he had spoiled it all. He wanted to take her in his arms and comfort her as one would a child. He had always felt that she was like something very precious and delicate that might break, and he had frightened and troubled her and he did not know how to put it right.

"We seem to have lost Tim," she said, when at

length the box was packed away again. "Will you help me find him?" It was a forlorn request, and as a change of subject useless, for at this moment Tim, no diplomat, rushed out of the house with a bound and came towards them joyfully. He had no silly sorrows and this was the life for him.

"Come on, Tim, we'll go into the orchard."

Una opened the door in the stable yard and they went through the orchard and kitchen garden with a shadow between them which had never been there before, both conscious of it and trying to banish it away.

"Don't you think my dogs will have a lovely time?" Una asked, showing Tony the woods and the golden fields.

"You aren't really going to have a dog farm?"

"Oh, yes." She looked frightened again, as though this too might be snatched away.

"But they'd never let you," said Tony in a gentle and persuasive voice. "You're so young."

"You've got to begin some time, though. I'm not awfully young and I mean to do it. They'll let me . . . because I don't really like town. And then there's Wenlock. It wants somebody belonging to it."

He did not argue with her any more, for what could he say to that? For a brief hour he had been in her dream and now he was shut out.

They turned back, but as one accord avoided the house and its friendly ghosts, and crossed the rose-garden. Instinctively they were seeking protection from each other in Kit, but the hammock was empty.

Kit, finding the wind cool under the trees, had sauntered away to the inn for her coat, laudably intending to see the village on the way back and leave them to themselves until tea-time.

Mrs. Wardell had brought out basket chairs, and Una took one of them, Tony flinging himself on the grass beside her and racking his brains for some nonsense to bring back her smiles.

He fished out his pipe, and in searching for matches came upon the onyx ring. The next moment he was sitting up and had slipped it into her hand.

"Lorenzo," he said. "You were advertising for the blighter."

"Oh, I wasn't," exclaimed Una in a horrified tone. "Truly I wasn't, Tony. Take him back. My father did that. He asked where the ring was, so I made out I had lost it and in sheer kindness of heart he advertised for it and didn't even tell me."

"I guessed it was something like that," said Tony, beaming with relief at having found something to say at last. "Not at first, though. You didn't know I called at your house about the advertisement, did you?"

"But that was about a pink ring and a fair girl," retorted Una, a smile dawning.

He laughed.

"Rather neat tale that, wasn't it?" he said. "Did your mother really swallow it?"

"She pretended to."

"Sporting sort of parent she must be. You know, I made the most frightful breaks, too. I thought she was your sister."

"B . . . but you'd seen her before," stammered Una in a puzzled tone.

"Never. I don't go about much, you know, and I didn't even realize she was Lady Anne Swithin. Called her 'Mrs.' on the telephone . . . another awful break."

"But, Tony, you made a statue of her."

"Of your mother? Never in this world. Whatever made you think so?"

"You said you did," cried Una, sitting up and gazing at him, "in the Gardens that day when I was so cross. You said you knew you'd been an idiot, but you hadn't had an idea Lady Swithin was any relative of mine."

"Yes, but that wasn't your mother, child. It was that old aunt in Florence . . . oh, lord, I hope she's not a favorite aunt. Is she?"

"No!" said Una violently.

"Thank heaven for that. If Whiskers wasn't a friend of mine I'd say she was a cat. As it is, I call her a catamaran, which doesn't mean in my vocabulary anything like what the dictionary says it does, either."

"But she's not Lady Anything. She's Miss Swithin, and you did admire her . . . you know you did. You got awfully romantic and made a little statue of her and took it to her hotel."

"What?" shouted Tony, and rolled in the grass, in a gale of laughter. "Hang it all, Una, she didn't say that?"

"Yes, she did."

"Good God! Oh, well, I suppose I was rather

rude to the poor old girl, and that makes us quits. Why, I was in such a rage with her for pouncing on Lorenzo and snaffling him before my eyes that I went back to the studio determined to make a comic figure of her *en pounce*. Only," said Tony mournfully, "the damned thing wouldn't pounce and I thought she'd be quite flattered with it, so being rather keen on the ring I raced off to her hotel to see if I could do a deal with her, Lorenzo for her image. It was there they called her Lady Swithin. I didn't know her from Adam, or Eve. And I'm dashed if when she saw her beastly portrait she didn't pounce on that, too, then thank me effusively, and when I asked about the ring, say she'd sent it away.

"Still, she was sending it to you," he added, "and she was doing me a good turn after all. I might never have met you. . . . I might have dashed on that day before the fight began if I hadn't seen it on your hand."

"And Tim would have been killed," said Una in a husky voice.

"Not he."

Tony's hand closed over hers and held it fast, but she didn't attempt to draw it away, and suddenly, as though out of the blue, he saw the whole thing . . . the fool aunt telling her maudlin tale and then his turning up with exactly the same sort of gift. No wonder she wouldn't have it, the darling. It was an insult . . . an outrage.

He stole one look at her face, saw the tremulous smile, then gathered her into his arms.

"My little dear, my sweet," said Tony. "I'm almost every kind of a blithering fool, but not that kind, darling."

Una buried her face in his coat.

i

I WAS terribly afraid you might not be able to work in the country," said Una with a happy sigh.

"Was I really in the scheme?" asked Tony, hardly able to believe his ears.

"Yes . . . not at first, though, until I came out here yesterday, and then I found out. I couldn't tell whether you cared for me, but I meant to see."

Her directness enchanted and amazed him. She loved him, and so she had come for him calmly and without a fuss to see if he loved her. Was there anywhere in the world another girl like this? But Tony, for a multitude of reasons, could not share her confidence in this dream of theirs.

Confused and mistaken as she had been in so many things, Una had always been strong of purpose. She was neither possessive nor demanding, and if he had not loved her she would have gone on her way without complaint, but since the miracle had happened all was well. There was no obstacle she could not overcome. Tony, on the other hand, with his ups and downs of temperament, his natural diffidence enhanced by unsympathetic handling in his youth, knew only that he held the most precious thing in the world in his arms, and that his claim to her, in the eyes of practical people, would be small if not actually ridiculous.

"My little darling, have we really a hope?" he said. "I'm a poor ass with no money to speak of and a very doubtful sort of talent. I'm afraid your father and mother will very quickly send me packing."

"Money doesn't matter," said Una calmly. "The dogs will begin to pay after a little while. Not at first, of course, but I have plans. It will be all right. Mother will give me Wenlock, especially now there's you."

"You haven't told her about me, have you?"

"No, but she sent her love to you," said Una triumphantly, "and told me to tell you it was very tactless of you to call her 'Mrs.' Swithin. You could make a perfect statue of her, Tony. I'll ask her to sit to you if you like."

"She'll probably make mince-meat of me first," said Tony, "because, my loveliest, no decent chap lives on his wife. She'll tell you so."

"How much money have you got?"

"Only three thousand."

"Then how would you be living on me? We'll have Wenlock and your thousands, and whatever father can allow me. I must cost him hundreds living at home, so he'll save money if you marry me. And now and then you'll sell a statue and I'll sell a dog. It won't cost us much to live with fruit and vegetables and eggs growing on the place, Tony, and we'll have the car to get about in. And then I shall take in boarder dogs whose owners are away. I know plenty of dogs that will come regularly, and Benyon will send us others. He said he will help, and I'm going to ask him to be our visiting vet. . . . There's somebody coming."

"Only Kit," whispered Tony, holding her closer. Then he stared defiantly into his sister's face, which was carefully wreathed with a smile of surprise.

"We're engaged, Kit," said Una.

"You look rather engaged," returned Miss Corcoran cheerfully. "Tony, stop goggling and let me wish her luck."

Tony, getting up, said doubtfully: "I've been trying to persuade her they'll never agree."

"They will, Kit. They must," cried Una. "Don't you let him worry, because I know it will be all right. I'm going into the house for a moment. I won't be long."

She ran off, and Tony looked at his sister.

"I didn't mean to speak to her here," he said. "It's not fair. I meant to wait, but I suppose it's this heavenly place, and you cleared out and left us."

He glared at her as though she had committed a crime and Kit retorted coolly: "Say one word more, my lad, and I'll cling to you both like a leech for the rest of your stay. Don't be an ass, Tony. Lady Anne Swithin is neither a fool nor a snob, or Una wouldn't have so much freedom. And the governor will have to do his duty by you for once. I'll see him directly I get back to town."

"Damn it all, I'll see him myself," cried Tony. "I'm not going to let you do the dirty work." He flung himself into a chair. "You needn't look like that," he added. "Do you think I don't know you've always stood between us?"

"Well, see what I've got out of it," said Kit.

"Precious little."

"I wouldn't call Freddy little, though I dare say I should call him precious if I were made like that," remarked Kit, placidly lighting a cigarette. "Because if I hadn't left home and clung to you, my little lamb, I shouldn't have met him, so after all you haven't lived in vain. Cheer up."

Tony flung a cushion at her. Kit, always practical, said "Thanks!" and sat on it.

ii

Una, from the drawing-room door, was calling Tony, and he rushed off at such a rate that Tim awoke from his dreams and gave chase, thinking there was sport afoot. The two lovers of Una reached her side by side, and she looked from one to the other with a little smile. It was to Tony, however, that she gave her hand, drawing him into the room.

"I brought her out," she said, and showed him on a table under the two old portraits the little figure which an hour ago she had refused. "They like her, Tony."

His arm crept round her, and he drew her close. Under the eyes of the kindly ghosts, the child of their blood lifted her face to his kiss.

iii

Kit, meanwhile, on a loose page of her sketching book, was drafting a letter.

"Dear father,

"Your son and daughter propose to marry. The man of my choice is Frederick Carstairs, the sculptor, and though you despise the breed, he is successful, which should appeal to a business man. His work is in the Tate Gallery, and if I don't put my foot down he will probably go and get knighted one of these days. A good investment, don't you think?

"Tony has done us really proud, for he hopes to marry the only daughter of Lady Anne Swithin, whose father was the Earl of Wenlock, political I think and Liberal, your crowd. I tell you this in confidence for Tony means to see you himself and I'm not permitted to interfere. Fight it out between you, by all means, but first let me tell you why you lost a daughter.

"You never cared for Tony, so don't deny it. You were never fair to him. Without a shred of excuse you destroyed the first beautiful thing he made, and I, who am said to be like you, count injustice the deadliest sin.

"If there is any likeness between us I suggest you pay him for the damage you did. I value it at £5000 and I am a business woman. If this is above the market price for daughters, dad, good-by.

"Kit."

In due course Kit was to receive a reply to this letter, which, for convenience, may be set down here.

"Dear Kit,

"An astute business woman should know that to demand money with menaces is a criminal offense. However, if only that I may claim the likeness you mention, the debt shall be paid. The market price for daughters has gone up during recent years. Your figure does not touch it.

"If you survive me, though it seems doubtful unless you desert the life of crime on which you have apparently embarked, you will find in my will, dated the week you left me, no trace, I trust, of the deadliest sin.

"Your affectionate father,
"P. Corcoran."

i

ANNE had received Brent's tidings of the goings-on at first with nothing but amusement, telling the agitated woman not to be absurd.

Kisses of any portent were not, even in these days, exchanged by young people in the hall with the servants looking on, and the talk of the ring was undoubtedly merely a joke between Una and Bill France, who were friends. Besides, Bill's affections had for years been engaged with Robby Lyne. The thing was ridiculous.

Yet, having hung up the receiver, Anne felt vaguely disturbed and she went back to the drawing-room of the Drews' old-fashioned house with a thoughtful face. For suppose Bill, feeling Robby lost to him by her latest escapade, had been caught on the rebound by Una? The notion was unpleasing, not that she disliked Bill, far from it, but because there was an element of second-handness in such a romance, and the child was young. Anne wanted the winds set fair for her daughter when she sailed out on the great adventure. And then, why Wenlock? She had never heard Una mention the old place in her life that she could remember, and it was certainly in no state to house guests after being empty for months. A week-end at Wenlock did sound like one of the fairy-tales some daughters tell, but surely not hers?

Anne, with a start, remembered their day together on Thursday, and the strange brilliance of the girl's face. Had it, after all, been due to something more than the fun of being nineteen?

Mrs. Drew, sitting bolt upright in a high-backed chair, listening to the click of the billiard balls in the next room, looked up at her returning guest with shrewd old eyes.

"Worrying news, eh?" she said. "Out with it."

She did not expect any response to this invitation, for Anne had never told her anything, which only went to show, thought the old lady, that there was plenty to tell. "She might be my own daughter, she keeps things so dark," Mrs. Drew often told herself, triumphantly.

Her carefully laid plan had succeeded. Jeremy and Anne were here together under her eyes, but the shadow between them, which she had sensed at Judy's party and felt herself strong to dissipate, was there no longer. Even Jeremy was a delightful guest. He seemed to have renewed his youth, and the senior partner, who had seen the change follow immediately upon his own homily of some days ago, was once more aware of the amazing perception of his wife. Swithin had needed a good blowing up. She had been right, as usual. He did not tell her so, however, nor had he told her of the interview. He was not the man to acknowledge that he had followed any woman's advice. And Mrs. Drew, wistfully glad that all was well with Jeremy and Anne, yet humanly regretful that she had not after all been able to serve her darling, supposed that she had been a sentimental old fool and imagined the shadow.

A sentimentalist, she acknowledged herself to be, without repentance. Words had no terror for her, and life had not given her so many pleasures that she should relinquish this one as a vice. Ironically, she would never know that she had done for Anne exactly what she had set out to do. Old Drew's talk with Jeremy, which she had inspired, coming on the heel of a dozen minor irritations, had led the younger man to voice his trouble at last, and to find that, like so many human troubles, it existed only in his imagination.

Anne had no suspicion of Mrs. Drew's affection for her. One cannot perhaps see oneself as a public and private darling at the same time and keep one's sense of humor. The first rôle had been thrust upon her almost at birth, and while it had not spoiled her it had inevitably made her a little insensitive to the second. She loved Jeremy and Una warmly, but without excitement, and had always been calmly confident of their affection, but she was as unconscious of the girl's selfless adoration as she had been of the cause of Jeremy's unrest. The scene a few nights ago had opened her eyes to the latter, and, being neither dishonest nor a fool, she saw that in a sense she had failed him. It was a disturbing thought. For the first time her self-confidence was shaken, and in this mood Brent's disclosures about Una certainly troubled her a little. How could she be sure, after all, what the girl would or would not do?

Sinking into a chair beside her alert old friend, Anne found herself reversing the habit of years and confiding in her at last, not as the other fondly hoped to seek comfort and reassurance, so much as to obtain a disinterested view of Brent's story. Mrs. Drew was no gossip, nor would she take the attitude of her own generation. She was still obstinately the champion of youth at sixty-five.

"It was Brent," said Anne. "She had a wild story that Una was seen kissing Bill France in the hall, and that she has now gone off for the week-end with him."

"What, as publicly as that?" inquired Mrs. Drew with scorn.

Anne laughed her relief.

"I know. I told her she was being absurd . . . and yet . . . am I merely thinking my goose a swan?"

"Better than thinking your swan a goose, my dear, as Brent appears to do. The girls of today are not such fools. Besides, where then does Roberta Lyne come in?"

Anne, explaining her own alarm in this context, suddenly recalled Judy's talk of Robby and her masked man, and Una's unexpected "I don't believe it." Was it possible she and Bill were going in search of Robby? This idea, though wild enough, was so much more acceptable than the other that she was afraid to trust it, for wasn't it almost safer to be a deceived parent than a self-deceived? And yet why either?

"I'm being absurd about the child," thought

Anne. "I am behaving exactly like her grandmother."

Pulling herself together, she said to Mrs. Drew:
"Probably she has gone off with Judy somewhere,
but I confess I should like to know if it is Wenlock,
for Judy is more scatter-brained than the youngest
of them, and Una has no business to be sleeping in
a house that has been shut up for months, after her
illness. They'll probably never think of that."

"Why not telephone to Wenlock and find out?"
suggested the old lady briskly. She rose to her feet
and folded her knitting away. "Come, we'll put a
trunk call through to the village post-office or the
inn and ask if Miss Swithin is at the hall. Villages
always know more than their prayers."

"I might drive over there in the morning, as we
can't be more than thirty miles away," hesitated
Anne. "It happens that I ought to see the old place.
The agent has been clamoring for weeks that I
should, so I could do it without arousing Jeremy's
suspicions. I shan't worry him with Brent's melodrama and spoil his holiday. Men are such babes."

"Bless them, yes. In the meantime, my dear, you
want a night's rest, so we'll telephone and make
sure. If the child is really trying to contract pneumonia in a damp house, you can drive over in the
morning and bring her here. Better leave the inqui-
ries to me."

Mrs. Drew was in high feather. She loved to
stage-manage and she was serving Anne at last. Her
sharp old voice awoke the sleepy local exchange,
and in due time linked her with Wenlock post-office.

That fount of knowledge informed her that Miss Swithin was at the inn, and put through her call, eager to serve the visitor. The whole village was by this time united in the desire to see Lady Anne's family once more in residence at the hall. For the same reason the inn was voluble. Miss Swithin and the other young lady and gentleman had gone out not ten minutes since to hear the nightingales, but would be back by ten o'clock. Was there any message, or would madam like a messenger sent after them?

"Not at all, thank you," said Mrs. Drew. "It is of no importance."

Hanging up the receiver and repeating the message to Anne, she added: "Nightingales and not pneumonia, and three is a crowd, my dear. No occasion for alarm, after all."

Anne laughed.

"Judy and Bill, I suppose, or even Robby and Bill, with Una to play propriety. Well, thank heaven for your common sense, for I should certainly have worried all night. I'm an ordinary parent, after all."

ii

She would have given up the proposed drive to Wenlock on the morrow, had not Jeremy changed her plans. He had had some letters forwarded from town, and when they were alone that night, he said to her uneasily:

"I was a fool to advertise for that ring of Una's. My mother has seen the advertisement and now she writes to reproach me for letting Una wear it until it was made smaller. It wasn't returned, by any chance, I suppose?"

Anne shook her head.

"You were a donkey, for, after all, as Una told you, it's her loss."

"I know. Mother does fuss, but it's merely because she is naturally careful herself, Anne. If the beastly thing had only been returned," said Jeremy, "I could have pointed out to her that she was fussing without cause."

He was so eager and apologetic that she knew he was trying to make amends for upholding his mother's interference in the past. He had even maintained a noble silence about Robby's escapade, but Anne had no faith in miracles. The interference would go on and continue to be a source of irritation between them until his absurd sense of obligation to his family could be removed. She decided that she had better see Wenlock, therefore, since she was so near, for in the end she supposed it would come to selling the place. Jeremy's talk of failure the other night had no doubt been part despondency, but at least it seemed to suggest that he would not have £5000 to give away.

Driving through the old familiar lanes next morning, Anne knew a vague regret that she had seen so little of them all these years.

"It is my own fault," she said to herself. "I should have kept Wenlock open in spite of Jeremy and his absurd pride. The doctrine of peace at any price is sheer indolence really. Why, this quarrel has actually done him good. We must have another."

Though she spoke half in mockery, there was an underlying truth in her self-condemnation. If Wenlock was to be lost to her in the somewhat ignoble cause of buying them immunity from old Mrs. Swithin, it was because she had not long ago insisted upon a frank understanding with Jeremy and an open instead of a secret share in their financial responsibilities. She had simply spared his feelings in the interests of peace, but how futile and how weak! Real peace, she thought, is knowing yourself.

As the car drew near Wenlock, she began to look about for Una and her friends, for her anxiety of the night before, though lessened, was not allayed. Suppose, after all, the child had lost her heart to Bill France? She could tell him what she thought of him, and Judy also for lending her aid. But what could she say to Una? Nothing at all. All her maternal doubts gave her no such right as that. She even knew a moment's fear that the culprits might have taken themselves off, alarmed by the telephone call of the night before; and when the car drew up before the house and she saw the excited figure of her daughter running to her across the grass, she drew a breath of relief. Culprit or not, Una's pleasure was plain.

The girl had not connected the telephone call with Anne. It might have been Bill or Robby, or even more likely Brent, nosily anxious to find out if she were at Wenlock after all. Her mother's appearance, therefore, was a joyous surprise, though Tony denied the adjective and wanted to run for his life.

"No, no, it's all right, really, Tony, because she likes you," Una had assured him, and was off like the wind to welcome Anne.

"Oh, mother, you must be a thought-reader," she cried, drawing the visitor into the house.

"Must I?" said Anne, endeavoring to look stern. "Let us hope not for your sake. What do you mean by running away from home?"

"Well, you and father ran away from me," returned Una reasonably.

"Oh, I see. It was revenge."

"No, but it seemed a good chance," said her daughter, in a cautious voice.

Anne laughed.

"Very neat, my bright rascal, but suppose you tell me what this is all about? Where are Judy and Bill? Well, why are you looking like that? Isn't it Judy and Bill?"

Una shook her head and smiled.

"No. I suppose you saw them in the garden, and I'll bring them in and introduce them in a minute. They are friends of mine. You see, I came out here for a drive on Friday, and it was so jolly I went back and collected them for the week-end. Better than matinées, and I knew you wouldn't mind."

Anne looked round the long faded room, with its jars of bright flowers, then back to her daughter glowing in the middle of it. In just this spirit of excitement the funny child had taken possession of her on Thursday and bought her a hat. She had suddenly grown up, thrown off the armor of childhood, and this was a new Una, who spoke to her as a friend. It had not even entered her head that her mother was really at this moment a spying parent, and in comic gratitude for this dispensation Anne found herself answering politely:

"Not in the least, but I didn't know you were fond of Wenlock, Una."

"Yes, I am . . . very. I . . . I want you to give it to me, mother."

"Give you Wenlock?"

She had asked for nothing all her life, and now she asked for Wenlock. Anne looked at her daughter in dismay.

"Do you mean now, or some day?"

"Now . . . for a dog farm."

"But, my blessed child, what do you know of dog farms?"

"I know quite a lot," declared Una calmly. "I've always wanted to have one, and I've been studying it up for years."

"You always were a queer little scrap," said her mother.

"I know . . . a changeling."

Anne's old habit of talking nonsense to the child rebounded on her at sight of her daughter's solemn face.

"You're no changeling, you're a Challice," she corrected. "Your great-grandfather bred dogs at Wenlock half his life."

"Oh, mother . . . then it's Fate!"

Una sat down, elation in every line of her, and in spite of herself Anne smiled. She remembered Tim, the poor stray grown under Una's hand to Tim the aristocrat, and it was the normal course, she supposed, for the girl to be restless in this restless era and want some occupation.

"If you'll give me Wenlock, or let me have it rent free for a few years, I'll call you Anne," offered Una suddenly.

"But why should that be an inducement?" inquired her mother, bewildered.

"You wanted me to once and I refused. It was a long time ago. . . . I was about seven at the time."

"Child, your memory is terrible. I suppose I thought it would be amusing then; you were so old and wise, but isn't that sort of thing rather overdone nowadays? Why did you refuse me, by the way?"

"Oh, I don't know." The girl was offhand. That old incident, which had seemed so valiant at the time, had lost its significance at last, because she saw that her mother had neither noticed nor understood.

Anne sensed at once the flatness that succeeds elation, and suggested hastily: "Suppose you tell me what you really want to do . . . to put someone in charge and come out from time to time and superintend, is that it? Though Wenlock is too large, I should have thought."

"Not really, because I meant to live here and do it all myself, and I know you can't let Wenlock easily. I would look after it," explained Una.

"But, my dear, you can't retire from the world and bury yourself in the country at nineteen. It's not to be thought of. We can't spare you for one thing, and you couldn't possibly run the place alone."

"I shan't be alone," was the surprising answer. "I . . . I'm going to be married." Pink as great-grandfather Challice, but quite collected, Una met her mother's startled glance.

"To a dog farmer?" inquired Anne faintly, at last.

"No . . . He's a sculptor and dreadfully clever." She was across the room in a moment, seizing Tony's little figure and bringing it back to place it in her mother's hands.

"He can make statues here and help me with my dogs, because he has a little money, though not much, and you said yourself that he was a nice rascal."

"So that is the highway robber? Where did you meet him, my dear?"

"He saved Tim's life that morning from the Alsatian, and we've been friends ever since. His sister is Kit Corcoran, who designed that frock for you. They're both here with me. You'll like them." She held out her left hand and showed Anne the onyx ring. "He had it because I gave it to him, and there wasn't a pink one or a fair girl either. I'm wearing it till he gets back to town and can buy another."

Anne, still with her eyes on the inanimate Una, took the hand of the living one and held it fast in her own, the beauty of the boy's creation and the strength of this child of her flesh significant within

her. This was their own adventure, and what right
had she to doubt or protest? Yet she must make a
pretense of both.

"Go and bring the scoundrel to me," she ordered,
looking stern.

Una, running off, paused at the door to say: "I
told him you'd be nice to him."

"Rash of you," said her mother, but she smiled.

iii

Anne was alone in the old room, so familiar yet
unfamiliar, which her daughter had awakened to
life. The long windows were open at both ends and
a little wind rustled the curtains and filled the air
with the scent of grass under a morning sun. It
was hard to believe this was a house for months
deserted. The chairs pushed carelessly about, a
woollen coat flung over one and a silk scarf on
another, an open box of sweets on the table, showed
youth in possession, carefree, as youth should be.
The bells of Wenlock church, very old and tremulous, as though fearing their use long past, played
to the drowsy silence what had once been a tune;
but they had lost it in the mists of years, that pr___,
peremptory melody, and their notes ran after each
other seeking it in vain. Just so had they sought it
when Anne was a child, and for a moment she lost
the illusion of time, until the sound of young voices
in the garden recalled her to the little figure in her
hands.

It was a lovely thing the boy had made . . . a
touch of genius in it surely, and this flame was to

be nurtured by Una and her dogs. A mad, unpractical scheme.

"She's too young," protested Anne, replacing Tony's gift on the table beneath the two old portraits and seeing them for the first time. "And yet I was married at nineteen. I'd have done it myself."

Fate Una had called it, but wasn't it rather history repeating itself, a Challice once more breeding dogs at Wenlock, an only daughter of nineteen imprudently marrying the most ineligible of all the men she knew?

Anne found herself hoping the rascal was indeed a nice one, knowing that hope her only stronghold.

"Mother, here's Tony. Can't I come in too?"

They were there in the doorway like two tall, eager children, hand in hand, and Tony was saying coaxingly: "Of course you can't. You leave this to me."

"Be off with you," supplemented her mother, hiding a smile. "You shall be called when the battle's over."

Young men in love! She was used to them for the best of all reasons. She had learned to recognize the first symptoms and the safest method of effecting an early cure. But she herself had been the object of these adorations, and this boy was the lover of Una, who only the other day, it seemed, had been a round-eyed scrap in her arms. It was fantastic.

His looks at least were in his favor, and also the fact that he was obviously alarmed. But, she thought, "That is simply because I want to like him and it won't do. I must be firm." So she said to him suavely:

"You seem to have found quite a number of my belongings in Kensington Gardens, one way and another."

"I know exactly what you must be thinking of me," admitted Tony.

"And what am I supposed to be thinking?"

"Oh, well, that I'm a fortune-hunter at the very least."

"If you are," observed Anne drily, "you are hunting in the wrong quarter. Una's father is a hard-working barrister, with a rather expensive wife and no fortune. I'm not expensive from choice, but because, having had a title wished upon me, the world makes me pay for it. You are proposing to marry into quite an ordinary family, you see, and not among the rich and great."

"Oh, I say, thank the lord for that," exclaimed Tony, beaming.

Anne who had been watching him covertly, stifled a desire to laugh.

"Why?"

"Because I'm terrified to death of the rich and great." Tony, rather red in the face, looked appealingly at his Una's mother. "I've loved her from the first minute," he said. "Nobody could help it, and for weeks I didn't even know who she was. Of course when I found out I thought I hadn't a hope. I've been trying to persuade her you'll never allow it."

"Faint heart?" quoted Anne.

"No, it isn't, now I know she cares. If you won't consent, we'll wait, or," said Tony recklessly, "do without it."

"Thank you for warning me," returned Anne amused. "I always did admire the bold burglar who sends a note in advance saying he's going to rob the house on such a night. Have you suggested this interesting alternative to Una?"

"Good heavens, no." Tony looked abashed. "I'm always talking through my hat, Lady Anne," he stammered apologetically. "She wouldn't do it. She's too fond of you, and I wouldn't ask her. I know she's awfully young, but I'll work like blazes, I will really, to take care of her. I suppose I had no business to speak to her while Kit and I were her guests out here, but I lost my head in this lovely place. And then," added Tony, in eager extenuation, "you see, we'd had a bit of a misunderstanding."

"Ah, that would be fatal, of course," said Anne, and suddenly she laughed. "It's all right, my dear boy, I don't blame you, but you'd better come and sit down and tell me all about yourself. Remember, I have to break it to Una's father that she wants to marry a complete stranger."

She drew him into a chair beside her, asked for a cigarette and told him to smoke his pipe if he preferred it. Tony attempted to obey but his hands were shaking so idiotically that he presently gave up the attempt.

"I'm nobody, of course," he admitted.

"Oh, good! Neither am I," confided Anne to

comfort him. "Won't you tell me about your people?"

"My father is a partner in the firm of Corcoran and Spence. They import tea, so of course he has a soul above artists," said Tony bitterly. "My mother was one, but he made her give it up. She died when I was six. Naturally when he couldn't knock it out of me, he despised me. Luckily Kit and I had a legacy and were able to leave home, and we've shared a studio up to now. I have about three thousand pounds. . . . Still I'm going to see my father and perhaps he'll do something for me."

"But won't he think it rather a cool request after your desertion of him?" asked Anne in surprise.

"He was glad to be rid of me. He said so."

"Don't you believe it! Parents are a much misunderstood people."

He smiled but shook his head.

"Not mine. He would have sent me to Oxford if I would have gone into the firm afterwards, but he wouldn't give me a penny to study the work I wanted to do. I had to get a clerical job so that I could pay for night classes and he never spoke to me again though I was living in the house."

"You seem to have been an annoying kind of son, you know," said Anne.

"Yes, but wasn't it his own fault? What business was it of his what I did with my life as long as I led a decent one? All the same, I have to think of Una now, so I shall go and see him," finished Tony with decision.

"I have rather misled you perhaps," said Anne

slowly. "Una will not be penniless, you know."
History was repeating itself with a vengeance, she
thought, Jeremy going to his people for money to
marry her, and now this boy tackling an irate father
on Una's account. What was the matter with the
men? Was it their insatiable sense of possession or
their vanity? It was folly to talk of partnership in
marriage while this old worn-out code persisted. It
had been fair enough in the past when women were
pretty ornaments and no more, but the girl of today
had a right to her part in the struggle. She was not
made for cotton-wool. "Don't go to your father,"
she urged. "I will see that Una has enough to give
you both a fair start."

"It's amazingly generous of you, Lady Anne,"
said Tony gratefully, "but how could I let you? I'd
deserve every beastly thing my father ever thought
about me."

"I warn you this is dangerous ground." She shook
her head at him. "I married a man who has persisted in ignoring my money, and if I thought
you were going to be equally idiotic, I should
run off with Una at once to the other end of
the world."

"But I won't. I should love her to have piles of
money, but you wouldn't really like me to count on
that. Una wants to go in for dogs and I believe
she'd do well with them. I'm going to help her on
the business side and go on with my own work meanwhile, but my profession doesn't bring in much at
present and I ought to be in a position to provide
necessities at least. Besides, I'd rather demand

money from my father as a right than accept it as a gift."

"You don't think he's so bad then, in spite of all your protests."

"He's fond of my sister," admitted Tony, "and she is determined to speak to him. I can't allow that naturally. I've got to get in first."

"And if he refuses you after all, what then? You'll expect Una to wait until you've made enough to keep her, I suppose."

"No, we'll live on my capital and hope for the best, but I'd like anything you can give Una to be settled on her, Lady Anne, if you don't mind," said Tony diffidently.

Anne threw back her head and laughed. She liked him, he was so young and earnest and absurd. The irate father was merely a giant to conquer for Una's sake, and even his refusal of his sister's aid was in the picture. "The girl would probably do it so much better too, if I'm any judge of my sex," she thought. "But of course he's perfectly right in theory. Theory and practice are like relations-in-law. They so rarely agree."

Tim entered the room at this moment, tactfully suggesting the picture of his anxious mistress outside. Anne rose to her feet.

"I should like to meet your sister, and as I haven't much time and want to look round the place while I'm here, perhaps we'd better declare a truce for the moment," she said with a smile.

"You've been awfully kind to me, Lady Anne."

"Ah, well, I was young myself once," she returned with a twinkle in her eye and was charmed when he took the platitude seriously. "Besides, I realize better than you can do what is before you, my boy. You have to see Una's father yet."

"She says he will do whatever you say."

"What? Am I to be called a managing woman to my face? Come along out of this before there's bloodshed," cried Anne gayly. She led the way to the window, then paused a moment to say: "Be good to her, Tony. Remember, if you are jealous of her money I shall disinherit the pair of you. Don't be too proud to let her help your career if she can."

"I'm an ass in a lot of ways," said Tony, "but not such an ass as that. She's helped it already, simply by being alive . . . you don't know."

Anne patted his arm.

"I know," she said. "And here she comes. I'm afraid your sister is being scandalously neglected."

At sight of them in the doorway Una came runing.

"It's all right, isn't it . . . she's going to let us?"

"Let you indeed," protested her mother. "You issue an ultimatum and then pretend it was a polite request. You're a hussy and there'll be no wedding in my family for six months at least. Let me tell you that."

"Isn't she perfect?" said Una excitedly to Tony and he smiled, holding something more perfect in his arms.

iv

Anne drove away from Wenlock leaving the three young people in possession. She had not attempted to break up the little party though it had been clear they expected it.

"I can't have the village suspecting the young devils came here by stealth," she thought. "And after all, why spoil their fun?"

Alone at last, she faced her problem. She had set out this morning determined to sell Wenlock and buy immunity from Mrs. Swithin's interference, but Fate, Una, and Tony had intervened. The child must have the old place if she wanted it, and Anne had had several glimpses of her feeling for it during their tour of inspection. "Wenlock ought to have somebody belonging to it," she had argued eagerly, "and I'd be better than a tenant, mother." She had even told the story of the cheque from her Uncle John and enumerated the various possessions she meant to sell for Wenlock. "Presents, you know. . . . I've always had more than I can do with. And then I thought perhaps you and father would give me an allowance for a year or two, because I must cost no end living at home."

Anne looking into the eager face had answered: "Oh, dear, yes, you have been a very costly rascal, but like Tim, I think, cheap at the price." She knew well the value of that tribute in her daughter's eyes.

Una and her dogs and Tony and his statues at Wenlock! Yes, it was a better fate for the old place, after all, than selling it for a peace that was problematical at the best. Anne, who had carelessly failed in any sentimental attachment to her old home, yet saw a kind of fitness in her daughter's love for it.

"She's more of a Challice than I am," she thought, "my darling changeling. Oh, dear, what shall I do without her?"

Had Una but known it, this was her hour. The close companionship between them, silent and un-demonstrative on the girl's side, casual and amused upon Anne's, took on for the latter a new signifi-cance, now its inevitable end was at hand, and the thought of the house, with Una gone from it, brought a pang of dismay. It was altogether too desolate for contemplation, but she thought: "This is mere selfishness. I'm not losing her, after all."

Jeremy she knew would not really mind this early marriage, however much he might think it his duty to protest, because thereafter he would have her to himself. He was happy now, but for how long, she wondered, knowing his mother's shafts would in-evitably continue. Still life was full of compromises and she had had to make fewer than her share, per-haps. Anne decided that she could at least make this one for Una's sake. Wenlock should be put in order and part of her income go to keeping it up for the child. The burden of their obligation to Mrs. Swithin must remain.

Anne, driving back to the Drews', recalled sud-denly the onyx ring, and smiled. One triumph at least she was taking to Jeremy out of a morning of dismays. The ring was found. He would be able to tell his mother she had fussed without cause.

That evening while the nightingales sang in Wenlock garden to the two who walked there, not many miles away a man was whistling under his apple trees.

"Listen to him," said Robby. "He's as happy as Larry again."

"Yes, but look here, Robby, you can't bury yourself out here. It's not natural." Bill's arm crept round her and she did not draw away. "I've never looked at another girl. It was always you," he said.

"Ass!" said Robby.

THE END